Praise for Ken Oder

"Secrets, passion, love and violence; they're not for the weak of heart or body...I couldn't put it down, and I can't wait for the next one."

- Pamela Fagan Hutchins, USA Best Book Award winner and author of the *What Doesn't Kill You* romantic mystery series

"...a work of art, or poetry, or beauty and all of the above. Oder takes you back in time to a place in a rural Virginia town and gently reveals parts and pieces of its topography and people. The story is not a gentle one...but it is simply beautiful."

- Rebecca Nolen, author of *Deadly Thyme* and *The Dry*

"...masterfully crafted, brimming with the sort of spellbinding wisdom that takes your breath away. Cast from characters who could easily be our friends and family, this story confronts the darker side of human nature with unflinching precision. It reveals that the line dividing right from wrong isn't always clearly defined, that an undeniable symbiosis exists between joy and heartache."

- Daniel Wimberley, author of *The Pedestal* and *The Wandering Tree*

THE JUDAS MURDERS

KEN ODER

SkipJack Publishing

Printed in the United States of America.

This book is a work of fiction. Any references to historical events, real people, or real places are used fictitiously. Other names, characters, places, and events are products of the author's imagination, and any resemblance to actual events, places, or persons, living or dead, is entirely coincidental.

Oder, Ken.

The Judas Murders / by Ken Oder.

First edition.

ISBN (first edition : paperback) 978-1-939889-95-9

ISBN (e-book) 978-1-939889-94-2

1. Appalachians (People)--Fiction. 2. Appalachian

Region, Southern--Fiction. I. Title. II. Series:

Oder, Ken. Whippoorwill Hollow novels ; 3.

First Edition: November 2018

Editor: Meghan Pinson

Cover design: Bobbye Marrs

To Cindy

Contents

Chapter One

THE MURDER OF BETTY LOU MUNDY

February 19, 1967, Sunday morning

A SHAFT of early morning sunlight broke through pine branches and fell across the gate of a picket fence that fronted Leland Mundy's property. Sitting in a patrol car parked on the side of the road with the engine idling and the heater whirring full blast, Sheriff Coleman Grundy stared at a crimson stain on the gate post. He broke open his service revolver to find two bullets in the chamber. He loaded four more rounds from his belt loop, holstered his gun, and cut off the engine.

When he opened the door to climb out, a wall of cold air hit him and a spear of pain stabbed him in the lower back. He winced and stood up straight, pressing his fist against the base of his spine. When the pain eased off, he looked at Leland's house, a little yellow clapboard box with a screened porch that barely accommodated two rocking chairs. Through the dark screen, Cole could make out Leland, a middle-aged bear of a man, sitting in one of the chairs, staring off into the distance. He didn't look at Cole or acknowledge his presence in any way.

Cole limped over to the gate. As he'd suspected, the stain was blood. He passed through the gate and stopped. Betty Lou Mundy lay on her back ten feet away. He walked over to her. Her robin's-egg-blue eyes looked up at him, glassed over and lifeless. A heart-shaped bloodstain crusted the front of her blouse.

Cole looked over at Leland again. He was still staring straight ahead.

Pressing his hand to his back, Cole eased down to one knee and put his fingers to Betty Lou's throat, knowing he would feel no pulse. Her flesh was cold, damp, and rigid, like soft plastic. He wiped the moisture off on his pants and looked her over. A sheen of frost covered her hair and clothing. Her clothes and makeup corroborated the gossip he'd heard, that she'd been stepping out on Leland. All the gray was died out of her chestnut hair. She'd blacked her eyes with too much eyeliner and painted her lips cherry red. She wore a black leather jacket over a red blouse that was too tight and cut too low, and a black tube miniskirt, too short. An attractive woman pushing fifty, trying hard to look twenty-five.

He peered at the bloodstain that soaked her blouse from her left breast down to her black leather belt. The entry wound was a small hole about two inches above the nipple. A small-caliber bullet, he guessed. He saw streaks of blood on her thighs and drops of it on the toes of her black spike high heels, one of which rested on its side in the frost-covered brown grass by her bare foot.

He took off his hat and swiped his hand over his bald head, thinking. Someone shot her while she stood by the gate. She leaned on it for support. Then she staggered into the yard. Her chest wound dripped blood on her thighs and the tops of her shoes, and she fell where her corpse now lay.

Her dead eyes gazed at him, as though pleading for help. Her mother had had those same blue eyes. Hazel Emley died of natural causes a couple months ago on Christmas Day, which now seemed like a blessing.

Cole put on his hat and stood up with some difficulty. He

glanced at Leland, then went back to his car, sat down behind the wheel, and radioed dispatch to send the medical examiner, a forensic technician, and two deputies. When he climbed out of the car again, another stabbing back pain weakened his knees. He grabbed the door and pulled himself up to stand straight. He grimaced and pressed his fist against the small of his back. The pain lasted longer this time, and when it eased off it left him weak and dizzy. He leaned against the car, breathing hard.

He was worried about Leland. He wasn't sure he could manage any trouble Leland might cause, but he knew he needed to approach him. The now familiar thought flitted across his mind that filing for retirement might be best for the county. He squinted at the slants of amber light that sifted through pine branches to streak Leland's tin roof and screen porch, and kneaded his back while letting out a long, slow breath. Best for the county, perhaps, but not for him. Thirty years as sheriff. No hobbies. No outside interests. Now that Carrie was gone, he wouldn't know what to do with himself.

He pushed his hat back from his face and ran his hand over his brow, which was damp with sweat despite the cold, and looked at Leland. It would take an hour for his men to drive out from Jeetersburg. If Leland took a mind to run off into the Shenandoah National Park, he'd be long gone before the first patrol car arrived.

Cole pulled his hat down low over his eyes and walked through the gate and over the concrete stepping stones to the porch, carrying himself as tall and straight as he could manage. He stopped just shy of the screen door.

Leland sat motionless in a rocking chair to the right of the front door, seemingly unaware of Cole's presence. Cole looked him over. Nothing in his hands. No bulges in his clothing. No weapon on the porch.

Cole put his hand on the butt of his service revolver. "I'm fixing to join you on the porch, Leland."

Leland looked at Cole with a blank expression. "Suit yourself."

Cole opened the screen door and stepped up on the porch. The door slapped shut behind him. Sweat glistened on Leland's brow and his thinning blond hair was damp. His big, rough hands clenched the arms of the rocking chair. He wore a dark gray work shirt and pants, like he had just come home from a plumbing job. There was an auburn smear on the chest of his shirt. Betty Lou's blood, Cole guessed. A sweet odor came off him, a distinctive flowery smell, not the kind of scent you'd expect a burly man like Leland to wear.

An empty bottle of Jack Daniel's sat on the concrete beside Leland's chair.

"You been drinking, Leland?"

"All night long."

"You shoot Betty Lou?"

"No."

"Who did it?"

"I don't know."

"How long's she been laying out there?"

"She was there when I come home." Leland delivered his answers in a flat tone, like he was discussing the weather or laying pipe for a sewer line.

"What time did you come home?"

"Bout seven."

"Where you been all night?"

Leland hesitated and then said, "Drove the back roads. Parked at the dam and drank my whiskey. Came home when it ran out."

A cold wind whispered in the pines and pushed through the screen mesh. Cole pulled the fur collar of his jacket tightly around his throat and snapped the top button. Leland wore no coat or hat or gloves. "Ain't you cold, Leland?"

He shook his head.

Cole studied him. His face was the color of oatmeal, his eyes clouded, his mouth pulled down at the corners.

"You have any guns in the house?"

"Winchester 64. Twelve-gauge shotgun."

"Any handguns?"

"Not in the house." Leland swiped his hand over his mouth. A tear beaded in his eye and ran down his cheek. "They say . . ." He faltered and then cleared his throat. "They say she's been seein a man in Jeetersburg." He took in a deep breath and let it out through his mouth. He looked up at Cole, his eyes full. "You hear anything about that, Cole?"

"No, sir," Cole lied.

Leland's chest heaved and tears slid down his face. He reached for something behind him. He'd placed a small pistol to his temple before Cole realized he'd withdrawn a gun from his back pocket. Cole threw himself on Leland and grabbed his gun hand. The rocking chair tilted backwards, struck the wall, and fell over on its side, spilling Leland and Cole on the concrete floor in a tangle.

They rolled over, grappling for the gun, and Leland ended up on top, astride Cole. He was bigger, stronger, and younger than Cole and a knife of pain stabbed Cole's lower back and twisted inside his spinal column as they wrestled, but somehow Cole managed to pull the gun away from Leland's head. It fired into a window and shards of glass fell behind them. They kept fighting for control and the gun fired again, splintering a plank in the wall.

Cole's back pain sharpened and Leland's gun hand slipped out of his grasp. He clawed at Leland's hand, but Leland managed to place the barrel of the pistol against his temple. The gun fired, and he collapsed on top of Cole.

Cole pushed Leland's heavy body off of him. Leland fell over on his back, his mouth open, his eyes closed, a trickle of blood draining from a small bullet wound just above his ear.

Cole tried to sit up but couldn't. He rolled over on his side by Leland, withdrew a kerchief from his pocket, and pressed it against Leland's wound with one hand while he put the fingers of the other to Leland's throat. He felt the faint beat of a pulse.

Blood soaked the kerchief and slid down Cole's wrist and forearm in a slick warm line. He wrapped the kerchief around

Leland's head and tied it tightly over the wound, but blood still seeped through and pooled on the concrete.

He knew his men were still forty-five minutes away. After they arrived and called for an ambulance, it would take a good while for the rescue squad to reach the place. Cole stared at the steady drip of blood from the soaked kerchief. He had to make the call for medical assistance now or Leland would have no chance.

He rolled over on his stomach and fought his way up to his hands and knees with his lower back on fire. His head lolled down between his shoulder blades, a string of drool sliding from his mouth to the floor. He took a deep breath and brought one foot underneath him to create the leverage to stand, but a bolt of pain shot from his back into his leg and he couldn't do it. He went back down on all fours, breathing hard, trying to muster the strength for another try.

"Hello?" An old voice, tentative and fearful.

Through the porch screen, Cole saw Bessie Tilden, the tall elderly widow who owned the house next door, standing in the yard clad in a skunk-fur coat, her gray hair in curlers and rabbit-faced house slippers on her big feet.

"Cole, is that you?"

"Yes, ma'am. I need your help."

Bessie put a hand to her chest. "I saw Betty Lou over there. She's . . . I think she's dead."

"Yes, ma'am. I'm afraid so. I need you to call my office, ma'am."

"I called your office a while back when I heard a gunshot. Then I heard more gunfire a few minutes ago. Are you all right, Cole?"

"No, ma'am," Cole said, still down on all fours. "Fact is I'm doing right poorly. I can't seem to get up from here. I need you to call my office right now, ma'am. Tell em we need an ambulance. Leland's been shot."

Bessie's eyes widened. "Leland's hurt?"

"Yes, ma'am. He's in a bad way. Call my office right now. If we don't get an ambulance out here lickety-split, he won't make it."

She sucked in her breath. "All right, Cole. Fast as I can." She hurried over the stepping stones, paused near Betty Lou's corpse, then hobbled on through the gate and along the road toward her house.

Cole lay down beside Leland and tightened the cinch on the bloody kerchief.

Chapter Two

THE WATCHERS

JUST AFTER DAWN THAT MORNING, an hour before Sheriff Grundy discovered Betty Lou's corpse, a man using the alias Ray Middleditch sat down beside Thurman Bowie on a fallen white pine at the summit of Bobcat Mountain and looked down over the Mundy property.

Bowie peered at the front yard through his rifle's high-powered scope. "Who you figure killed the woman?"

Ray stared at the corpse through his field glasses. "I don't know."

Ray's eyesight for distance had dimmed with age to the point that he'd become an unreliable shot at a hundred feet, so he had gone looking for help. He found Bowie on a firing range in Buck County. A tall, rail-thin scarecrow in his twenties with a knife-edged nose, receding chin, and greasy shoulder-length blond hair, Bowie didn't look like much, but he could shoot the eyes out of a crow at three hundred yards.

Ray checked out Bowie's credentials at a crafts shop that was the hub of all gossip in Buck County. The shop's owner, a grossly obese old woman named Eva Deatherage, sat on a stool beside racks of handmade quilts and recited Bowie's resume. He spent his youth in reform school for assaults on his parents and their neighbors. When he turned eighteen, he shot a man to death. He spent a year in county jail awaiting trial, got off on self-defense, and promptly broke into an elderly widow's house in the middle of the night, beat her half to death, and stole a fistful of cash and a bottle of Canadian Club. The county sheriff found him at daybreak, passed-out drunk in a ditch across the road from the widow's house. Sentenced to six years in the Richmond Penitentiary but released after four, Bowie came home last summer. "Couple days later," Eva said, "Thurman's daddy up and disappeared." She gave Ray a knowing look.

A half hour with Bowie over a jar of moonshine corroborated Eva's report. Dumb as a rock, mean as a timber rattler, and dirt poor, Bowie was tailor-made for Ray's needs. Ray offered him five hundred dollars for two long-range kill shots, and he jumped at the chance.

The unforeseen downside to Bowie surfaced after they struck the deal. He talked incessantly, a continuous stream of stupid blather that made it impossible for Ray to concentrate.

"The woman must have been hell on wheels," Bowie said. "Got you mad enough to kill her. Got some other man so mad he come along and killed her first." Bowie squinted at Ray. "What'd she do to you, anyway? You ain't never said."

Ray ignored Bowie and scanned the foot of the mountain in search of Leland Mundy.

"Can't be no lover's quarrel," Bowie said. "She don't look more'n forty-five. You must be what? Sixty-five? Seventy? She'd never drop her drawers for an old man like you." Bowie made a sucking sound with his teeth. "Course, you coulda paid for it, I reckon. How much did you pay?"

"Shut up."

Bowie propped his rifle against the pine and picked up his bottle, sixty-nine-cent Hombre, red wine with a smiling bandito on the label, bandoleers crisscrossing his chest and a rifle in each hand. Bowie took a swallow, wiped his mouth on his sleeve, and belched. "None of it's my fault. I can't help it some bastard horned in and killed the woman. And it ain't my fault the man ain't here. You're the one said he'd come out the house at daybreak. I held up my end of the bargain. You got to pay me my money."

"You'll get your money. Be quiet while I think this through."

While Bowie guzzled rotgut, a few blessed minutes of silence allowed Ray to ponder his next move in light of Betty Lou's murder. He had scouted the Mundys since New Year's Day. Every Sunday Leland left the house between eight and eight thirty and drove to Grace Church in Fox Run to attend the nine o'clock service while Betty Lou slept in. Leland didn't seem the churchgoing type, but Ray didn't have the time or interest to investigate what had driven him into the arms of the Lord. All Ray cared about was the predictability of his behavior.

That Sunday morning before dawn, Ray drove Bowie to Bobcat Mountain's summit, five hundred feet above Mundy's property. They set up in a stand of white pines where they had a clear view of the house and planted a shoulder-high tripod in front of a fallen pine. Ray's plan was for Bowie to shoot Leland when he came out of the house to go to church. If Betty Lou came outside, Bowie would take her down, too. If not, eliminating her later would pose no challenge. She was a soft target, but Leland was not. He owned an array of firearms and he was a good marksman. Blowing his head off from five hundred feet away avoided the risk of confronting him face-to-face, and the long-range shot would be difficult to trace. The law would find no sign of the shooter on the Mundy property, no footprints, no tire tracks, no evidence of any kind except a .30-06 bullet. Determining the trajectory of the kill shot and pinpointing its origin based on nothing more than a corpse with a gaping head wound would be almost impossible.

When Bowie took his position that morning, Ray anticipated a successful hit. Then came the dawn, when they saw Betty Lou's corpse lying in the yard. Leland's truck was not in the driveway, and Ray's carefully crafted plan evaporated with the morning mist.

He moved his field glasses over the terrain around the house again in search of some sign of Leland. Nothing.

"The man ain't here," Bowie said. "We might as well head out."

"Not yet."

A few minutes later, the groan of an engine rode the back of a cold wind up to the fallen pine. Ray trained his glasses on a bend in the road below the house. Leland Mundy's blue pickup truck came around the turn. It pulled in the driveway at the far end of the yard and braked to an abrupt stop. Leland got out of the truck and ran across the yard to Betty Lou's corpse.

Bowie placed the rifle in the crotch of the tripod and took aim.

"Hold off," Ray said.

"I got him square in my cross hairs. I can't miss."

"I said hold off. I want to see what he does."

Bowie pulled his sighting eye away from the scope and spat.

Ray watched Leland kneel beside Betty Lou. He embraced her and rocked her back and forth. He seemed to be crying.

"Let me shoot him fore he moves to cover," Bowie said.

"Not yet," Ray said, watching. Leland held Betty Lou in his arms for a long time, then got slowly to his feet and stood over her. After another long stretch, he left Betty Lou and walked toward the house.

Bowie took aim.

Ray put his hand over the scope. "Wait."

"He goes in the house I won't have a shot."

"Let him go."

Leland went inside the screened porch.

Bowie exploded. "God damn it! I would've blown his head clean off you hadn't stopped me. I want my money. Now! Pay up!"

Ray pulled a roll of twenties out of his pocket, counted off twenty-five Andrew Jacksons, and handed them to Bowie, giving him a good look at the rest of the cash before he put it away. "If you sit tight, there'll be more in it for you."

Bowie counted the cash and jammed it in his pocket. He shook his head and smiled. "I had you figured for a cheat there for a while, but I reckon you're a square dealer after all. You got more you want me to do, we can work a deal."

"Let's see what develops."

A patrol car came along the road and stopped in front of the property.

"Somebody called the law," Bowie said. "We best get out."

"Stay put. He can't see us from down there."

Ray watched Sheriff Coleman Grundy walk across the yard to Betty Lou. He knelt beside her, looked her over, went back to his car, and climbed inside.

"If you want me to kill the law," Bowie said, "it'll cost you another five hundred."

"He's calling for backup. We'd better hold off."

Cole got out of his car and walked across the yard to the porch. It looked as though he talked to someone and then went inside. Shortly after that, two little pops, ten seconds apart.

"What was that?" Ray said.

"Small firearm. It ain't the law's gun. Selk County lawmen carry a powerful weapon, Colt Python, six-inch barrel, .357 Magnum. Talks loud."

Twenty seconds more and another pop. Then nothing.

"Mundy shot the law," Bowie said.

Ray doubted it. Cole was too careful for that.

A few minutes later, a tall old woman in a bulky black fur coat crab-walked down the road and across the yard.

"Want me to shoot the old lady?"

"Let's see what she does."

The woman stood at the porch, talking to someone inside. Then she shuffled back to her house as fast as her bent legs would carry her.

The old woman's calling an ambulance, Ray guessed. Cole must be down or he'd make the call.

"What do we do now?" Bowie said.

"Wait for the sheriff's backup and the rescue squad. See what they do."

Bowie took a swig of Hombre and belched a long, guttural croak.

Ray looked at him ruefully. His patience with Bowie had run out without his firing a shot. Ray stood and stretched his legs, stiff from the cold. "I've got to take a piss. Watch the road and call me if anything happens."

Ray walked up the slope to his truck on the summit. He leaned over and massaged his left knee. The morning's activity had inflamed his arthritis. The doctor said all the cartilage in the joint had worn away, bone grinding on bone with every step he took.

He straightened up, took a piss, zipped up, opened the truck's door, and groped on the floorboard under the seat until he grasped a cold steel barrel. He glanced at Bowie to make sure he wasn't looking, then put the Colt Python .357 Magnum in the big side pocket of his winter coat.

He withdrew a bottle of Cutty Sark from the glove compartment and took a short pull. It lit a warm flame in his stomach. He turned the bottle up twice more, small swallows, enough to dull the pain in his knee without slowing his reaction time. He stowed the whiskey in the glove compartment, returned to the pine, and sat beside Bowie.

Bowie took another swallow of rotgut. The bottle was three quarters gone.

"How much can you drink before you can't shoot straight?" Ray asked.

"Long as I'm standin, I'll hit my target."

Could be true, Ray thought. Set the trap carefully. He looked down at the house and waited.

Soon, the wind carried the faint sound of a siren. An army-green patrol truck cleared the bend in the road and stopped in front of the house. A deputy climbed down off its running board, ran a hand over his bristly red hair, reached inside the truck for his hat, and put it on. In his midthirties, average height, and muscular, he fit the description of Chase Dooley. Ray had never met him, but he'd heard plenty about him. A foster kid who served time in reform school, a bad boy until the army got hold of him and sent him to Korea. Cole had snapped him up when he came home. By reputation, he was tough and street smart with no quit in him.

Dooley went through the gate, paused at Betty Lou's corpse, and headed toward the porch. Ray set his field glasses on the pine and put one hand in his coat pocket. "Kill that one," Ray said to Bowie. "Split his skull in two and I'll pay you a thousand."

Bowie tossed his bottle of Hombre into the bushes. "He's a dead man." He positioned his rifle on the tripod and put his eye to the scope.

Ray placed his Colt Python's silencer against Bowie's temple and squeezed the trigger. *Thump.* The top half of Bowie's head exploded in a crimson mist. His carcass lurched violently away from the gun, as though he'd been hit above his ear with a sledge hammer. Bowie's legs stiffened straight out like an underwater frog-kick. He fell on his back, knocking over the tripod and throwing his rifle down the hill.

Ray leaned over him, placed the silencer over his heart, and fired again. His arms and legs twitched; cords of muscle in his neck flexed; and he went still.

Smoke curled from the silencer. Ray set the gun on the pine and looked down at the house through his field glasses. Dooley was nowhere to be seen. Inside, Ray guessed.

More sirens. An ambulance rocked into view and pulled up to the porch. Two EMTs unloaded a gurney and hauled it inside the screen porch.

A minute passed before they emerged with Leland on the gurney. They hadn't pulled the sheet over his face, but he looked dead. He had blood in his hair and he wasn't moving. The EMTs loaded him in the van, went inside again with the gurney, and came out with Cole, Dooley trailing alongside. The EMTs carried him into the van and sped away.

Ray watched Dooley walk over to Betty Lou and kneel beside her.

Ray lowered his field glasses. He would learn nothing more by staying there. He might as well return to the rental house. Think things through. Reformulate his plan.

He looked at Bowie's corpse at his feet. So much for the idea of working with a second man. Ray had sure as hell learned a hard lesson with this dumb ass.

He searched Bowie's corpse for the five hundred dollars and pocketed it. He looked through Bowie's wallet. Three one-dollar bills. Bowie's driver's license, birthdate January 3, 1943. Ray did the math. Twenty-four years stupid. A couple of photos, a skinny toothless old hag and a fat young woman with buck teeth. Ray shoved the wallet in his pocket.

He retrieved the rifle and looked it over. A .30-06, bolt action, fitted with a Leupold scope. A fine weapon in pristine condition. He propped it against the pine, picked up the tripod, and put it beside the rifle. He'd make good use of them down the road.

He looked at the corpse again, thinking. People didn't climb Bobcat very often. The body might go undiscovered for a while. There was a patch of dense brush near the truck. Bowie probably didn't weigh more than a hundred fifty pounds, less with most of his head blown off. Ray supposed he could drag the bony carcass that far without further crippling his arthritic knee.

He grabbed Bowie's still warm hands and pulled his body up the slope.

Chapter Three

A DEAD MAN'S ALIBI

March 1, 1967, Wednesday afternoon

TEN DAYS after Betty Lou Mundy's murder, Sheriff Coleman Grundy pulled into the old schoolyard across the road from Grace Church about four o'clock on a Wednesday afternoon and parked in front of the Fox Run Schoolhouse, an abandoned yellow two-story stone building with padlocked heavy wooden double doors and windows boarded up with sheets of plywood. The schoolyard was a barren desert of powder-dust, save for a sickly locust tree near a rusty swing set.

Across the road Cole saw Reba Emley, Betty Lou Mundy's sister, kneeling beside a grave inside the wrought iron fence that separated the cemetery from the churchyard. The grave looked fresh, its mounded soil still iron red. Betty Lou's grave, Cole guessed.

Reba placed a long-stemmed rose at the foot of the shiny new headstone. She lingered there and then seemed to notice Cole's patrol car across the road in the schoolyard. She took a last look at the grave and walked along the fence toward the cemetery gate, disappearing from Cole's view behind the pine trees that surrounded the church.

Carrie's grave lay behind those trees. Cole stared at the pines until the cold seeped into the car. He started the engine and turned on the heater.

Reba's souped-up black Chevy Impala emerged from the pine grove and rumbled over the church's driveway to the road, sunlight glinting on the twin white racing stripes on its hood. It crossed the road and coasted into the schoolyard, its muscular engine thrumming. Reba parked beside Cole and got out of the car.

A wave of cold air blew into the patrol car when Reba opened the door and sat down. Her perfume grabbed Cole's attention right off, a distinctive odor, floral, like violets, mixed with something earthy, leather or oak moss. The fragrance seemed familiar to him, but he couldn't place it.

Reba looked like a younger version of Betty Lou. Big heavy-lidded baby-blue eyes, a strangely sensuous hooked nose, and a pouty mouth with full lips painted cherry red, all framed by chestnut hair cut chin length. She wore a sable coat over a beige blouse and a black skirt. The skirt and coat stopped at midthigh.

"Afternoon," Cole said.

Reba slipped the gold chain strap of a little black purse off her shoulder and clutched it in her lap. "Thanks for comin. I heard tell the doctors made you stay down for a while. I hope drivin over here don't aggravate your back." Her voice was raspy and she spoke with a lisp.

"They gave me a shot that numbed it up pretty good. It's coming along fine."

"I'm sorry I called you off your sick-break, but I don't trust no one else." She withdrew a pack of cigarettes from her purse and lit up. She set the pack on the bench seat between them. Kool Filter Kings, menthol.

The acrid smoke overwhelmed her perfume. Cole cracked his window to give it somewhere to go.

Reba's hand trembled as she brought the Kool to her lips. A streak of eyeliner on her cheek told him she'd been crying. He looked across the road at the grave. "I'm sorry about Betty Lou."

"Betty Lou's buried on the other side. That one's Leland."

He mulled that over, putting it together with the long-stemmed rose. The implication didn't shock him. She had a reputation for sleeping around. Still, an affair with her sister's husband seemed brazen, even for her.

"When I heard about it on the radio," she said, "I went straight to the hospital. The doctors wouldn't let me go in his room, so I stood in the hall and looked at him through the window." A tear slid down her cheek. "The machines kept him breathin for a while, but I knew he wouldn't make it. When you know someone real good, you can tell. You can feel it."

Cole studied her. He'd heard she was a spitfire who didn't care about any one man. It appeared the gossip was wrong. "I'm sorry I couldn't wrestle that gun away from him."

"From what I hear, you tried your best."

Cole sighed heavily. "I'm afraid my best wasn't good enough."

"Neither was mine," she said bitterly.

He looked at her curiously.

She blew out a chain of little smoke rings. "You go to school here?"

He shook his head. "I grew up in Jeetersburg."

"Me and Betty Lou went here. Four little rooms with potbelly wood stoves. Hot as hell next to em. Cold as a icebox two rows back." She puffed her cigarette and stared at the padlocked doors.

She was working herself up to tell him something about the murder, he thought. He waited her out, allowing her to come to it on her own terms. The patrol car's engine vibrated and the heater whirred. A cold wind blew across the schoolyard. The locust tree's spindly branches clattered and little twisters swirled in the powdery dust.

Reba stubbed out her cigarette in the car's ashtray. "Leland didn't kill Betty Lou."

"How do you know?"

"He was in bed with me when she was shot."

"He told me he parked at the dam and drank all night."

"He was with me. He showed up at my trailer Saturday night at supper time, bout eight o'clock. I fried him a steak. We drank whiskey and watched TV. Went to bed bout ten. He didn't leave my place till six thirty the next mornin. People in the know tell me Betty Lou was shot sometime between four and six. If that's true, Leland couldn't have killed her."

People in the know. Walt Ballard, Cole thought, one of Cole's deputies and Reba's third ex-husband. When he applied for a job with the sheriff's office, people warned Cole that he talked too much, especially with a snoot full of shine, but Cole sensed an undercurrent of untapped talent in the man, so he took a chance on him. He panned out to be an average deputy, but when Reba left him last year, his job performance took a nosedive. Cole guessed he'd told Reba about the Mundy case to curry favor with her.

"You sure it was six thirty when Leland left your place?" Cole asked.

"I'm sure."

"Any chance he left during the night and came back while you were asleep?"

Reba gave Cole a wry look. "I didn't sleep. Neither did he."

Cole chewed on that for a while. Then, "How long you and Leland been carrying on?"

"Since last summer."

"How did it get started?"

"I was sittin at the bar in Carter's Tavern on a Saturday night. He come in by himself. We talked and I let him know I was interested. He followed me home. After that, we hooked up off and on till the night Betty Lou was shot."

"What does off and on mean?"

20

She lit another Kool and pulled so hard on it she burned down half an inch of ash. "Means he came to see me when he couldn't stand it no longer. In what they call 'moments of weakness.'"

He heard the bitterness in her voice. She had wanted more from Leland, he guessed. "One-night stands?" he said, to see how she'd react.

She glared at him, but the anger died quickly and resignation took its place. "Leland saw it that way, I reckon. Bout once a month he'd show up at my door lookin hangdog." She blew out a stream of smoke. "He'd leave in the mornin and I wouldn't hear from him till the next time he came along."

"Anyone see you with him?"

"People saw us at Carter's Tavern that first time, but I never heard no talk about it. The other nights, he came to my trailer and we didn't go out."

"If he parked at your trailer, someone should have seen his truck."

"My lot has a shed around back. He parked in it so no one would see. He always came after dark and left before dawn. He didn't want anyone to know about us."

"Did Betty Lou know?"

"He didn't want her to know." She put the cigarette out in the ashtray and put the pack of Kools in her purse. "Said he didn't want to hurt her feelins." She bit off the words.

Cole looked across the road at Leland's grave, wondering if Reba's story was a lie concocted to exonerate him.

When they hauled Cole away in the ambulance the morning of the murder, he left Chase Dooley in charge of the investigation. With the help of Shirley West, a state medical examiner, Chase gathered a lot of evidence that pointed to Leland as the murderer.

Shirley determined the cause of death to be a .25-caliber bullet that pierced an aorta. Ballistics tests established that the gun Cole tried to take away from Leland that morning was the murder weapon, a .25-caliber Browning pistol commonly known as a Baby

Browning, four inches long, ten ounces in weight. Chase traced the pistol to Jenkins Gun Shop in Jeetersburg where Leland purchased it two years before the murder. The pistol bore Leland's fingerprints on its ivory handle, a partial print from Cole's index finger on the barrel, and no one else's prints.

Bloodstains on the cuff and chest of Leland's shirt matched Betty Lou's blood type.

As Walt had apparently told Reba, Shirley pegged the time of death as between four and six Sunday morning. Bessie Tilden, the widow who lived next door, told Chase she heard a lone gunshot shortly before five. Although Leland told Cole he parked at the dam that night and drank until dawn, Chase found no tire tracks or any other sign that Leland had been there.

The morning of the murder, Leland told Cole he'd heard Betty Lou was seeing another man, so he had motive, and discounting his unverified story about drinking all night, he had opportunity. The case against him was rock solid.

Cole studied Reba. The sun was setting on her side of the car. A soft orange light limned her dark hair. He saw no signs of dissemblance in her demeanor, but a woman who carried on a secret affair with her sister's husband had to be capable of telling lies with a straight face, and the way she laid out her story, there was no witness or independent fact that could corroborate it.

And yet he could think of no reason for Reba to lie. Leland was dead. Her alibi would do him no good.

"You believe me, don't you?" she said.

Cole looked down at her hands folded in her lap, small with delicate fingers tipped with red acrylic nails. The last wisps of cigarette smoke drifted out Cole's window, and the fragrance of her perfume took over. He breathed it in, a flowery scent, sweet but earthy. His strong sense that he'd encountered it before returned, and a sudden recollection of the morning of the murder swept over him in a rush. Standing in the little enclosed space of the screen porch, he'd picked up a sweet floral scent coming off

Leland, memorable because it didn't fit for a rough-as-a-cob working man.

"What's the perfume you're wearing?"

Reba looked puzzled. "It's French." She withdrew a little bottle of cut glass from her purse and handed it to him. "Leland liked it. I wore it whenever we got together. It seemed right to wear it this afternoon when I come to see his grave."

"Jolie Madame by Balmain" was scrolled across the label over an ink-black sketch of a smiling woman with long curly hair. Cole pulled the stopper and held the bottle to his nose. He recognized it as the scent he'd smelled on Leland the morning of the murder. Jolie Madame must have rubbed off on him when Reba held him in her arms that night and lingered on him through the morning.

Cole thought through the perfume's implications. It supported Reba's claim that Leland spent the night with her, but it didn't prove he was with her when Betty Lou was killed. Reba's trailer was a forty-five-minute drive from Leland's house. He could have slept with her that night but left her trailer earlier than she claimed.

Cole handed the bottle back to Reba. "Come down to headquarters in the morning. Meet with me and Chase Dooley. We'll go over everything in detail. Take your statement."

She clenched her jaw and looked out the window at the schoolhouse.

"What's wrong?"

"I need to get me a lawyer first."

"Why?"

"There's more to the story than I told you. Some people might take it the wrong way."

"You'll have to tell us everything. Lawyer or no lawyer."

"Could be. We'll see, I reckon."

"If you're worried about your own neck, why did you come forward in the first place?"

"I heard y'all were about to close the case and put the killin on Leland."

"Walt Ballard."

"Don't matter where I heard it. The point is I know Leland didn't kill Betty Lou." Her eyes were full. "I won't let Leland go down as a murderer. I don't want him to be remembered that way."

This relationship was much more than an illicit affair, Cole thought. She was in love with Leland. All the way. Head over heels. Which gave her a powerful motive to kill the woman who stood between them.

"I'll get me a lawyer tomorrow," Reba said. "If he says I can give you a statement, I will." She got out of the patrol car, rounded the Impala, and climbed inside. The engine roared and she spun out of the schoolyard kicking up a trail of dust, sped up the road, and disappeared around a turn, tires squealing.

Cole looked at the red mound over Leland's grave. There was a lot more to learn. Pursuit of the truth required energy and will, which were once Cole's dominant traits, but no longer. He was lonely; he was old and tired; and his body was failing. He stared at the pines that blocked his view of Carrie's grave. After a long while, he started the car and drove out of the schoolyard.

Chapter Four

THE MEDICAL EXAMINER

March 1, 1967, Wednesday evening

COLE LEFT the schoolhouse and headed home, stopping at Kirby's Store in Fox Run to buy a couple of Moon Pies and a Brownie, a makeshift supper. By the time he left there and drove into Whippoorwill Hollow, night had fallen and a crest of maroon, violet, and purple clouds colored the western horizon, the last remnants of the sunset.

Twelve miles from the store, he turned onto his gravel driveway. Thirty years ago, he and Carrie had built a little cottage halfway up the slope of Butter Ridge on a flat ledge over Little Bear River. He still rented the bottomland pasture to a neighbor for grazing, and tonight as he drove past the cattle gathered under spreading oaks along the riverbank, moonlight paled their black backs to gray.

When he crested the steep slope to his house, his headlights washed over a midnight blue Cadillac in front of his car shed. Cole pulled up beside it and got out of his car. On the front porch, a mane of snow-white hair and a full beard were rocking back and forth, disembodied in the dark.

The pain in Cole's lower back graduated from dull to bother-some as he limped across the yard to the foot of the steps.

"About time you showed up." Randall Hotchkiss was wearing a three-piece tweed suit. "I've been sitting here for the better part of an hour."

"Why didn't you call and tell me you were coming?"

"I didn't know I was coming till I came."

Cole grasped the railing, pulled himself up the steps, crossed the porch to the front door and unlocked it. "Let's go inside."

"Not worth the trouble."

"It's cold."

"I'd rather sit out here. I won't keep you long."

Cole knew why Randy had come to see him. If the roles were reversed, Cole wouldn't want to go inside and visit either, so he relented and took a seat in the rocker next to Randy.

Randy was cradling a gallon mason jar in his lap like a precious treasure. The tangy scent of his preferred poison, a strong screw-driver mix, wafted up from the jar's open top.

"That won't help," Cole said.

"Nothing helps." Randy raised the jar to his lips and took a long pull. He set it back on his meaty thigh and swiped his sleeve across his mouth. His chest rose and fell in labored wheezing breaths, his huge belly straining against his vest. "I suppose Shirley West told you. The state let me go."

As the state's assistant chief medical examiner, Shirley made recommendations for the appointment and removal of examiners in the western district, and her recommendations were always approved. She had called Cole that morning to notify him that the state had terminated Randy's thirty-year tenure as Selk County's local medical examiner. "I'm sorry," Cole said to Randy.

"No, you're not."

Cole let that stand. It was true.

Randy took another swig and was quiet for a while. Then,

"Shirley said she found strands of my hair and fibers from my suit on Betty Lou Mundy's corpse. She asked me how they got there. I told her I was so drunk I don't remember what I did that morning. That seemed to be the last straw. She said she had no choice but to fire me."

Cole looked out at the cattle standing under the oaks. A light breeze carried the river's faint hum up to the porch.

"I told her the truth," Randy said. "I don't know what happened. I want you to tell me what I did."

"I wasn't there. I was down with my bad back."

"You left Dooley in charge. He's like a son to you. He tells you everything."

"I don't see what good it does—"

"We go back a long way, Cole. When I was on my game, we were best friends. Tell me what I did."

Cole rubbed his palms on his pants legs. "Dispatch couldn't find you for hours. When you finally showed up at the Mundys' house, you were drunk." Cole fell silent, hoping Randy wouldn't push it.

"Tell me the rest of it. Tell me what I did when I got there."

Cole took in a breath and let it out. "Chase said you were talking nonsense. Crying and blubbering. Didn't seem to know where you were. You fell on your face. Crawled over to Betty Lou on your hands and knees." Cole hesitated and then said, "You passed out on top of her."

Randy took a big swallow from the jar. "I don't remember any of it." He ran a trembling hand across his mouth. "What did I say when I was crying?"

"Chase said it was gibberish. He couldn't make any sense of it."

Randy seemed to think about that. Then he said, "Is Dooley the one who ratted me out?"

"He told Shirley you were down with a cold. She didn't believe him. She called me. I told her the truth. You want to blame someone, blame me."

A tear rolled out of Randy's eye and disappeared in his beard. He lifted the jar, but Cole put his hand on it and pushed it down.

"You wanted to hear the truth. Crawl out of that jar and face up to it."

"Facing the truth isn't my strong suit."

"It used to be."

Randy blew out a short, heavy breath and leaned back in the rocker. "I was a good doctor in my day."

"One of the best."

"If I could just go back to the time . . ." His voice broke. He tucked his chin and squeezed his eyes shut, his shoulders shaking.

Cole took the jar from Randy, stepped over to the porch railing, poured the yellow mix onto the ground, and threw the jar into the night. It thudded on the turf and skidded across the yard to come to rest under a tree by the driveway. With the twist of the throw, a needle of pain pricked Cole's lower back. He limped back to the rocker and sat down.

Randy's wheezing came on strong and then tailed off. A chill wind blew across the porch. Cole zipped up his jacket.

Randy struggled to button his suit jacket, but it wouldn't reach around his girth so he abandoned the effort. "How did you get past it?"

"What?"

"Carrie's murder. How did you get over it?"

Cole paused for a long moment. "I didn't get over it. I never will."

Randy gave Cole a baleful look. "How do you go on?"

"I get up in the morning. I put on the uniform. I go to work."

Randy looked off at the night. "Hardly seems worth it." He grasped the arms of the rocking chair and pushed his heavy frame up to stand. He walked unsteadily across the porch to the top of the steps.

"Randy."

Randy stopped and looked back at Cole.

"I can't bring Carrie back, but you've still got a chance. Samantha left you because you're a drunk. Sober up and beg her to come home."

"Samantha," he said in a hoarse voice. "Seems like so long ago." He descended the steps and weaved across the yard to his Cadillac. The headlights came on and the engine fired up. The big car made a wide circle in the driveway, almost colliding with the corner of the car shed, and headed down the hill.

Cole went inside and limped across the parlor and down the hall to a little home office. He sat down at his desk and grabbed the radio transmitter. "County One to dispatch."

"Hey, Cole." The grainy voice of Molly Ruebush, the county's most experienced dispatcher.

"Who's on patrol in Whippoorwill Hollow?"

"Chase is on till midnight."

"Randy Hotchkiss just left my house. Tell Chase to pull him over. Take him home and put him to bed."

"Will do."

Cole hung up and took off his jacket. He pulled out his shirttail and unhooked his back brace so he could massage a spot high on his right hip, over the bone his doctor referred to as the iliac crest.

Carrie's image came to his mind's eye as it always did in idle moments. He saw her as clearly as the last night her head rested on the pillow beside him, her brown eyes, the splash of freckles over her cheeks and nose, her dimples when she smiled, her red hair streaked with gray. His perfect recall of her aspect apparently wasn't typical of widowers three years gone. Cole's neighbor, Joe Willis, said his wife's face faded away a few weeks after she died. He carried her photograph in his wallet to remember what she looked like. Cole wondered who experienced more pain, Joe because he couldn't recall his wife's image or Cole because he couldn't forget.

He got up and walked slowly down the hall to the kitchen. When he opened the cabinet above the sink and withdrew the bottle of pain pills, he stared at the wall phone for a few moments, thinking about calling his son, Peter, a doctor at Philadelphia General Hospital. Probably busy, he thought, and he had nothing new to say to him. He'd call some other time, he told himself. He took two pills and limped down the hall toward the bedroom.

Chapter Five

THE WIDOWER

THREE YEARS before Betty Lou Mundy's murder, in 1964, Sheriff Grundy's wife came home from grocery shopping on a warm sunny afternoon in June. Just as she reached the top of the porch steps with a bag of groceries in one hand and her house key in the other, a man opened the front door and fired one round into her chest. The force of the blow threw her off the porch and Carrie landed on her back on the flagstones at the foot of the steps, her heels on the bottom step, her arms above her head. Her groceries fell in the crotch of a big boxwood bush by the porch. Her keys landed on the lawn to her right.

The bullet perforated her chest wall, severed an artery, and remained lodged in her spine. Shirley West performed the autopsy. "She didn't suffer," Shirley assured Cole. "She died almost instantly."

Other than the bullet that killed Carrie, Cole's men recovered nothing helpful from the crime scene. No prints, tracks, or clues of any kind.

Even though nothing was stolen from the house, Cole's men thought the murder might have been a burglary gone bad.

Cole didn't think so. The shooter's precise aim didn't bear the mark of panic. Cole believed her murderer was seeking revenge against Cole. Either he came to the house to kill Cole, or he killed Carrie knowing it would cut Cole's heart out.

Cole's thirty-five years of law enforcement had spawned a lot of enemies; his list of suspects was long. He spent more than two years investigating them and cleared the last man just before Christmas. Three years after the murder, he had no suspects and no leads, and he knew nothing more about Carrie's murder than he knew the day she died.

Cole met Carrie when he was fifteen and they were married for forty years. He had never been intimate with another woman.

After her murder, he took an indefinite leave of absence from the sheriff's office. He wouldn't talk to the county's grief counselor or to Reverend Chatham. He refused to book an appointment with the psychologist his doctor recommended.

Their son came home the day before the funeral. Peter and Cole had never been close. They stood together at the graveside service without looking at or talking to one another, and Peter flew back to Philadelphia the next morning.

TWO MONTHS after Carrie's funeral, on a warm night in September, Cole sat in an Adirondack chair under a sweet gum tree in his front yard watching the light of a full moon pierce the shade trees and dapple with pale yellow more than twenty birdhouses he'd made by hand at Carrie's request. She loved birds so much she turned the yard into an aviary.

He looked out at the bottomland where fireflies winked over the river and crickets sang in the weeds. Whippoorwills called from the forested slope behind the house.

Headlights on Whippoorwill Hollow Road turned onto Cole's driveway and climbed the hill. An old blue Ford pickup came to a stop in front of the car shed and Deputy Toby Vess stepped down off its running board. Tall and lean, he walked across the yard with long slow strides and sat down next to Cole in Carrie's chair.

Toby took off his hat and ran his hand over his close-cropped gray hair. "Pretty night," he said.

In his late sixties, he had served as Cole's right-hand man for thirty years, and he was a good friend, but Cole wasn't in the mood for company. "I don't mean to be rude, but I need to be alone. I'd appreciate it if you'd leave me be."

"I understand. I won't stay long." Toby fiddled with his hat and cleared his throat. "My wife died when I was twenty-eight."

Cole looked at Toby incredulously. Toby had never hinted that he'd been married.

"It was forty years ago," Toby said, "when I lived in Windmill Point on the Chesapeake Bay. Her name was Connie Patel. We were married for six years."

Cole struggled to find his voice. "How did she die?"

"Influenza. There was no vaccine for it back then. No cure. No treatment. All the doctor could do was make her comfortable and hope for a miracle. She fought hard, but her lungs filled with fluid, and she couldn't breathe." Toby's eyes glistened, but his voice remained clear and steady.

"How come you never told me?"

"Didn't want you to know. Didn't want anyone to know. I was a deputy in Lancaster County when she died. I tried to kill myself with whiskey. Drank my way out of my job. My father pulled me out of it. Sheriff Musgrove grew up in Irvington and was good friends with my dad when they were boys, so he offered me a job in Selk County as a favor to him. I wanted to make a clean start. When I signed on, I asked the sheriff to give me his word he wouldn't tell anyone. He never told a soul, as far as I know."

They fell silent. A cow in the pasture lowed. An airplane droned across the night sky high above them.

Toby put on his hat. "You'd be coldhearted if you didn't think about Carrie on pretty nights like this, but if you think about her all the time, it'll kill you. You've got to get up and go on. Mix with people. Go back to work." He got up out of the chair, walked across the yard to his truck, and drove down the hill to the road.

Cole returned to work the next day, and over time, he settled into the rhythm of the job again. He got up every morning and went to work. He walked on, step by step, but he was not the same man.

Chapter Six

THE BROKEN HEART

March 2, 1967, Thursday morning

THE DAY after Reba Emley talked with Sheriff Grundy at the old schoolhouse, she drove in to Jeetersburg to meet with a lawyer. Thirty-three years old and six feet tall with hazel eyes, an aquiline nose, and curly, shoulder-length black hair, Rachel McNiel sat at her desk in a dark blue suit jacket and skirt and a white blouse while Reba sat across from her in a black leather miniskirt and a red sweater with a deep V neck, her legs crossed, smoking a cigarette.

Reba recounted for Rachel her meeting with the sheriff. When she finished, she said, "I didn't tell him everything. There's a lot more to the story."

"What did you hold back?" Rachel asked.

Reba took a deep draw on her Kool and stubbed it out in a silver tray. She opened her purse and withdrew a miniature revolver. She held it in her hand and looked at it for a moment, then placed it in the center of the desk.

Rachel looked it over. An old pistol, small enough to fit in the palm of a woman's hand. Its pearl handle was scratched and worn, its snub-nosed barrel as dull as pewter; no trigger guard.

Reba said, "I tried to kill Betty Lou with that gun." Her jaw was clenched, her lips pressed together.

"When?"

"Twenty years ago."

"Why?"

"She stole Leland from me."

Rachel took a moment to digest that. "How did she steal Leland from you?"

Reba lit another Kool, pulled mentholated smoke deep into her lungs, and blew a long stream toward a picture window that looked out on Lighthorse Street. "I met him first. Him and me fell in love. We planned to get married. We were tryin to find a way to raise the down payment for a little house on Beale Street." Reba's hand shook as she lifted the cigarette to her lips and inhaled again. "One night, out of the blue, he said he didn't love me anymore. Said he was heartbroke about it. Said it wasn't nothin I did wrong and I didn't deserve to be hurt so bad. Cried. Hugged me. Packed his bag and left me." She propped her elbow on the arm of the chair, held the cigarette at eye level, and stared at it. No tears. A hard look on her face.

Rachel watched gray threads of smoke drift toward the ceiling and waited for Reba to continue.

"You know Luther Boaz?" Reba asked.

"The building contractor?"

Reba nodded. "Betty Lou was his secretary back then. One of my girlfriends was his bookkeeper. She said Luther called Leland into the office about a plumbin job. Him and Betty Lou struck up a conversation when he found out she was my sister. My girlfriend said Betty Lou gave him a real heavy come-on."

"How old were you then?"

"Nineteen. Leland was twenty-three. Betty Lou was twenty-four."

"Did Betty Lou know about you and Leland when she came on to him?"

"She knew. She didn't care." Reba's voice was strained.

"You said you tried to kill her. When? How?"

Reba breathed out a swirling gray cloud. "Bout a year after they got married they bought their house out in the hollow. I got drunk and drove out there. Parked by the road and sat in my car lookin at it, thinkin it should be me and Leland livin in it. I took that gun and went inside. Found Betty Lou in the kitchen, fryin up supper. I fired all five rounds at her." She drew on the cigarette. "It's hard to hit your mark with that little gun, and I was drunk. I only hit her once."

"What happened then?"

"She stood there squeezin the wound on her leg, lookin at me like she couldn't believe it. Leland came runnin in the kitchen, sat her down, tended to her wound, called the rescue squad." Staring out the window, Reba's eyes glistened. "He looked at me like he hated me. Told me to get out. Real cold-like." She blew out a heavy breath. "So I went home. Went to bed. By myself. Like always. Cried till daybreak."

Rachel gave Reba a moment. Then, "Did the police arrest you?"

Reba shook her head. "Leland and Betty Lou told people she shot herself by accident. He come to my door a couple days afterwards. Told me I had to back off. Claimed him and Betty Lou cared about me, but if I tried to hurt her again, he'd come after me for it. Made me promise I would stay away from her. I cried. He hugged me. Said he was sorry, but he couldn't help it that he loved Betty Lou more than me. Kissed me on the forehead, and went away. I stayed away from them after that. I never spoke to him again until I saw him in Carter's Tavern that night last summer."

So Reba's hatred for Betty Lou wasn't mutual, Rachel thought. She looked at the revolver. "Where did you get this gun?"

"Betty Lou gave it to me."

"When?"

"Long time before I shot her, when I was ten years old."

"Why did she give it to you?"

Reba looked out the window. She seemed to be debating in her mind whether to answer the question.

A gentle breeze blew across Lighthorse Street. The white and yellow limbs of the sycamores lining the sidewalk swayed. "You know about my momma?" Reba asked.

"I heard rumors."

"The rumors are true. She was a whore." Reba put the cigarette out and folded her arms over her chest. Her shoulders trembled. "I think she sold Betty Lou."

Rachel paused. "You really think your mother could have done that?"

"Momma would do anything for the right price."

Rachel took a moment to adjust to that. Then she said, "What makes you think your mother sold her?"

"Betty Lou ran away from home when she was fourteen and never came back. The day she ran off, she gave me that gun. Wouldn't tell me why she wanted me to have it. Took me out to the field behind our place. Showed me how to shoot it. Watched me practice with it. Said to keep it close."

Rachel pushed her chair away from her desk, crossed her legs, and took a moment to think it through. "So you think Betty Lou gave you the gun because she thought your mother would sell you, too."

Reba nodded. She uncrossed her arms, clasped her hands in her lap, and looked down at them.

She wants to stop the conversation there, Rachel thought. Rachel would, too, but she had to know everything to represent Reba competently. "Did your mother sell you, Reba?" she asked gently.

"I won't talk about that."

Rachel pulled her chair up to the desk and leaned forward. "I know it may be hard to talk about, but I can't do my job if I don't know the whole story."

"It's got nothing to do with Leland's murder."

"It's my job to decide what's relevant. That's why you hired me."

"I won't talk about it. That's my final word."

Reba looked as tight as a coiled spring. Rachel decided to let it go and come back to it later.

"You said Leland followed you home from a bar last summer," Rachel said. "With the history between the three of you, I'm surprised he did that."

"I was surprised, too. I'd finally given up on him after he told me to stay away from him and Betty Lou, and I'd tried to move on with my life." She smirked. "Didn't do so good at that, what with three broke marriages and all."

Rachel stared at her pensively. Past forty, single, childless, lonely, with no man on the horizon. The thought flitted across Rachel's mind that she might find herself in the same place in ten years unless she changed her ways.

"That night last summer in Carter's Tavern," Reba said, bringing Rachel's attention back to her, "I figured I had nothin to lose so I threw out a line and Leland bit down hard on the bait. I was excited. I thought maybe he'd leave Betty Lou and take up with me again, but after we made love, he said he was sorry and he shouldn't have done it. He left my trailer fast as he could, and I thought that was the end of it. But he kept comin back."

Reba wrapped her arms around her shoulders. "That last night, the night before someone killed her, he seemed worse off than before. He made love like he was desperate. Three go-rounds. When he was spent, I told him I couldn't go on with him showin up whenever he felt like it. Said I had to know what he planned to do about me and him. Told him he owed me. Shamed him. The shaming is what pulled it out of him, I reckon. He said Betty Lou had been cheating on him. Said he knew she was with a man that very night. Claimed this wasn't the first man. Told me she was with a man last summer when I hooked up with him at Carter's Tavern, a different man, and it sounded like there might have been others before that."

"Why did he stay with her?"

A look of defeat came across Reba's face. "I tried to get him to leave her. I told him she didn't deserve him. Told him I loved him, and I'd make him forget her." Reba paused, her eyes beading with tears. "He said he couldn't leave her because it wasn't her fault. He claimed she couldn't help herself because of the way Momma treated her. He told me he cared for me, but he loved her more, too much to leave her. Said he was weak because every time she pushed him away he gave in to his needs and took advantage of me."

Rachel pushed a box of tissues across the desk. Reba took one and wiped her eyes. "Leland cried that night," she said. "Just like he did twenty years ago when he threw me over for Betty Lou. When he drove away that mornin, I knew he wouldn't come back."

Rachel considered everything Reba had told her. She had a powerful motive to kill Betty Lou, and she'd tried to do it once before. Her story about sleeping with Leland at the time of the murder was uncorroborated and unverifiable. Not a good mix.

"Too many people know about your old relationship with Leland for it to go undiscovered," Rachel said. "The sheriff will learn that Leland left you for Betty Lou and that you were angry about it. Does anyone know you shot Betty Lou with this pistol?"

"Walt Ballard."

Rachel grimaced. Ballard was known for his loose tongue, and he was a deputy. Rachel had to assume he would tell the sheriff.

Rachel looked at the portrait of a young woman in a Victorian gown that hung on the wall across from her desk. The girl was twirling an umbrella, strolling past a park bench under a maple tree with russet leaves. It was a serene image that sometimes eased Rachel's mind and helped her think more clearly in tense times.

The best course of action might be to tell the sheriff everything before Ballard did, if he hadn't reported what he knew already. "Touch the open wound," Burton Jaffee, Rachel's old mentor, used to say. "Better to expose the weakness of your case on your own terms than to have your adversary cast it in its worst light." That usually made sense, but it might not work here. Reba had withheld part of the story and Rachel couldn't make an intelligent decision about disclosure without knowing all the details.

"Let's go over everything from the beginning," she said. "When and where did you first meet Leland?"

Reba lit another cigarette and drew hard on it.

Chapter Seven

THE WITNESS

March 2, 1967, Thursday afternoon

WHILE REBA WAS GOING over her story with Rachel the second time, Sheriff Grundy drove out to Whippoorwill Hollow to interview Leland Mundy's neighbor, despite his doctor's orders to rest his back. Bessie Tilden had told his deputy she heard a gunshot the morning of the murder, but she clammed up when he asked follow-up questions and refused to meet with Chase Dooley again. Now that Reba had cast doubt on Leland's guilt, Cole was determined to make Bessie tell him whatever she might know about the murder.

The sun hung low over the field across the road when Cole parked his patrol car in front of Bessie's house at the foot of Bobcat Mountain. She and her husband, Milton, bought the four-acre lot in 1946. They moved into the farmhouse and sold the small cottage next door to Leland and Betty Lou Mundy a few weeks later. Three months after Milton retired from thirty years as a rural mail carrier, he died of a massive heart attack. With help from their daughters and their husbands, Bessie had managed to retain the farmhouse and eke out a meager living from Milton's government pension.

The place had seen better days, Cole thought as he limped over the concrete stepping stones to the porch. Strips of yellow paint had peeled off the wood siding and patches of rust were spreading across the tin roof.

Bessie opened the door when Cole rapped on it. She'd teased her silver hair as big as a five-gallon bucket and troweled a thick layer of makeup onto her face. Charcoal eyebrows arched over her eyes and neon-pink gloss shellacked her lips. She'd always favored loud outfits, but that afternoon she'd outdone herself with lavender wool slacks and an orange blouse with purple flowers on the sleeves. She looked like an aged circus clown.

"Afternoon, ma'am. You look mighty pretty," Cole said politely.

She scowled at him. "What do you want?"

"I have some questions about the murder."

"I told that young deputy all I know. I don't want to talk about it any more."

"I'm sorry, ma'am, but I'm afraid we have to talk about it." He stepped into the house.

"I didn't invite you in, Cole!"

He took off his hat and jacket and hung them on a rack by the door. He gestured toward a sitting area in front of a window looking out at the front yard. "Have a seat, ma'am."

"I said I don't—"

"I said take a seat."

Her eyes brimmed with tears and her chin quivered. She bowed her head for a few moments and then gave Cole a cross look. "I made a pot of coffee a while back. I expect I'll need a cup if you won't leave me be."

"Suit yourself, ma'am, but I'm not leaving here till we talk."

She shook her head disgustedly and walked across the room. She passed through a swinging door to her kitchen.

The woman is eighty-five, Cole told himself. Age takes its toll on a person's good humor, as he had learned all too well since he turned sixty and everything went to hell.

He looked around the room. An upright piano stood against the opposite wall, an arrangement of family pictures hanging above it. He walked over to them.

On the top row, Milton Tilden posed under a soft light in a World War I army uniform. He was a tall skinny young man then, with sandy hair, a big nose, and a toothy grin. Another photograph showed a young Bessie in a wedding gown and Milton in a tuxedo standing in front of a church. Another showed Bessie in front of Monticello, Thomas Jefferson's home, bundled up in a skunk-fur coat, a fad back in the twenties when Cole was a boy. He vaguely recalled that she wore something like it the morning of the murder.

Pictures of the Tildens' daughters, grandchildren, and great-grandbabies filled out the middle and bottom rows. The one exception to the family theme hung in the lower right-hand corner: a photograph of a young Leland Mundy standing in front of his screen porch wearing blue coveralls, squinting into the sun, smiling. Betty Lou was not in the picture.

Bessie backed through the swinging door carrying a tray with a coffee pot and cups. She walked unsteadily across the room.

"Let me take that for you, ma'am." Cole set the tray on the coffee table and helped her sit down on the sofa. He sat in a rocking chair.

She poured coffee with a trembling hand. The light coming through the window tinted her silver hair blue and unearthed liver spots and gullied creases under her coating of makeup.

She handed Cole a cup, and he took a sip. He set it down and withdrew a pencil and notebook from his shirt pocket. "What time did you wake up the night of the murder, ma'am?"

Bessie pinched her lips together. "I talked to that young man, Dooley. I have nothing more to say."

"Yes, ma'am, but Chase tells me you were rattled and wouldn't say much. The murder had to have come as a shock to you. Now that some time has passed, you'll remember more about what happened. Let's start with the gunshot. You told Chase you were awake when you heard it. What time did you wake up?"

Bessie didn't respond.

"I'm not leaving here till you answer my questions, ma'am."

She made a sour face. "Four in the morning."

"What woke you so early?"

"Milton's prostate gave him fits before he died. He got up several times a night to answer the call a nature. Always woke me up, clunking around in the bathroom like a big ole bear. Waking up at night turned into a habit I can't break. Four o'clock was when he made his last run. That awful night, I woke up at four, like always, and couldn't get back to sleep."

"I see, ma'am. You told Chase you heard gunfire about four forty-five."

"That was the time on my bedside table clock when I heard the shot."

"What did you do then?"

"I went to my bedroom window and looked out at the road in front of Leland's house, where it sounded like the shot came from. I couldn't see anything except the car's headlights shining through the fir trees."

Cole paused. "You didn't mention a car to Chase, ma'am."

"What?"

"You didn't tell Chase about seeing a car."

She put her hand to her brow. "My word. I could have sworn I told him."

Bessie's sighting of a car intrigued Cole. Chase had found the tire track of a big car or light duty pickup on the shoulder of the road about twenty feet below the gate, but couldn't discern a tread pattern. The forensics team estimated it could have been left there any time during the week prior to the murder, so Cole had thought it wasn't related to the killing. Bessie seeing headlights that night changed his opinion.

"Where was this car?"

"In front of Leland's house near the gate."

"What did it look like?"

"The fir trees blocked my view. All I saw was its headlights."

"Did you see it drive off?"

"Oh," she said, furrowing her brow. "I'd forgotten, but you're right. After the gunfire, it went up the hill."

"Then you must have gotten a look at it."

She put her hand to her lips and looked at the floor. "It was big. A dark color. Blue or black."

Cole thought of Reba's black Impala with its racing stripes. "Did you notice any details about it, any unusual markings or paint patterns?"

"Nothing like that, but one of its taillights was burned out." She shook her head. "No. Wait. That might have been the car I followed home the other night." She shook her head feebly. "I don't know."

"Was the sound of the engine quiet or loud?"

"Normal, I guess. I don't remember."

"Could you see the driver?"

"I couldn't see inside the car."

Cole puffed out his cheeks. If she'd told Chase about the car the day of the murder, she might have remembered more.

Bessie seemed to sense Cole's frustration. "In all the turmoil, I must have forgotten to tell that young man about the car." She touched the rim of her hairdo self-consciously. "When you get old as I am, you forget things. You can't even trust what you think you remember. When my sister, Clara, was my age, she saw a man in her bedroom every night knocking down the walls with a ball-peen hammer. Of course, it was all in her mind. My nephew had to put her in a home. She didn't know who she was those last few months." Bessie stared into space, looking fearful.

"Are you sure you didn't see anyone out there by the gate, ma'am?"

"It was too dark. There was no moon that night."

"What did you do after the car drove away?"

"I called your office."

"What did you do after that?"

"I couldn't go to sleep, so I made coffee and sat at the kitchen table until the sun came up. When I heard more shots, I went over there and found Betty Lou in the yard and saw you on the porch."

Bessie was a textbook case of an unreliable witness. Cole was reasonably certain she'd seen a car at the gate, but much less confident it was dark-colored with a broken taillight. Given her faulty memory, he thought he'd probably gotten all he could expect to learn from her. He asked a general question to close the interview. "Is there anything else you can tell me about the murder, ma'am?"

"I can tell you Leland didn't kill her," she said vehemently. Her eyes filled with tears. "He was like a son to me, took care of my house, mowed the grass, cleaned the gutters. He watched after me and wouldn't take a penny for it. He was a good and decent man. And he loved Betty Lou. Don't ask me why. God knows she didn't deserve it." Bessie's face hardened. "She was nothing but a brazen tramp!"

Cole was surprised by the animosity in Bessie's voice. "Why do you say that, ma'am?"

"She cheated on Leland for years!"

"How do you know that?"

Bessie stared down at her coffee and ran her finger around the lip of the cup, seemingly reluctant to answer the question. Then she took a deep breath, went to the piano bench, lifted its lid, returned to the sofa, and thrust an envelope at Cole.

He took a kerchief from his pocket and grasped it. It was smudged, soiled, and yellowed with age. Its sealed flap had been ripped open. He spilled its contents on the coffee table. A color photograph fell out faceup. Betty Lou Mundy sat on the edge of a bed stripped of its covers except for a sheet. She looked to be in her twenties. She was naked, her hands cupping her breasts and thrusting them toward the photographer, her knees pressed together. Her face was flushed and she was smiling.

48

"Where did you get this?"

"I stole it from Betty Lou."

"You stole it? When?"

"A long time ago."

"How long ago?"

"I don't remember exactly. Fifteen years ago or more."

"How did it come about that you stole it?"

"I went over to their house one morning to give them an angel food cake. Leland was at work. Betty Lou made coffee and we sat at the kitchen table and talked. The telephone rang and she went in the living room to answer it. One of those trashy magazines was sitting on the table, *True Detective* or something like that. I flipped through it and out plopped that envelope. I thought it was strange it didn't have an address or a stamp. I knew it was none of my business, but I stuck my nose where it didn't belong. I looked inside and found that picture and a note."

"Where's the note?"

"I lost it long ago. I don't know where it went."

"What did it say?"

"The man who wrote it said he hoped he and Betty Lou could get together again the next time Leland was away from home." Bessie hesitated. "Had some dirty talk I won't ever repeat to a living soul."

"Was it signed?"

"Papa Bear."

"You have any idea who Papa Bear was?"

"None."

"How did you end up with the envelope?"

"While Betty Lou was on the phone, I decided to leave because I didn't want to socialize with a woman like her. I put the magazine back on the table the way I found it, and I took the envelope with me because I didn't want Leland to find the photograph. It would have broken his heart."

"Why did you keep it for all these years?"

"I kept it so I wouldn't forget who Betty Lou really was. She came over here all the time, sat in the kitchen with me and sweet-talked me and acted like she cared about me, but that picture showed me the real Betty Lou, a liar and a cheater." She took a sip of coffee. "For Leland's sake I hoped she'd straighten up, but she never did." She wiped her lips with a napkin. "You should be looking for one of the men she slept with. With all her filthy carrying-on, it's a wonder someone didn't kill her years ago."

"Do you know the names of any of the men she took up with?"

"No."

He looked at the photograph and thought about Papa Bear. A man from fifteen years ago almost certainly had nothing to do with the murder, and even if he did, Cole probably couldn't trace the old photograph back to him. Without much hope that it would ever lead to anything, he slipped the photograph into the envelope and put it in an evidence pouch.

"I may have more questions later, but that's all for now, ma'am." He stood. "Thank you for your help."

She retrieved his hat and jacket. He thanked her again and went outside, and she shut the door behind him.

Chapter Eight

THE ATTACK

COLE GRASPED Bessie's porch railing and descended the steps. His back had gotten worse. At the foot of the steps, he leaned over and propped his hands on his knees. His doctor said leaning over opened gaps between his spine's lumbar joints, easing the pain of spinal stenosis by relieving pressure on nerves in his lower back. The doctor was right. The pain went away, but as soon as he straightened up, it returned. He cursed under his breath and limped across the yard toward his patrol car.

Cole stopped just outside a row of hedges bordering the road, gripped Bessie's rusty mailbox, and leaned over as far as he could. He lifted his head and looked at the box. Flaking white paint with black letters, "M. Tilden." Below that, "358 W.H. Rd." Pockmarks from a load of bird shot. Rust clotted in the little pits.

His back felt better. He straightened up and it hurt again. Holding on to the mailbox, he leaned over again. He looked over the top of Bessie's hedgerow at Bobcat Mountain rising up behind her house. A light breeze moved through the fir trees halfway up the slope.

His back pain went away. He straightened up and it returned. It was maddening. He heaved a sigh and started to take a step toward his patrol car when the shriek of a blue jay on Bobcat pierced the silence. He stopped and looked up at the mountain. The jay shrieked again, drawing Cole's eyes to a big white pine about a quarter of the way up the slope. A heavy wind moaned in the trees as it blew across the face of Bobcat. A sliver of brilliant blue broke through the green and a light flashed just below it, blinding Cole. When he raised his hand to shield his eyes, his back clenched. His leg gave way and he listed to his left, grabbing the mailbox to stay upright. At that moment, a shot rang out; air rushed by his right ear; and a thump and a whoosh sounded behind him.

He twisted around to see his front tire flattened, the car's front end sagging down over the blown tire. Cole sank to his knees as the thunderous shot echoed through the hollow. BOOM, Boom, boom. A few seconds later, a second shot exploded, decapitating the mailbox and splitting the wooden post on which it was perched. The metal box hit the side of the patrol car as Cole raised his hand to fend off a covey of splinters.

He got down on his belly and army-crawled around the patrol car to its far side. He got up on his knees behind the front fender, drew his service revolver, and peeked over the car at the mountain. A third shot shattered the windshield and bits of plate glass stung his face just before he ducked down.

He crawled on all fours to the rear of the car, took off his hat, and peered over the back fender. The white pine where he'd seen the blinding light was about seventy-five yards away. He was a good shot with a handgun, but not that good, and the pine's branches were thick, concealing the shooter. He could throw a scare into him, though. He braced his hands on the car and aimed at the base of the pine. He fired three shots in rapid succession.

The shooter returned fire. A bullet plowed a furrow in the asphalt ten feet down the road to Cole's right. He ducked down and looked over at the bullet's stripe in the road, way off the mark for a shooter with a scoped rifle.

He peeked over the car's trunk and trained his gunsight on the big pine, waiting for another flash of light, a swatch of color, a glimpse of movement, anything that would betray the location of his assailant. Ten seconds passed. Twenty.

Bessie's front door opened. She half-crouched in the doorway, looking dazed and confused. "Cole?"

Afraid she might come out to the car, Cole stood and waved at her. "Get back inside! Get back!"

Light flashed under the pine and another shot exploded. A bullet broke a window on the passenger side and thumped into the front seat just as Cole crouched down.

Cole peeked over the rear fender at the house. The door was closed, and Bessie was nowhere in sight. He braced his hands on the trunk and fired two shots at the spot where he'd seen the flash of light. A branch of the pine broke off and fell, exposing a patch of tan clothing. Cole fired another shot and the swatch of tan melted into a thicket of green fir.

Cole pulled bullets from his belt loops and reloaded his gun while he watched the pine. He caught a glimpse of tan to the right of the tree and then it disappeared.

Cole trained his gun on that spot and watched for the man. A full minute passed. No flashes of light. No movement in the trees. No sound. Nothing.

He crawled to the car door, opened it, and radioed dispatch to report that he was under fire and needed backup. Thinking of Bessie, he requested an ambulance with orders for the driver to wait at the bend in the road below Leland Mundy's property until Cole gave him the all-clear.

He crept back to the rear of the car and watched the big pine. No sign of the shooter. He wanted to go after the bastard, but there was no cover between Bessie's house and the foot of the mountain, and the shooter's position pinned him down. He resigned himself to waiting for help.

Five minutes. Ten. Then he heard an engine fire up below him at the bend in the road. Tires squealed and the roar moved south toward Fox Run. The son of a bitch was running. Abandoning caution, Cole jig-jogged awkwardly down the road, hoping to get a look at the vehicle. He stopped at Leland's driveway. He saw nothing and the engine had already faded away.

His back throbbed. He leaned over for a few moments, then straightened up, holstered his gun, and walked back to his car. He leaned against it and worked his hand under his back brace to rub his iliac crest.

A jay shrieked, drawing his attention back to the tall white pine. A blaze of blue burst from the tree and flew west into the red setting sun. The blue speck grew smaller and smaller until it melted into orange and maroon clouds.

Cole stared after it. If the jay hadn't cried out, he wouldn't have turned and stumbled, and that first shot would have split his skull like a ripe melon, but the perfect timing of the bird's call meant nothing, he told himself. There were thousands of jays in the hollow. And yet . . .

A siren wailed. Cole turned toward the sound. Chase Dooley's patrol truck sped around the bend in the road and climbed the hill toward Bessie's house.

Chapter Nine

THE CONTRACT

ON A HOT FALL afternoon six months before he tried to kill Sheriff Cole Grundy at Bessie Tilden's house, Ray Middleditch turned off a state road outside Cheraw, South Carolina, onto a gravel road. A half mile into a pine forest, the gravel road petered out and a dirt road carried on from there to an abandoned brick manse sitting in a neglected field. Ray parked beside a falling-down outbuilding and walked toward the porch, sweeping the weeds ahead of him with a walking stick, watchful for snakes. He pushed his way through shrubs that had grown chest-high across a brick walkway, stopped at the foot of the porch steps, and looked up at the place. Its front door was missing and the windows on each side of it were busted out, dark holes that looked like gouged-out eyes on either side of a gaping mouth.

He climbed the steps. Cane chairs were strewn across the porch, lying on their sides. Ray righted the sturdiest one and sat down on it. He tipped it back on its hind legs to lean against the crumbling brick wall and looked out over a field of thistles to the edge of a forest. Crickets sawed in the weeds and cicadas clacked from the tree line.

In a short while, the cracked windshield of an old battered black Studebaker glared in the sunlight as it cut a path through the weeds and stopped beside the outbuilding. A tall, slim man got out of the car and fought his way to the porch through the overgrown shrubs. He was in his sixties and had thinning gray hair; he wore a blue business suit and oxblood wingtips.

"Boss," Ray said, nodding to him.

"Jim," Boss said. He brushed off his jacket and trousers, picked up one of the cane chairs next to Ray, and sat down on it.

"Changed my name," Ray said. "For professional reasons. I'm Ray Middleditch now."

Boss half smiled and crossed his skinny legs, his pants cuff riding up to expose a black nylon tube sock. "How have you been?" Boss said.

"Not great. Haven't been able to find regular work since Dillon fired me."

"I'm sorry about that. Dillon promised me he'd keep you on when I sold him the company, but he changed his mind. He claimed your skills didn't fit his needs. There was nothing I could do."

"So he told me," Ray said, not entirely convinced.

"Perhaps I can make it up to you. I have a special project for hire."

Ray smiled sardonically. Special project was Boss's code phrase for a shady deal. "So that's why you wanted to meet in the middle of nowhere. Why you drove up in an old rattletrap car no one would think you own."

A breeze mussed Boss's wispy gray hair. He smoothed it down with a delicate lily-white hand. The word prissy crossed Ray's mind, but he reminded himself that the package was deceiving. Ray had learned that the hard way.

"This project is an ugly matter," Boss said. "No one can know I'm associated with the dirty work required to resolve my dilemma."

"What sort of dilemma?"

"Salacious allegations toxic to my reputation."

"What kind of dirty work?"

"Homicides."

Ray paused. "How many?"

"Five."

Ray paused again. "Who are they?"

Boss handed Ray a list of names and addresses.

Ray looked it over. "Why do you want these people killed?"

"The old lady's been blackmailing me since July. She regards me as her retirement plan. Big monthly payments. Big enough that she knows I want to relieve myself of them. She claims she told the others about me and they share in her bounty. She says they'll expose me if anything happens to her, but I think she's lying to keep me from harming her."

"What makes you think she's lying?"

"I know her and the others. She doesn't trust them, and they don't trust her. They wouldn't shed a tear over her demise. In fact, they'd dance on her grave. My guess is she hasn't told them anything."

"Then why kill them?"

"I could be wrong. There's a small chance they know what the old lady knows. I can't take that chance."

"What does the old lady have on you?"

"That's none of your concern."

Ray thought it over. He didn't like it. "I have a history in Selk County. I'd have to dig in there for a good stretch of time to take them all out. Someone might recognize me."

"You'll have to work around that problem."

Ray shook his head. "The risk is too great."

"I've set the compensation high to account for that."

"How high?"

"Ten thousand dollars per head, fifty thousand in total, all cash, twenty-five up front, twenty-five when all five are dead. I've got the first installment with me."

The big numbers produced the desired effect, but Ray sensed that Boss wanted this deal badly enough to pay more. "Fifteen per head."

"Twelve."

Another counter might succeed, but provoking a man like Boss was a dangerous gambit. At twelve, Ray would make sixty thousand dollars, more than he could earn in two or three years even if he found a regular job, which seemed unlikely. "You'll cover reasonable expenses?"

"Like what?"

"I'll have to rent a house and buy a truck. I'll need a scanner to monitor police radio transmissions. Nothing unusual beyond that. Living expenses, food, gas, and the like."

"All right. Sixty thousand plus expenses."

"Deal."

Boss went out to the Studebaker and returned with a brown paper bag. "Here's the first thirty thousand. Cover your costs as you work the project. When you're done, I'll reimburse your expenses and pay the remaining thirty."

Ray nodded. "I'll need some time to set this up."

"How long?"

"Couple months. Once I've begun, I'll want to space out the killings to make them appear unrelated. Cole Grundy's shrewd. If he thinks he's dealing with a serial killer, he'll bring a lot of heat to bear."

"Dispose of them however you like, but kill the old lady first. She's the one milking me. Just in case I'm wrong about her and the others working together, make it look like she died of natural causes. That way, if the others have information against me, her death won't cause them to go public."

Ray nodded.

"A word of caution," Boss said. "I realize you have a score to settle with Grundy, but he's not part of our contract. Once you've completed my project, you can do as you please with him, but not before. I'm paying you to serve my interests, not to advance your personal goals. Understood?"

"I'll keep my emotions in check. I always do."

BUT SIX MONTHS after that meeting, Ray lost control of his emotions, broke his promise to Boss, and tried to murder Cole before completing the contract. By the time Ray got back to his rental house after shooting at Cole from Bobcat Mountain, night had fallen. He took an ice pack out of the freezer, slipped it into a cloth sleeve, hiked up his pants leg, and strapped the sleeve around his swollen knee.

He swallowed four arthritis pain pills, a quadruple dose. The bottle told him not to mix alcohol with the medication, but the hell with that. He poured a tall glass of Cutty Sark over ice. He sat down wearily in a wicker chair on the glassed-in back porch and sipped the blended scotch.

He let out a long breath and looked out at the night. Moonlight glistened on a broken-down rail fence at the far end of the yard. Beyond it, a dilapidated apple-packing shed stood on the edge of a defunct orchard, the branches of its trees barren, gnarled, and broken.

He took another swallow of scotch and thought about the afternoon's fiasco. He had thought he could still hit a medium-range target with a rifle if the conditions were right—an unsuspecting victim, the scope finely adjusted to compensate for his failing eyesight, the rifle braced on a tripod, little or no wind—but he hadn't test-fired Bowie's .30-06 beforehand. He was accustomed to placing his sighting eye close to his .30-30 Winchester's scope because it didn't recoil, but Bowie's weapon kicked like a mule. When he fired the first shot at Cole, the scope pounded the socket of his sighting eye and the barrel jumped two feet in the air. He swiped the blood out of his eye and took aim again, but it was no good after that. He flinched before every shot and missed by wide margins. He was lucky he got out of the hollow alive.

He ran the cool surface of the glass across his brow. Boss had been right when they met in October. Ray should have completed the contract before he turned his attention to Cole. Three of his five targets were already dead. Everyone thought the old lady died of natural causes. Someone else killed Betty Lou, which drove Leland to suicide, so no one could pin their deaths on Ray. Bowie's corpse, an unplanned side product of the project, still lay undiscovered on Bobcat Mountain. Ray was not implicated in anyone's death and the law didn't even know he was in Selk County. He had no reason to eliminate Cole now.

Hatred had distorted his judgment. It festered like a thorn under his skin, inflamed and poisonous, and it made him too eager. But that was unwise. Stalking Cole required patience. Killing him would tax all his skill, energy, and guile. The better course was to finish the contract and come back to Cole when he could take his time.

He took a big swallow of Cutty Sark and concentrated on the next hit.

Chapter Ten

A KETTLE OF VULTURES

March 2-3, 1967, Thursday night–Friday morning

AFTER THE ATTACK on Sheriff Grundy, Deputy Chase Dooley worked all night at Mrs. Tilden's property gathering evidence. When he arrived on the scene, he and the sheriff found Mrs. Tilden crying softly on the floor beside her piano with her hands covering her ears. She didn't seem to know where she was and the sheriff couldn't calm her down. When the rescue squad showed up, the sheriff told them to take her to Dolley Madison Hospital.

Deputy Toby Vess arrived a short while after the ambulance drove away, and he convinced the sheriff to go home and ice his back. The sheriff briefed them on the shooter's attack, and then Toby drove him home.

It was dark when the county's senior forensic technician arrived in his van, but Frank Woolsey was determined to collect as much evidence as possible during the night so he and Chase drove to Kirby's Store in Fox Run to borrow a generator and lights. By the time Toby Vess returned to Mrs. Tilden's house, they had rigged up the lights and were searching for bullets in and around Cole's car.

Toby had just come off a double shift, so he left at ten and Chase managed the crime scene through the night. By four in the morning Frank and Chase had found a bullet embedded in the road, two lodged in the car's frame, and another that had cracked the wheel well of the blown front tire. Then Chase located the entry point of a bullet in the engine head. By the time Frank dug out that last bullet, dawn had broken.

Chase sent Frank back to headquarters with the bullets and climbed Bobcat Mountain to investigate around the big white pine where the sheriff saw the shooter. The sun was up and the light was good when Chase reached the spot. A few feet below the bole of the tree, he found a patch of scuffed-up pine tags, and in front of that, three half-inch-square indentations in the soil, each about two inches deep, set in a wide triangle. He stared at them for a while before it came to him: a tripod. Chase looked down at the property below. From that spot, the shooter had an unobstructed view of the sheriff's patrol car less than a hundred yards away. A challenging shot with a handgun, but a sure hit with a scoped high-powered rifle sighted with a clear eye and braced on a tripod. The sheriff was lucky to be alive.

As the sun rose higher, a shaft of light pierced the pine canopy to fall on a piece of metal a few feet up the slope. Chase climbed up to it. A shell casing lay embedded in the pine tags. He picked it up with a kerchief and inspected it. It looked like a .30-06 long casing. He put it in an evidence pouch.

On the other side of the tree, he found a trail of disturbed pine tags heading south. He walked along it above the Mundys' house and then down to a graveled area next to a bend in Whippoorwill Hollow Road. Tires had made troughs in the gravel, but there were no treads there or on the shoulder. No boot prints either.

He walked the road back to the Tilden house and climbed in his truck, planning to take the shell casing to headquarters, when he saw a large kettle of vultures circling over Bobcat Mountain, forty or fifty birds, their wings tipping, banking in the wind, around, back, around again, dropping, rising, dropping again. A few disappeared below the tree tops.

Chase wondered what sort of carrion could have attracted so many buzzards. It had to be a large carcass, he thought, a white-tail deer or a black bear, but big game rarely ventured out of the sanctuary of the park so soon after hunting season.

He counted the birds. Twenty-three in the air, and twenty or more had dropped out of sight into the pines before he started counting. More descended while he watched and the others circled ever lower.

His curiosity piqued, he wanted to take a look, but the only way up there by truck was an old logging road. It would take him an hour to drive out of the hollow, around the mountain range, and back to the mouth of the logging road on Bobcat's other side. It wasn't worth the time, and he was too tired from working all night to climb the mountain on foot again.

Nothing up there could be related to the attack on the sheriff, he told himself. The summit was a good five hundred feet above the tripod prints, and the trail indicated that the shooter fled down the mountain, not up it.

Chase watched the last of the buzzards disappear below the treetops. He stared at the summit for a while longer, then cursed, got out of the truck, and walked across the Tilden property to the woods.

By the time he scaled the mountain, the buzzards were jousting in a patch of dense brush near the summit. They were big, ungainly black birds with red heads, squawking, flapping their wings, thrusting hooked sharp beaks at one another. They were in such a frenzy that shouting and waving his arms didn't drive them off. He fired two shots in the air and two more in the ground near the birds before most of them took flight. Even then, four hopped up the slope to the end of the old logging road and stood glaring at him with their beady eyes and hunched shoulders, like a quartet of undertakers.

When he approached the brush, the sickeningly sweet scent of decay knocked him back. He covered his nose and mouth with a kerchief before he started pulling away giant creeping vines to find a dead man in the undergrowth. The top of his head was blown off and there was a dry hole in his chest. Dried blood matted his blond hair and crusted what was left of his head and face. The buzzards had been at him for a while. Dead a week or more, Chase guessed.

The undertakers on the summit squawked as Chase searched the dead man's pockets. No identification. Nothing. He stepped out of the brush and looked around. Scuff marks in the pine tags ran from the patch of brush down the slope. He followed them. As he passed a clump of bushes, the sun glanced off a wine bottle. He picked it up with a kerchief. Hombre, its label said. Clean and unsoiled, the bottle hadn't been there long. He set it down by the bushes for retrieval later.

He followed the scuff marks around a fallen pine to its lower side. Bits of bone were scattered on pine tags there. A large concave piece picked clean of blood and tissue appeared to be part of a human skull. Rodents and birds had scratched in the soil all around it. They'd probably made off with more than they'd left behind.

Chase looked at the brush where the corpse lay and pieced together what he thought had occurred. The man had been killed where Chase stood, a bullet to the head and another to the heart. The killer dragged the corpse up to the patch of brush, leaving behind the trail of scuffed pine tags.

Chase scanned the terrain below him. Imprints in the tags caught his eye. He knelt beside them and a chill went up his spine. The same tripod that had stood down below had been set up here on the summit.

Chase took in the view. From that spot, a shooter could take aim at a target on the Mundy and Tilden properties and the field across the road. A long-range shot, three hundred yards, requiring a marksman. But a Baby Browning had killed Betty Lou, not a high-powered rifle. Chase stared at the Mundy property for a long time, trying to deduce a connection between the corpse in the brush and Betty Lou's murder or the attack on the sheriff. He could not.

Raucous squawking brought him out of his thoughts. The quartet of vultures had returned to the corpse. They flapped their wings and lunged at one another, fighting for dominance over their prize. Chase drew his gun and headed up to the corpse.

Chapter Eleven

THE PHOTOGRAPH

March 3, 1967, Friday noon

COLE'S back was sore the morning after the attack. He planned to take the day off, but without the distraction of work, he couldn't keep his mind off Carrie. He took a pain pill at ten o'clock, strapped on his back brace, and drove in to Jeetersburg to sheriffs' headquarters, a two-story brick building on the outskirts of town with a large lobby in the center of the first floor and two long wings stretching away on either side.

He parked behind the building and went to the county's lead forensic technician's office on the ground floor in the east wing. Frank Woolsey was a short, stocky man in his early sixties, bald with a fringe of long gray hair gathered into a ponytail that dribbled down his back, a moustache waxed and twisted into points like twin silver toothpicks, and intense green eyes under bushy gray eyebrows. When Cole walked in, Frank was behind his desk sipping a cup of coffee. His eyebrows darted upward at the sight of Cole. "Thought the doctors told you to stay home and rest your back."

Cole sat down across from Frank. "I'm on light duty."

"Light duty like dodging a killer's bullets?" Frank grumped.

"Light duty like sitting here talking to you," Cole said in a tone that warned Frank off the subject. "What did you find at Bessie's place?"

"Five bullets. Thirty-aught-six longs."

"The most popular hunting rifle in the county. Won't narrow the search much. You find anything at that big white pine?"

"It was too dark to search the mountain last night. Chase is up there now."

"Keep me up to speed. In the meantime, take a look at this." Cole spilled Bessie's envelope and photograph out of the evidence pouch onto Frank's desk.

Frank emitted a low whistle. "I always thought Betty Lou was a helluva looker, but I never got this good a look at her."

Cole explained the photograph's history. "Can you track down the photographer?"

"Fingerprints from fifteen years ago are long gone," Frank said. "Color photographs were more rare back then than today. That might help us narrow down where it came from." He squinted at it. "Faded with age. Poor quality. Background is browned out in the upper right corner." He withdrew a magnifying glass from his desk drawer and held it over the photo. "There's a bedpost to her left. A door on the wall behind her. Looks like a closet door." He put the glass down. "The picture's so old I doubt we can identify the photographer, but maybe we can find that bedroom. We'll need to make an enlargement. How about I ask Rupert Dilbey to help me?"

Dilbey owned a camera shop in Jeetersburg. "Good idea," Cole said.

Frank scooped the photograph and envelope into the pouch. "I'll get on it."

COLE'S OFFICE was on the second floor directly above the lobby. A square blond-oak desk sat in front of file cabinets along one wall across from a conference table and floor-to-ceiling windows with a view of Beacon Hill, a rocky knoll that rose up out of the flatlands around Jeetersburg.

At noon, Mabel Lucas, Cole's secretary, sat across the desk from him, her legs crossed, a yellow pad in her lap, her pen poised over it. Forty years old, as tall as Cole, big-boned with a round face, black eyes, and coal-black hair gathered into a tight bun on top of her head, she wore a shapeless high-necked black dress that fell to midcalf, white socks, and black and white saddle shoes. With a photographic memory and an IQ Cole guessed was higher than any two of his deputies put together, Mabel was one of Cole's best resources. He had offered her a promotion to deputy four times in the five years she'd worked for him. She'd turned him down each time, saying she had enough on her plate with seven children, thank you very much, so he'd done the best he could to tap into her outsized talent by loading her up with assignments far beyond normal secretarial duties and paying her way above scale.

She told him about Chase's discovery of the corpse on Bobcat Mountain.

Cole was surprised. "Any connection to Betty Lou?"

"Chase said he doesn't know yet."

Cole looked out the window. A cluster of billowy clouds floated across the sun, casting a shadow over Beacon Hill. He thought the man's murder was almost certainly related to Betty Lou's killing and the attack on him. All three took place over a short span of time in a remote, sparsely populated, generally peaceful area.

"Frank is headed up there now," Mabel said. "Shirley West is on her way from Roanoke." She flipped a page on her yellow pad. "I checked with Dolley Madison about Bessie Tilden. The nurse said she's dehydrated and exhausted, but she should recover in a day or two. I sent her flowers with a card from you."

Mabel turned another page and tapped her pen on the pad. "I went through the files you gave me." Cole had asked her to review Leland's plumbing company records. "Found something interesting. Leland started a big plumbing job in Greene County for Carter's Construction Company on May twenty-eight, 1965. He worked on it through the end of September. Receipts from a motel in Stanardsville show he stayed up there every weeknight that summer. That job caught my attention because he started it close to the date he bought the murder weapon. Jenkins Gun Shop's record of the sale of the Baby Browning to Leland is dated June third, 1965. I'd been puzzled about his purchase of that little gun before I looked at his business records. He owned a Winchester rifle, a double-barrel twelve-gauge shotgun, and a .357 Smith and Wesson handgun. Seems clear he favored powerful weapons, but Jenkins's sales clerk told Chase he asked for the smallest revolver they had in stock."

It only took Cole a moment to pick up Mabel's line of reasoning. "You think he bought it for Betty Lou?"

"The timing fits. He bought it five days after he started a job that required him to be away from home weeknights. They lived way out there by the park with no one nearby who could help Betty Lou if someone took after her. I figure Leland gave her the Baby Browning for protection because she wasn't comfortable handling his guns."

Cole stared out the window. A shaft of sunlight pierced the clouds. A dozen crows flew in a line across the face of Beacon Hill, their wings glistening like black jewels as they passed through the wedge of gold.

Cole thought about the little revolver and Betty Lou. Bessie's theory that an illicit lover murdered Betty Lou might make more sense than he'd originally believed. "Bessie says Betty Lou's been cheating on Leland for years. She thinks we should look for one of the men she took up with."

Mabel's black caterpillar eyebrows came together. "I see what you're thinking. The Baby Browning was small enough to fit in her purse. If she was promiscuous, she would have been smart to carry it with her in case one of her boyfriends turned bad on her. And if one of them turned real bad, he could have taken her gun away from her and killed her with it."

Cole adjusted his lumbar pillow and leaned back into it. "Leland told me he heard she was seeing a man in Jeetersburg. We need to know who that man is."

"Chase has been trying to identify him. He talked to Lee Beaumont yesterday. He's the contractor Leland worked for the week before Betty Lou's murder. He said he saw Betty Lou carousing with a man he didn't know in Kelly's Place on a Saturday night in January. Chase talked to Kelly McNiel. She said she'd talk to the staff and check her records. She called this morning and asked to meet with Chase to tell him what she found out. Chase'll be on Bobcat the rest of the day, so I told her you'd come by her office at two this afternoon." Mabel placed a manila folder on Cole's desk. "Chase's notes about his talk with Lee Beaumont."

Cole rolled the boyfriend theory around in his mind. It didn't feel right to him. "We may be sliding off track. The evidence against Leland is powerful: Betty Lou's blood on his shirt, his prints on the Baby Browning, the fact that he had it in his pocket when I found him on the porch. Reba's story that he was with her at the time of the murder could be a lie."

Mabel swept threads of hair that had broken loose from her bun away from her face. "Could be, but there's evidence that points away from Leland, too. The tire track near the gate, the headlights Bessie saw after she heard a gunshot, and the big dark car she saw driving away. If Leland killed Betty Lou, who drove that car and what was he doing at the gate at the time of the kill shot?"

Cole tried to adjust his thinking. "Maybe a boyfriend followed her home that night. Called her out to the gate. They argued. She pulled the gun. They struggled for control. He shot her, accidently or in a fit of anger." Cole pondered the razor-thin foundation supporting such speculation. "I don't like it. A string of maybes with no proof backing it up."

"No proof yet. Like you said, we need to find the man she was seeing." Mabel looked at her watch. "It's almost one. I'll leave you alone so you can prepare for your meeting with Kelly." She went to the door, stopped, and looked back at him. "Any idea who attacked you?"

"All we know so far is he fired a scoped thirty-aught-six rifle."

Mabel looked concerned. "We know more than that. No one knew you were headed to Bessie Tilden's place yesterday except the dispatcher, so we know your attacker had to be watching you. He followed you to Bessie's house, climbed a steep mountain carrying a heavy firearm, and lay in wait. He invested substantial time and energy in trying to kill you. He'll likely try again."

"I hope he does. I'll be ready for him."

She pursed her lips. "Be careful, Cole." She lingered in the doorway and then walked away.

Cole stared after her. He looked up at a large, framed photograph of his predecessor, Sheriff Robey Musgrove. His jowly face sagged and dark bags drooped under his bone-tired eyes. He'd been a hard charger all his life, but when his wife died of a heart attack, he faltered. About six months before his term expired, Robey announced that he would not stand for reelection in the fall. He endorsed Cole as his successor, and because of that, no one ran against him. Robey died in his sleep of a brain aneurysm the following year. He was sixty-three.

Cole was thirty-two when Robey stepped down, young and energetic, his potential as yet unrealized, his life filled with promise. Robey's rapid decline had puzzled him back then. Now he understood it. Carrie had been dead three years, and the pain of her loss had not diminished.

Now, in his eighth term as sheriff, Cole was sixty-two, and Chase was almost ready to take the baton. A more experienced deputy like Karson Deford could handle the job, too, but Mabel might be the best of the three. She was doing half Cole's job now. If he could convince her to take a job in the field, she'd be more than ready in a year or two.

He looked at the doorway. The familiar dull ache pulsed in his lower back. He pulled out his shirttail and rubbed the sore spot. Mabel cared more about his safety than he did, he thought.

Chapter Twelve

THE ACTOR

March 3, 1967, Friday afternoon

AFTER COLE REVIEWED the notes Mabel gave him about Chase's search for the man Betty Lou was seeing before her murder, he drove into Jeetersburg to Kelly's Place, the most popular restaurant/bar in southwestern Virginia. He had known the owner, Kelly McNiel, all his life. Carrie and Cole and Kelly and her husband, Charley Hix, were good friends until Charley walked out on Kelly and their daughter without warning twenty-five years ago.

When Charley disappeared, Cole couldn't square the abandonment with the man he knew. He'd thought he could talk some sense into him, but no one knew where he'd gone. Cole put out a statewide alert with instructions not to approach and to report his whereabouts to the Selk County sheriff's office. Three days later, a state trooper spotted Charley's car at a motel in Danville a hundred miles southeast of Selk County.

It was almost midnight when Cole got there. Charley's green Oldsmobile had paled to the color of pea soup under a yellow floodlight perched on a telephone pole at the end of a rundown motel's long row of rooms. Cole walked across the lot, the gravel crunching under his boots. He stopped in front of the last metal door, whose number 30 hung upside down from a loose rivet. Its dull pink paint was pocked at the base like someone had tried to kick it in with steel-toed boots.

He rapped on the door. A light came on inside. The door opened an inch, and Charley peered at Cole through the slit.

"You and me need to talk," Cole said.

"I have nothing to say to you."

"I'm not leaving here until we talk."

Charley stared at him for a few moments and then shut the door. Cole heard him moving around inside the room. A minute later the chain lock rattled and the door opened. Charley stood in the doorway in an undershirt and wrinkled black slacks, barefooted, his curly black hair pressed down on one side and sticking up on the other, his face flushed. "What do you want?"

"You owe a good friend an explanation for what you've done to your family."

"What I do with my life is none of your business," Charley said angrily.

Cole dug in. "I'm not going away until we talk."

Charley looked back inside the room and then at Cole.

"Give me five minutes," Cole said. "If I can't talk some sense into you by then, I'll leave you alone."

Charley gave Cole an aggravated look. "Five minutes," he said. He crossed the room, sat on the edge of the bed, and lit a cigarette. "Not a second longer."

Cole stepped inside. The room smelled like a wet dog. A bedside table lamp cast it in dim light. Twisted and tangled sheets lay on the bed. The bedspread and blanket had been thrown on the floor. Brown spots stained the paper-thin carpet. The paint above the bathroom door was peeling.

Cole sat in a chair to the right of the front door.

A rip in the lampshade painted Charley's face with a vertical yellow stripe. "Say your piece and get out," he said.

"Jerry Beesecker told me he offered to buy your business last winter. You turned him down and said you'd never sell out. Monday morning you showed up in his office unannounced and said you'd take his best offer if he cut you a cashier's check that day. He asked why you changed your mind. You gave him no answer."

Cole paused, hoping Charley would engage, but he didn't say anything.

"Kelly told Carrie she woke up Tuesday morning to find your note on the kitchen table. All it said was you didn't love her anymore. She said you took all the proceeds from the sale of your business and left her with nothing."

"I inherited my business from my father," Charley said. "Kelly had no ownership interest in it. Besides, I gave her the house. I left the deed on the kitchen table with my note. I guess she forgot to tell Carrie about that." Charley inhaled and blew out a stream of smoke. "How is this any of your concern? It's not a crime to quit your business and leave your family."

"It's not against the law. That doesn't make it right."

Charley scowled. "Right? I don't know what's right. More to the point, I don't care what's right."

Cole searched Charley's face for some remnant of the man he knew, but the man sitting before him was a stranger.

"I've known you all my life," Cole said. "The man I know couldn't break Kelly's heart and leave his little girl without a daddy. What's going on, Charley? What happened to make you run off like this?"

A thump came from inside the bathroom, followed by a murmur. A line of light came through the crack at the base of the bathroom door. Charley glanced at Cole and then looked away.

"I see we're not alone," Cole said.

Charley put his cigarette out in a tray on the bedside table and leaned forward, his forearms on his knees, his hands clasped together. "It's why I left," he said in a gravelly voice.

"You're throwing your life away," Cole said. "Is she worth it?"

"I'm not throwing my life away. I'm taking control of it."

They were quiet for a long while, Cole staring at Charley, Charley looking down at his clasped hands.

Charley came out of his thoughts and stood up. "Your five minutes is up, Cole. Don't come looking for me again. I'm through with Kelly and Rachel and you and everybody else I knew. I don't want to see or hear from any of you again."

Cole had his explanation, and Charley's tone left no room for argument. There was nothing more Cole could do. He went to the door, then looked back at Charley. "You're not the man I thought you were," he said. He gave Charley a long last look and left the room.

AT THE TIME Charley left Kelly, Cole didn't think she could survive his betrayal, but she'd done much more than that. She filed for divorce, reclaimed her maiden name, and gave it to Rachel. She made barely enough to support them by waiting tables at Bodine's Bar, but when the owner drove the business into the ground, Kelly somehow convinced First Virginia Bank to loan her the funds to buy it out of bankruptcy. She renamed it Kelly's Place, built it up into a thriving business, and parlayed the profits into a network of valuable holdings that included controlling interests in a construction company, a real estate firm, a mortgage company, a furniture store, and a portfolio of distressed properties she remodeled and sold. Now sixty years old, Kelly was by far the most successful businesswoman in southwestern Virginia, and arguably the most successful businessperson, period.

Kelly's Place was a long, low white-brick structure sandwiched between a storage facility and a garden-office complex. Cole drove down the paved alley behind the buildings and parked in an asphalt lot behind the restaurant.

Pausing at the back door, he tried to recall when he'd seen Kelly last. She undoubtedly came to Carrie's funeral, but he was in shock that day and didn't remember much about it. He searched his memory. Her daughter's graduation ceremony at Jefferson State University Law School, he thought. Eight years ago he and Carrie sat with Kelly in an outdoor amphitheater and watched Rachel cross a stage in a cap and gown. He didn't remember much about Rachel or Kelly that day. He remembered only Carrie. He could still see the sunlight kissing her red hair and her dimpled smile as the law school dean boomed out, "Rachel Devon McNiel, summa cum laude."

Cole swallowed hard and went inside.

Chapter Thirteen

KELLY'S PLACE

March 3, 1967, Friday afternoon

KELLY MCNIEL WAS at her desk looking at the file she had prepared for Cole. His knock came at two o'clock sharp. She called out, "Come in."

Her office was in the rear corner of the building. A maple secretary and matching chairs sat on a cardinal and green oriental rug. French doors opened onto a small courtyard with a copper birdbath and a yellow wooden bench shaded by a walnut tree, all enclosed by a grape-stake fence that butted up against the brick wall of the building next door.

Cole stepped into the room, took off his hat, and came around the desk. She stood and they hugged. She stepped back and smiled at him. "It's been too long."

"For sure." He looked her up and down. "You look the same."

"I am the same. Out of sorts and ornery." She laughed.

"I don't know about that," he said with a shy smile.

She pointed to the chair in front of her desk. "Have a seat

He sat down.

She did, too, and looked him over. He was a good-looking man, big shoulders, deep chest, strong arms, one of those rare men whose baldness improved his looks. His broad forehead drew attention to his warm brown eyes, square jaw, and strong chin, but he didn't look well. He'd gained weight. His face was pale and drawn; his eyes sunken and dark.

"First time I've been in here," he said, his sad eyes moving around the office. "It's nice." He looked up at an oil painting hanging on the wall behind Kelly. "She looks like you."

Kelly looked up at the portrait. A tall, slim middle-aged woman with an aquiline nose, striking hazel eyes, and auburn hair in an olive tweed jacket and long, tight skirt leaned casually on the high back of a wing chair, her direct stare conveying confidence and worldliness.

"Rachel found it in Boston when she summer-clerked for a law firm there," Kelly said. "It's a self-portrait by Polly Thayer. Rachel says it reminds her of me because she looks like she doesn't give a damn what anybody thinks." Kelly laughed again.

He gazed at the portrait with a somber expression. "She could be your twin."

"Maybe twenty years ago. Thayer was forty years old when she painted it."

"You haven't aged. You look just like her."

"You're nice to say so."

His eyes fell to his hat in his lap. He fingered its brim absent-mindedly.

Kelly was struck by the change in his manner. It was under-standable. The way Carrie died would have killed a lesser man. She was glad Cole survived, but his transformation was hard to witness.

"Are you all right, Cole?"

"I'm fine," he said too quickly. "Mabel said you have some information about Betty Lou Mundy."

"I put together a file of her bar tabs." She handed him a folder. "This is your copy."

He opened it. "Looks like the first night she came here was New Year's Eve."

"That's right. Blanche Tolliver waited on her. She says Betty Lou showed up about six thirty, sat in booth eight, ordered fried chicken, green beans, and creamed corn, and drank two glasses of white wine with her supper."

Cole raised his eyebrows. "That was two months ago. How come Blanche remembers so much detail?"

"It'd be hard to forget anything about Betty Lou that night. She walked in here wearing a red blouse cut low with a push-up bra to show everything she had up top, a skin-tight black leather miniskirt, red stilettos, heavy black eyeliner, blood-red lipstick. When I saw her, I told my people to keep a close eye on her. A woman who dresses like she wants to give it away to any man in the place can set off a hell of a bar fight."

Cole looked at the file. "The receipt for that night calls out sixty-eight dollars for drinks at the bar."

"When she finished her meal, she climbed up on a barstool beside Elwood Critzer and gave him a heavy come-on. She paid for their drinks and they left together."

"Elwood Critzer," Cole said, shocked. "Elwood's close to seventy years old, and I've never known him to take a drink, much less cheat on his wife."

"That fits what I saw of him. He didn't know how to drink, but he knocked down quite a few that night. I was tending bar when he came in. He showed up about six and went straight to the bar looking like his best dog had died. I tried to cheer him up, but he wouldn't talk. He was three drinks into it when Betty Lou put the moves on him. Other men tried to get her attention, but she wouldn't give anybody a chance except Elwood."

Cole shook his head. He flipped through the other receipts. "Looks like Elwood paid all the tabs after that first night."

"Larry Stillwell was the bartender on shift the next night, January one. He says Elwood met Betty Lou here about eight. They left together about midnight. Best I can tell from talking with the staff and looking at the bar tabs, they followed that pattern for the next several Fridays and Saturdays."

"I see here that Elwood paid a bar tab February eighteenth. The night of the murder." Cole looked down at the floor and let out a heavy breath. "What the hell was Elwood thinking?"

"A pretty woman wanted to take him to bed. From what I saw, that blocked out the rest of his brain waves."

Cole looked back up at Kelly. "Betty Lou ever come in here before New Year's Eve?"

"None of my staff remembers seeing her before then. My book-keeper checked records going back two years and found no receipts from her or Leland, but someone else could have paid her tab."

"What about Elwood?"

"He'd never set foot in my place till New Year's Eve."

Cole seemed to think over what she'd told him. "You hear any rumors about Betty Lou running around with men before she took up with Elwood?"

"Owning a night spot teaches you not to put much stock in rumors. I don't believe anything I hear and only about half of what I see."

The corners of Cole's mouth lifted slightly and a smile almost broke through. "I don't normally pay attention to gossip either, but I don't have much to go on in this case. I've heard she played around, but my source is unreliable."

Kelly pushed back from her desk and crossed her legs. "For what it's worth, which is probably nothing, I heard tales over the years that Betty Lou slept around, not the brazen way she behaved here in my place, but more discreetly, behind closed doors."

"Did the gossips name any of the men?"

"I never heard any names."

"Where'd you hear these rumors?"

"The place where all gossip in Selk County originates."

"Gertie Wilson's Beauty Salon."

"Tongues wag under the hair dryers, and Gertie passes along everything she hears."

Cole looked down at the folder and said nothing, seemingly lost in thought. Kelly's concern for him grew. A disturbing emotion washed over her. It was a stranger to her at first and she didn't recognize it. Then it settled in and she understood. Envy. She envied Carrie. A good man had loved her so much that he still loved her even though she was three years gone. There was a time, back when Charley first left her, when she would have killed for a man to love her like that, but fighting to make a life for Rachel had crowded out everything else, and now it was too late to pursue such a dream. Her eyes filled with tears and she bowed her head to wipe them away, bringing herself under control while Cole was still lost in thought.

A blue jay shrieked in the courtyard outside. She saw Cole look out the French doors at the jay on the lip of the birdbath. It dipped its beak in the water and fluttered its wings, its brilliant plumage sparkling in speckled sunlight. Cole's eyes followed the bird's movements and she knew what he was thinking.

She cleared her throat to make sure her voice would be steady. "Carrie loved blue jays."

Cole looked at her.

"They were her favorites when we were kids," she said. "Cardinals caught her fancy, too, but she liked jays the most. Mischief makers, she called them. She thought they were her soulmates."

Cole's eyes glistened. "Yesterday," he said, his voice husky, "a blue jay cried out to me. I thought maybe . . ." He looked down at the folder and swallowed hard.

"Have you spoken to Peter lately, Cole?"

He looked uncomfortable. "Not since the funeral. They keep him busy at the hospital. I don't want to bother him."

An awkward silence followed while Kelly continued to study Cole. She would have thought his son could have been of some comfort to him, but maybe not. Years ago, Carrie hinted that something had come between Cole and Peter when he was a little boy, but she wouldn't open up about it.

Cole put on his hat and pulled the brim down low, shielding his face from her view. He stood. "Thanks, Kelly. You've been a big help."

She came around her desk and gave him a hug. "Take care of yourself, Cole Grundy," she whispered in his ear. She leaned back and patted him on his chest. "Don't be such a stranger." She turned her back to him so he couldn't see the emotion in her eyes.

When she heard the door close, she sat down and wiped away tears. When she looked out at the courtyard, the jay was gone.

Chapter Fourteen

THE SNAKE

March 3, 1967, Friday afternoon

WHILE HER MOTHER and Cole met on the other side of town, Rachel McNiel was sitting across her desk from Reba Emley for the third time. Rachel had decided this would be a come-to-Jesus moment for Reba. Up to that point, Reba had refused to tell her whether her mother had sold her like she had her sister, and whether she'd ever fired the pistol Betty Lou gave her at anyone other than Betty Lou.

"Here's where we stand," Rachel said. "I can't protect you if I don't know everything. Answer my questions or I won't represent you. I won't charge you for our time together, and I won't divulge what you've told me to anyone unless you want me to talk to the lawyer who replaces me. So it's your call. What do you want to do?"

Reba lit a Kool. She blew smoke to the ceiling and glared at Rachel. "I don't want another lawyer. You're the only woman lawyer in town. It's easier to talk about Leland and Betty Lou with a woman."

"Apparently not easy enough to tell me the whole story."

Reba pulled hard on the cigarette once, twice, a third time. "I've never told anyone the things you want to know. No one knows. Not even Walt. Why do I have to tell you?"

"Because you're involved in a murder investigation. Your life is on the line. I won't stand beside you and risk that you'll lose it because I'm surprised by something you didn't tell me. That's my decision. It's final."

Reba stood and walked over to the window, her back to Rachel, smoking. A full minute passed. Rachel waited. Another minute. And another. Then Reba said something so softly that Rachel couldn't hear her.

"I'm sorry, Reba. What did you say?"

"There was a man," Reba said hoarsely. She turned around, walked slowly back to the desk, stubbed the cigarette out, and crossed her arms over her chest. "He wore a mask. He came at night in the dark." She sat down in the chair and sank back into it. "He did whatever he wanted to do."

Rachel's throat tightened. "How old were you?"

"Ten the first time."

Reba's answer kicked Rachel in the gut. "How long did this go on?"

"Two years."

Rachel fought off the tears she felt coming. "How often?"

"Couple nights every month. More in the summer." Reba's eye twitched. She swiped at it.

Rachel laid down her pen and wiped her eyes. "Did you tell anyone?"

"The man said he'd made a deal with Momma. If I told, they'd kill me and bury me where no one would find me."

Rachel leaned back in her chair and looked out the window. A yellow city bus rolled by on Lighthorse Street, smoke pumping from its exhaust pipe. "Your mother made this deal with the man after Betty Lou gave you the gun, right?"

"Yes."

"Why didn't you use it to keep him at bay?"

"I was afraid he'd kill me if I missed my aim. If I hit him and killed him, I was afraid Momma would do me in." Reba closed her eyes and pinched the bridge of her nose. "But after two years of what he did to me, I was so miserable I didn't care if they killed me."

Rachel hesitated to ask Reba if she'd fired the gun at the man, trying to game out the legal consequences of worst-case scenarios before she pressed on, but Reba's story came tumbling out like a waterfall anyway.

"I hid the gun under the pillow," Reba said. "When he got on top of me, I gripped the pistol and brought it down by my side. Took me a few minutes to get my courage up. Then I put it flush against his belly and fired. It made a little pop, like a toy cap pistol. He jumped off of me. Stood by the bed, holding his side. I pointed the gun at him but my hands shook so bad I couldn't pull the trigger." She took a deep breath and shuddered. "I was scared he would charge at me and take the gun away, but he just stared at me. The mask got wet under his eyes, and he said, 'Why?' Only thing he ever said to me out loud." She put her hand over her eyes, then dropped it into her lap, looking tired and spent. "I scooted off the bed and pointed the gun at him. Said, 'You come at me I'll shoot you dead.' He didn't move. He just stood there, his hand holdin his side, shakin his head back and forth real slow, makin chokin noises."

Reba lit another cigarette with a trembling hand. She drew hard on it and blew smoke across the room. "I yelled at him. 'You get out! Get out now and don't you ever come back!' He put on his clothes. Gave me a long hard look and left the house. I never saw him again."

Rachel gave Reba a few moments, and then said, "Did your mother find out you shot him?"

"Momma left the house that night when the man showed up. I

cleaned up the blood he dripped on the floor and burned the sheets, but she wouldn't have noticed the blood anyway. She came home after midnight with old man Gordon Slaughter hangin all over her like a dog on a bitch in heat, both of em so drunk they couldn't walk straight. They went back in the bedroom and slammed the door. Bout a week later, she asked me how it went down with the man that night, like she was suspicious about why he stopped comin around. I told her he did his business and left the house, same as always. She gave me a hard look but she didn't ask any more questions about it."

Rachel couldn't speak. She looked out the window. A middle-aged businessman clutching a briefcase walked along the sidewalk. Trash cans clattered farther down Lighthorse. A cardinal alit on a low branch of a sycamore, its feathers ruffled by a light wind.

"Do you know who this man was?" Rachel said, her voice low and menacing.

"He never said his name."

"What did he look like?"

"I don't know. He wore a mask. Black. Leather. It fit tight around his head with a zipper up the back and holes for his mouth and eyes."

"What color were his eyes?"

"Brown."

"How tall was he? What body style?"

"Tall. Thin. Butt-white skin."

"What color was his hair?"

"Black fuzz on his neck below the mask. Black hair on his chest and around his privates."

"How old was he?"

"It was hard to tell, but he didn't have any gray hair, and his skin wasn't wrinkled or sagging."

"Any scars, moles, birthmarks?"

"No."

"What did his voice sound like?"

Reba hesitated. "He didn't want me to hear his voice. He whispered," she said. "He hissed like a snake."

Rachel shivered.

Reba inhaled and blew smoke across the room.

"What type of clothes did he wear?"

"Nice clothes. Khaki pants. Gray slacks sometimes. Collared dress shirts. Twice he wore a suit. Black socks, the type that came up to his knees. Dress shoes. Shined up good."

"Did he wear rings or a watch?"

"He wore a gold wedding ring. Plain band." Reba looked grim. "I remember the first time I saw it. I felt sorry for his wife, whoever she was. Figured she was even worse off than me."

Rachel looked over her notes. A tall, thin man with brown eyes and black hair, probably under forty, middle class or better off, married. Not much to go on, especially thirty years after the fact. "You've never told anyone?"

Reba shook her head.

"You shot him and he went away. Why didn't you reach out to someone after that? A teacher, a friend, the police."

"Momma didn't go away. I was more afraid of her than him."

"The county would have taken you from your mother, placed you in a good home."

"I was twelve years old. I didn't know about county services. Besides, the way I came up, I didn't trust anybody. Couple years later, when I couldn't stand how I was livin, I ran away to the home for beat-up women that used to be on Stuart Street. They made Momma sign some papers givin me up and they put me in the Baptist orphanage on Fremont Road. I know now I was safe there, but back then I was afraid she might sneak in the place and kill me. Later on, when I got older, I blocked it out of my memory so I could go on with my life. Livin through it was bad enough. I didn't want to talk about it and relive it all again. And I never did till now." Reba blew smoke ceilingward.

Rachel tried to imagine the horror of Reba's childhood. She

could not. She looked down at her notes. Touch the open wound, her mentor Burton Jaffee had said, but she doubted Burton had ever handled a case like this.

"What do we do now?" Reba said.

Rachel pulled her thoughts together. "We'll go over the risks and advantages of disclosure. How much you reveal to the sheriff is your decision."

"What do you think I should do?"

"It's a hard call, but if I were you, I'd tell the sheriff everything. Now."

"Even the part about the man?"

"Especially the part about the man."

Reba's hand shook as she brought her cigarette to her lips. She inhaled deeply. "I don't know if I can do it. It's awful hard on me to talk about him."

"If you decide you want the sheriff to know, I'll talk for you."

Reba looked out the window, her eyes red and tired. "Wish I'd killed him that night," she said softly.

"If we can bring him to justice," Rachel said, "he may end up agreeing with you about that."

Chapter Fifteen

THE PIT BULL

March 3, 1967, Friday afternoon

AT THREE THAT SAME AFTERNOON, Ray Middleditch drove his truck into Saddleback Cove and turned off Whiskey Road onto a dirt road. The sky was clear and the temperature mild, a harbinger of the spring to come. Ray had taken off his winter coat and set it on the seat beside him, covering his .357 Magnum.

The truck heaved and swayed through scrub pines and dense brush to a clearing where a dilapidated frame house slouched in a barren yard between a caved-in shed and a dead mulberry tree. A rusty window screen lay on the porch roof. A gutter hung down at a slant across an upstairs window.

Ray parked at the edge of the weeds. He had never met Deputy Walt Ballard, but the man smoking on the stoop fit his description: forties, average height, stout with a beer belly, thinning brown hair, sad basset-hound eyes. The service revolver at his hip removed any doubt that Ray had located his next target.

The deputy stared at Ray with bleary, bloodshot eyes and Ray noted the gallon jug between his feet. His scanner had intercepted

Ballard's call to dispatch that morning claiming he was too sick to come to work. Drunk sick, apparently.

A face-to-face confrontation hadn't been Ray's preference. He had intended for Thurman Bowie to take Walt out, but blowing Bowie's brains out had left Ray no alternative but to kill him himself. A long-range shot still would have been preferable, but Ray's unsuccessful attack on Cole discouraged him from trying that gambit again. Besides, with the element of surprise on his side, the risk of a close-in kill shot was negligible.

That assessment changed when Ray started to get out of his truck and a huge brindle pit bull with cropped ears and a head as broad as a frying pan scrambled out from under the porch, barking furiously. Foam flew from his chops and his thick body quivered as his powerful jaws snapped.

Ray pulled his legs back inside the truck and shut the door. He considered aborting the effort, but he thought better of it. He couldn't drive off now that Ballard had gotten a good a look at him and his truck.

He eyed the space from the truck to the stoop: about fifty feet. From that distance, Ray would miss his target with a handgun one time out of two, and Ballard was known to be a reasonably good shot. He looked drunk, but Bowie claimed to be a crack shot when he was plastered. Ballard might be, too. Ray had to get closer. He rolled down his window. "Call off your dog."

"Buck! Down!" Ballard pointed to a spot in the dirt beside the stoop. Buck lay down on his belly and lowered his head, a low rumble coming from his throat, his yellow eyes trained on Ray from under his furrowed brow. "Shut up!" The rumble shut down, but the eyes didn't soften.

Ray saw a chain coiled up beside a stake a few feet from the stoop. "Can you chain him up? He don't look too friendly."

"What's your business here, mister?"

"Reba sent me."

This had the effect Ray had hoped for. Ballard's eyes widened. "Who are you?"

"Reuben Emley, Reba's uncle, her father's younger brother."

"She never mentioned no uncle to me."

"I moved to California a long time ago. Lost touch with Hazel and the girls. I hoped to come back here and reconnect in my old age, but looks like I showed up in the midst of tragedy. Hazel dead, Betty Lou murdered. Reba's all I got left." Ray donned a sad, wistful smile. "I was able to join up with her yesterday. Hadn't seen her since she was a little girl."

Ballard looked skeptical. "You say she sent you here?"

"That's right. She told me all about you. Asked me to come out here and have a sit-down with you."

A spark of hope flashed in Ballard's eyes. The rumors were true, Ray thought. Ballard was still a sap for his ex-wife.

"A sit-down? About what?"

"Chain up your dog and I'll come inside the house and explain."

"He don't need to be chained up. He does what I tell him."

Ray forced a smile. "I don't know. He looks like he thinks I'm a piece a red meat. I'd feel a helluva sight better if you restrained him."

Ballard flicked his cigarette into the dust, stepped off the stoop, and snapped the chain onto Buck's spiked collar. "All right, but he don't need it. He minds me good."

Ray picked up the Colt Python and jammed it into his belt at the small of his back. He opened the door and got out slowly, watching Buck.

A crisp wind blew across the clearing, ruffling Ray's thinning silver hair. From where he stood beside the truck, he couldn't determine the length of Buck's chain. He put his hands in his pockets and grinned, trying to look casual and friendly as he walked toward the porch. "I'm countin on that chain, by God. It don't hold him back, he'll chew my ass off."

"The chain'll hold, but he's a good dog. He won't come at you unless I tell him to."

Ray broadened his grin. "I sure-to-God hope so."

Buck glared at Ray and whined.

"Shut up, Buck!"

Ray had hoped Ballard would help close the distance between them, but the deputy stayed rooted to a spot between the stoop and Buck.

Ray stepped forward cautiously, his eyes darting back and forth from Ballard to Buck. Thirty feet. Twenty. Ray felt the barrel of the gun pressing against the base of his spine. Sweat trickled down his back. At fifteen feet, Buck jumped up and snarled. Ray froze.

"Down!"

Buck got down on his belly and whined.

"Stay!" Ballard smiled at Ray. "You don't need to worry now, mister. He won't go nowhere till I release him."

Ray looked from Buck to Ballard to the .357 Magnum in Ballard's hip holster. His eyes fell on the jug sitting on the steps. "What you drinkin?"

"Mule Kick. Cecil Garrison's brew. You want a taste?"

Ray smiled. "I wouldn't turn down a swallow or two."

Ballard leaned over to pick up the jug. Ray pulled the Python free of his belt. As Ballard straightened up, Ray aimed at the center of his chest. Buck jumped to his feet and snarled, causing him to flinch. Boom-Crack! The bullet hit the house, wide to the left of Ballard, who dropped the jug and reached for his gun.

Buck emitted a deep-throated cry that rattled Ray just as he fired his second shot. The bullet hit the house wide to the right.

Ballard's gun cleared its holster. Ray steadied his hand and fired a third shot. Ballard screamed, staggered to his right, and fell on the stoop, blood spurting from his right shoulder.

Ray glanced at Buck, who was barking furiously, but staying put.

Ballard tried to point his gun at Ray. Ray fired again, hitting him in the thigh. Ballard dropped his gun and grabbed his leg. Gritting his teeth, he choked out, "Sic him."

Buck bounded to Ray in two big strides. Ray's bullet creased the top of the dog's head just as Buck's front paws pounded into Ray's chest like twin hammer blows. Ray hit the ground, dropping his gun as Buck's jaws clamped down on his forearm like a pair of bolt cutters. The dog swung his big head back and forth furiously, jerking Ray's arm to and fro like the limb of a rag doll, threatening to rip it out of the socket. Ray scrambled backward, flailing at the dog's rock-hard bloody head with his fist. He fought his way up to his knees, fell, got up on his knees again, and scuffled backward, trying to pull his arm free. Buck's hot breath smelled like rancid meat; his yellow eyes were wild; his muzzle was frothed with foam and blood.

At great cost in blood and pain, Ray made a torturous retreat to his truck with his arm in Buck's jaws. The chain finally stretched taut. Buck's eyes and the veins in his neck bulged. Ray managed to get to his feet, summon all his remaining strength, and make one great thrust backwards. His shirtsleeve and what felt like most of the flesh between his elbow and wrist tore away as he pulled free of Buck's jaws and fell on his back out of reach of Buck's chain. Ray lay on the ground, screaming, holding his arm against his chest.

Buck ran back toward the house, turned, and charged full tilt at Ray. The chain and collar whiplashed him, his body flying into the air and then slapping down hard in the dirt five feet short of Ray. No sooner had the dog hit the ground than he jumped up, ran back toward the house, turned, and charged again. And again.

The son of a bitch won't quit, Ray thought. He's either going to break the chain, pull up the stake, or break his own neck.

Ray staggered to the truck, and climbed in the cab. Cradling his bloody arm against his belly, he slammed the door and rolled up the window. He leaned forward on the steering wheel, its rim cool against his forehead, and took his breath in short bursts. His arm was on fire. Blood soaked his lap and pooled on the seat beneath him.

He took off his shirt, pinned the body of it under his thigh, and tore off the right sleeve. He wrapped it around his left arm above the elbow, put one end in his mouth, and tied a knot with his right hand as tight as he could. Then he wrapped the rest of the shirt around his forearm.

He fell against the driver's door and pressed his face against the cool glass, looking at Ballard, unconscious on the stoop in a lake of blood. Buck stood beside him, licking his face. He would likely bleed out and die. In normal circumstances, Ray would put a bullet in his brain to make certain, but he sure as hell couldn't venture close enough for a kill shot.

Ray gazed at Ballard's .357 Magnum lying on the stoop beside him. It brought to mind some sort of problem, gnawing at the edge of Ray's brain, a risk, a danger lurking in the fog of his pain. He squinted at Ballard's gun, trying to concentrate his wits. Ballard's .357 Magnum. A Colt Python, like Ray's weapon. It came to him slowly out of the miasma of confusion.

He had dropped his gun.

The steel barrel glinted in the sun, lying in the dirt fifteen feet from the stoop. Well within the length of Buck's chain.

Buck nudged Ballard's head with his nose and whined.

Ray struggled to formulate clear thoughts about the Python. He had purchased it at a gun show outside Charlotte, North Carolina, five years before, using an alias. He had filed down the serial numbers, so they couldn't trace it.

He looked down at his bloody right hand. It was bare. A wave of panic washed over him. As he had told Boss, he had a history in Selk County. His fingerprints were on file in the sheriff's office archives.

Ray looked at Ballard again. Blood ran across the stoop and streamed down the steps to pool in the dust. He wouldn't survive to point the finger at Ray.

It didn't matter, though. Ray's cursed fingerprints would do him in. He stared ruefully at his gun, lying in the dust. Ironic, he thought. He had outsmarted investigators and lawmen through scores of hits over three decades only to be brought down by a crazed attack dog.

He looked down at his mangled arm. The tourniquet had stopped the bleeding, but he had lost a lot of blood before it staunched the flow. He felt faint and nauseous. He had to get away from there before he passed out. He started the truck and shifted into gear. As it lurched forward, the top of the steering wheel rose up to strike his face, and a thick black veil fell across his eyes.

Chapter Sixteen

THE MENTOR

March 3, 1967, Friday night

AFTER COLE GRUNDY left Kelly McNiel's office Friday afternoon, she couldn't concentrate on her bookkeeper's February report. Her thoughts kept drifting to Cole, his pale, drawn face, his sad eyes. He seemed so lost and lonely.

She knew how he felt. Her spirit was just as broken after Charley left her, but Kelly didn't have the opportunity to dwell on her grief. Her nine-year-old daughter's survival depended on her resilience. "Daddy's gone," she told Rachel back then, "but I love you and I'll never leave you. I promise we'll be happy forever after, like in all the fairy tales." At the time, she wasn't sure she was strong enough to keep her promise, but her determination to make a good life for Rachel steeled her through her fear and she overcame every obstacle she encountered.

In the process, she instilled in her daughter the traits that sustained Kelly in every crisis: courage, hard work, and an unrelenting will to win. Rachel was valedictorian of her high school class, ripped through Mary Washington in three years, and finished second in her class at Jefferson State Law School.

And when the best law firms in the country tried hard to hire her, Rachel turned them down because she wanted to emulate her mother and be her own boss. Kelly loaned her the money to open her own law firm and helped her convert a nineteenth-century Queen Anne Victorian into the offices of Rachel McNiel and Associates.

Even with all Kelly's help, the enterprise still almost failed at the outset for lack of a mentor. "There's a big difference between acing law school exams and practicing law," Rachel told her mother. "I need an experienced attorney to teach me how to be a lawyer, but no one in town will give up his practice to sign on with me."

Kelly came up with a solution that surprised Rachel and most everyone in the legal community: "Let's talk to Burton Jaffee."

Burton Jaffee was a drunk who closed down his own firm because he couldn't stay sober past ten o'clock in the morning. Rachel said as much to her mother.

"He's a drunk now," Kelly replied, "but he was a good lawyer in his day and he can teach you a lot. And it's not like we have a better alternative. He's the only lawyer who'll take the job."

"Why would he? He's been plastered since I was in high school. He couldn't care less about the law."

"He sits at my bar every night, crying over his scotch and soda about how his life has no meaning. We'll dry him out and put him behind a desk in the Queen Anne. Give him a chance to make a mark before he dies of liver cirrhosis. Besides, he can't turn me down. I'm carrying a hell of a bar tab on him."

Kelly's idea worked out better than she hoped. Burton Jaffee accepted Rachel's offer of a partnership and sobered up, off and on. Before he died of liver cirrhosis, he taught Rachel everything he knew about being a lawyer, which turned out to be considerably more than Kelly or Rachel anticipated. Now, eight years later,

Rachel was one of the most successful lawyers in southwestern Virginia.

Kelly smiled, recalling Burton's assessment of Rachel after their first month together: "Smart, tough, ambitious, courageous, and a major pain in the ass. Like mother, like daughter."

Kelly's meeting with Cole earlier that day had left her unsettled and depressed, but thinking about Rachel had cheered her up. She turned and looked up at Polly Thayer's self-portrait. When Cole had said the portrait looked like Kelly, she told him about Rachel's remark when she gave the painting to her: "She reminds me of you, Mom, because she looks like she doesn't give a damn what anyone thinks."

Kelly kept to herself Rachel's more personal comments, the ones that had touched her heart. "You can see it in her eyes," Rachel had said. "Nothing and no one can beat her down. She's got that look you had, Mom, when it was you and me all alone against the world."

Kelly's vision blurred. She turned back to her desk and wiped her eyes with a tissue. The hell with the bookkeeper's report. She needed a lift. She picked up the phone and dialed Rachel's office.

THAT NIGHT, Kelly and Rachel sat in a window booth sipping wine before their supper was served. Outside Kelly's Place, street lamps cast a yellow hue over maple trees that lined the sidewalk on Pendleton Street, and ivory moonlight gleamed on the gently rippling surface of a duck pond in Beauregard Park.

Kelly watched Rachel as she stared at her glass, twisting its stem, lost in thought.

"You okay?" Kelly asked.

Rachel forced a tight smile. "Long day at the salt mine."

"Something's wrong. What happened?"

"Nothing I can talk about. Attorney-client privilege." Rachel took a swallow of wine and looked up at Kelly with shining eyes. "Suffice it to say I saw the face of evil today."

"You've handled ugly cases before. What's different about this one?"

"A child molester."

Kelly sat back. "I see."

They were quiet for a while. Then Rachel said, "My client doesn't want to go after him."

Kelly searched Rachel's face. "But you do."

"I want him to pay for what he did. But it's not my call."

Kelly nodded. "What would Burton do if he were alive?" She was relieved to see Rachel smile.

"He'd convince the client to go after the molester. He'd hunt him down to the gates of hell. In those rare moments when he was sober, of course."

Kelly returned the smile. "Maybe that's what you should do."

Rachel's smile gradually gave way to a look of intense concentration and she stared off into the distance.

Over supper, they talked about Kelly's business and Rachel's cases. When the table was cleared they ordered another glass of wine.

Kelly caught Rachel's pensive stare. "Something on your mind?"

Rachel shook her head. "It's nothing."

"Come on. What are you thinking?"

Rachel looked out the window for a moment. "Are you lonely, Mom?"

A cold spot pooled in Kelly's stomach. "Of course not. I'm surrounded by people, business associates, employees, friends."

Rachel looked down at her glass. "Was there ever a man in your life? I mean after Daddy left us."

Kelly shifted in her seat. "Not a romantic interest, if that's what you mean."

Rachel looked out the window again. Kelly followed her gaze to a young woman walking a German shepherd under the street lamps.

"The business," Rachel said. "Is it enough? Does it make you happy?"

Kelly's throat tightened. "Of course I'm happy. I love my work." She paused. "And I've got you."

Rachel's eyes glistened. She reached across the table and touched her mom's hand. Kelly grasped it, her own eyes full. Then Rachel said, "Sorry. This is more about me than you."

Kelly flinched.

Rachel slid out of the booth. "Gotta go. Early court appearance tomorrow. Thanks for supper." She bussed Kelly on the cheek and hurried out of the restaurant.

"Like mother, like daughter," Kelly thought. She wiped her tears away and got up to mix herself a martini.

Chapter Seventeen

THE COLT PYTHON

March 3, 1967, Friday night

RAY MIDDLEDITCH AWOKE in the dark, slumped over the steering wheel of his pickup truck, his right arm draped over the gear-shift stick, his left limp at his side. He was bare-chested and cold. When he straightened up and picked up his coat with his right hand, a hot bolt of pain shot through his left arm and he cried out. He gritted his teeth and lifted his throbbing arm into his lap. His forearm was swollen to twice its size and white-hot to the touch. It felt as though he'd cooked it over a wood fire.

Fighting through paralytic stiffness and fearing he might pass out again, he draped his coat over his bare shoulders. Breathe, he told himself. Stay awake. You've got to get away from here. He took deep breaths. In and out. In and out. The dizziness passed slowly.

He looked out the windshield. Smoky clouds shrouded a yellow moon hanging low over a line of scrub pines. The truck was stranded in waist-high brush. Behind him Ballard's house loomed over the clearing like a hulking ghost, dark and quiet.

He started the truck, shifted into reverse, and backed out slowly. Five feet, ten, fifteen. The truck pulled free of the growth and regained the clearing. He flicked on the headlights. Cones of yellow flashed on the trench his truck had cut through the brush and bounced off the scrub pines beyond it. He shifted into gear, struggled to turn the sluggish steering wheel with one hand, and drove around the edge of the clearing to find the head of the driveway that ran back to Whiskey Road. His headlights washed over the wall of brush, lit up the dead mulberry tree, and fell on the house.

He braked to a stop. Ballard lay on his side on the stoop. Ray scanned the clearing. The dog was nowhere to be seen.

Fifteen feet this side of the stoop, the barrel of Ray's Colt Python shone in the headlights. He looked all around again. No sign of Buck, but the clouds over the moon had darkened the night. The dog could be in the shadows or under the house.

Ray looked at the gun and licked his lips. He eased the truck forward and stopped a few feet from it. Crusted blood stained Ballard's thigh and the shoulder and chest of his shirt. The end of Buck's chain rested beside his outstretched hand.

Ray shucked off his coat. He reached across his body with his right hand and opened the door. He eased out one leg, keeping his eyes on the dark space under the house. He stepped off the running board and held on to the door to steady himself. When the dizziness passed, he stood still for a full minute, his knees trembling while he looked under the house and all around the clearing. No Buck.

He staggered to the front of the truck, sliding his hand along the fender for balance. He stepped over to his gun, swayed, leaned over, propped his right hand on his knee, and steadied himself. He took a last look around, then grabbed the gun, straightened up, and gazed at Ballard's corpse. Make sure of the kill. Walk over to him, put the gun to his head, pull the trigger.

He couldn't do it. Ray was so weak he couldn't walk the fifteen feet to the stoop and back without support. The hell with it. He had his gun. The county wouldn't find his fingerprints. That was the important thing.

He shuffled back to the truck, climbed inside, and sat behind the wheel, breathing hard. His arm felt like someone had ravaged it with a chainsaw. He came perilously close to passing out again, but a full minute of heavy breathing cleared his mind.

He knew he couldn't survive without medical attention. He'd lost a lot of blood and his arm was badly infected, but he couldn't risk going to a doctor for fear it would be reported to the sheriff's office.

He leaned back in the seat and wept softly. The project was almost over. The old lady, Leland, and Betty Lou were dead. He'd killed Ballard. Only one hit left to go, and he couldn't finish. He leaned his head against the back of the cab and rubbed his temples.

An idea fought to free itself from the shackles of his pain. Something about Betty Lou and the old lady. Betty Lou had come to the old lady's shack after Ray killed her, and the drunk had followed her. Betty Lou and the drunk. Ray knitted his brow and peered into the night, struggling to push an elusive idea out into the open.

And then it came to him. He cursed himself for not having realized it from the outset. The drunk was the answer.

Drive to the rental house to get the drug, he told himself. Go to the drunk's house. Force him to treat the wound.

Ray sighed heavily. The effort would require all his strength and then some, but he would die otherwise.

He took several deep breaths, shifted the truck into gear, and drove it out to Whiskey Road.

Chapter Eighteen

TOBY'S DISCOVERY

March 3, 1967, Friday night

DEPUTY TOBY VESS was working the swing shift when dispatch reported gunfire at 42 Horsehead Road in Tinker's Mill, a rural town in northeast Selk County, a little after ten P.M. He knew the address all too well: Grover Sipe's house. Toby had responded to calls there four times in the last six months. In each case, Grover had drunk himself senseless and beat his wife while his two little boys cowered in the corner. The violence escalated with each incident, but Lurleen refused to press charges.

Toby told dispatch to notify the rescue squad and sped to Tinker's Mill, lights and sirens on. Five minutes later he slid to a stop in front of Grover's squalid yellow shack. The storm door had been ripped off its hinges and lay shattered in the yard beside the concrete stoop. The main door stood wide open. Toby hopped up on the stoop and entered the house, then stopped cold.

Grover and Lurleen sat at the kitchen table under a lightbulb dangling by a frayed cord. A sheen of sweat glistened on Grover's bald head and naked chest and belly. Lurleen's eyes were wide and fearful, one of them blackened and swollen. Her dress was on the floor and the broken strap of her slip exposed one sagging breast. Grover was gripping the trigger guard of a shotgun with one hand and pressing the mouth of the barrel up tight against Lurleen's chin. His other arm rested casually on the table in a pool of blood.

Tommy and Billy, eight and ten years old, short and chubby like their mom and dad, crouched in a corner behind a chair.

"Go ahead," Lurleen said through clenched jaws. "Pull the goddamned trigger! That's what you want, ain't it?" She sobbed. "Go ahead and get it over with."

Grover thrust the barrel against her chin, forcing her head against the wall with a thump. "You think I won't do it? You think I won't?"

"You won't," Toby said, his service revolver drawn and pointed at Grover.

When Grover turned to look at Toby, the mouth of the shotgun's barrel slid off Lurleen's chin. Toby crossed the room in three quick strides, jerked the shotgun out of Grover's hand, and hit him over the head with his service revolver.

Grover's head hit the table and bounced up off of it. He sat up straight, looking confused, and grabbed his round pate with both hands. Blood slid through his fingers. He held his hands up in front of him incredulously. He scowled at Toby. "Look what you done. You had no call to hit me. It was just the liquor talkin."

Toby threw the shotgun out the front door. "Get away from him," Toby said to Lurleen.

She lifted the flap of her slip to cover her breast and edged over to the corner with the boys. They came out from behind the chair and grabbed her around the waist, one on each side.

"Stand up," Toby said to Grover. "Hands against the wall. Feet spread apart."

Grover looked stunned. "What the hell you doin?"

Toby rounded the table, grabbed Grover's arm, jerked him up to a standing position, and slammed his face into the wall. "Hands against the wall!"

Grover did as he was told and Toby frisked his jeans. No weapon. Blood dripped from a deep long slit on the underside of Grover's meaty forearm.

"How'd you get cut?" Toby said.

"He drove his fist through the storm door," Lurleen said. "Showin off what a big man he is."

"It ain't nothin," Grover said.

A siren wailed and flashing lights splashed through the open door. Two EMTs rushed into the room, Larry Graybill and a young man Toby didn't know. Larry was tall and thin with a long face cursed with a perpetual expression of perplexity, as though he couldn't quite believe what was happening, but he'd proved to Toby long ago he knew his business. In his fifties with thirty years on the rescue squad, he was as good as they got.

Toby stepped back and Larry took charge. He sterilized and bandaged Grover's arm and head and checked his vitals while the young EMT, a baby-faced boy with sandy hair that fell to his shoulders, stood by idly, watching with saucer-wide eyes, apparently a new trainee.

"Is he all right?" Toby asked.

"He's lucky. If the wound to his arm was a half inch to the right, he would have bled out before he got to the table."

"You need to hospitalize him?"

"No. He'll be fine if he doesn't pick another fight with a storm door."

Larry went over to Lurleen and the boys to doctor Lurleen's eye. When he pressed her ribs, she cried out. He lifted her slip to expose a purple bruise the size of a grapefruit under her breast. He probed it gingerly. She flinched with each touch. "You've got a broken rib." Larry shook his head and looked at Toby. "You remember the Jayhews?"

"I can't forget them."

"Me either."

"Who are the Jayhews?" the trainee asked.

"Some people we knew," Larry said. "Long time ago."

Toby looked at Lurleen, whimpering, holding her slip over her breast, her black eye swelled shut, the boys clinging to her with blank faces. He turned to Grover, sitting at the table, looking utterly indifferent about the harm he'd inflicted on his family.

"Stand up," Toby said. "Face the wall."

"Why? You already ran your queer-bait hands all over me."

"Stand up!"

Grover scowled and stood slowly.

Toby unhitched handcuffs from his belt and pulled Grover's hands behind him.

"What the hell?" Grover said.

"You're under arrest."

"Wait a damn—"

"Don't lock him up," Lurleen cried out. "He didn't mean no harm."

Toby recited Grover's rights to him as he pulled him toward the door.

"You can't do this!" Grover yelled. "She don't do what I tell her. I had to teach her a lesson. It's my right. She's my wife, goddamn it."

"It's true!" Lurleen said. "It's my fault! I don't mind him like he wants me to." She ran over to Toby and grabbed him by the arm. "Please don't take him to jail."

Toby pulled her hand away.

"Please," Lurleen begged.

"She won't go against me in court, Vess," Grover said. "You know that. You got no case."

"He's right," Lurleen said. "I won't go against him."

"You won't have to go against him," Toby said. "I will. I saw him put the gun to your head."

Toby dragged Grover out to his truck and shoved him into the cab.

Larry came out to Toby's truck as Toby climbed in. "I didn't see what he did, but I can testify about Lurleen's injuries. I'll back you in court any way I can."

"I appreciate it."

As Toby pulled out of the yard, Lurleen stood at the front door with the boys still clinging to her, all three sobbing hysterically. Larry took her by the arm and led her and the boys toward the rescue squad van, the rookie EMT trailing along behind.

"You know I'll beat your bullshit charges," Grover said.

"We'll see."

IT TOOK TOBY two hours to drive to Jeetersburg, book Grover, and lock him down in the county jail. Then he called Ramona Beasley of Social Services on her home number, waking her from a sound sleep, and told her about Grover's assault. "Larry took Lurleen and the boys to Dolley Madison. They're in a bad way, and Grover won't be able to make bail so he won't be bringing home a paycheck for a good while."

"I'm on it. I'll head over there now."

AS TOBY DROVE north out of Jeetersburg, smoky clouds floated across a yellow moon, casting the pastureland along the road in a gray hue.

Two miles south of Fox Run, he slowed down at the site of the old Jayhew house and looked it over. Nothing remained but a stone chimney standing sentry over a pile of charred planks. Rumor had it that Cale Jayhew, the grandpappy of the family, burned the place down.

Toby sped up and drove toward Fox Run, thinking about Cotton and Linda Jayhew, a short, skinny young man and a waifish girl with big round eyes, and their two little girls. Toby had responded to calls from dispatch about violence at the Jayhew place seven times over a six-month stretch. Each time, Cotton was drunk on moonshine. Linda's injuries were minor at first, a purple spot under her eye, a split lip, a bruised thigh. Each time she claimed she injured herself. "I fell and hit my head." "I ran into the door." "I tripped on the steps."

The injuries grew worse, a broken nose, a nasty gash above her ear, a broken arm. Toby pressed her about Cotton. "He didn't do nothin. I'm clumsy. It's been my way since I was a little girl. Always gettin hurt cause I ain't careful." Toby knew better. Everyone knew better.

Larry Graybill led the rescue team that responded to the last three calls. "You ought to arrest the sumbitch."

"She claims he's not responsible. I don't have probable cause."

The last call came on a Saturday night. An old couple down the road had heard gunfire. Toby sped to the Jayhews' place with a sense of foreboding. No previous report had involved gunfire.

He parked on the shoulder and knocked on the door. No one answered, but the lights were on and the house was eerily quiet. The door was unlocked, so he went inside.

The little girls and Linda were facedown on the floor, each shot in the back of the head. Cotton sat in a recliner, his head blown off, a shotgun lying at an angle across his lap, the finger of his right hand still lodged in the trigger guard.

That was fifteen years ago.

Toby pulled off the road and cut the engine. He sat in the dark for a good while. He finally took off his hat and ran his hand over his close-cropped gray hair. Cale Jayhew was right to burn the place down. Toby would have done the same. He took a deep breath, started the truck, and drove on.

IN FOX RUN he turned left at Kirby's Store and headed into

Saddleback Cove toward his house. Four miles down Whiskey Road, he rounded a sharp turn and slammed on the brakes, wrestling his truck to a stop ten feet from a dog that was frozen in the headlights, its eyes glowing yellow. When it sprinted off the road, Toby got a side view of its brindle coat, thick chest, and sinewy legs. Walt Ballard's pit bull, the product of a dogfighting ring he busted, his only worthwhile achievement as a deputy since Reba Emley left him.

Toby sat in the truck staring at Walt's driveway. It was strange that the dog was running loose. Walt kept him on a chain because of his violent tendencies; the dog hated most every living creature but Walt.

Toby's gut told him something was amiss. He turned onto the dirt road and jostled over ruts through dense brush to emerge in Walt's clearing. He swung the truck around to point its headlights at the house.

Walt lay on his side on the front stoop, covered in blood, not moving. Toby radioed dispatch, jumped out of the truck, and ran to the stoop. Walt lay in a large circle of blood, his clothes soaked with it. Toby knelt and put his hand to his throat. There was a faint pulse. He rolled Walt over on his back and saw that the bleeding came from gunshot wounds to his shoulder and thigh. The shoulder had stopped bleeding on its own. Walt's belt cinched high on his leg had staunched a heavier flow of blood from his thigh.

A high-pitched whine came from the edge of the clearing. Toby looked up. The pit bull stood fifty feet away, staring at him. Toby drew his gun. The dog walked slowly toward him. Toby cocked the hammer. "Get back!"

The dog whined and crept forward. Toby stepped backward off the stoop, holding his aim. The pit bull stepped up on the stoop and licked Walt's face, then lay down and rested his muzzle on Walt's shoulder. A dark auburn stripe of dried blood ran down the middle of his huge head.

Walt made a choking sound. The pit bull jumped up and barked.

Toby thrust his gun at the dog. Walt heaved a deep breath and blew it out. Then he went still.

"Get away from here!" Toby shouted.

The pit bull jumped off the stoop and crawled under the house.

Toby stepped up on the stoop and knelt beside Walt again. He wasn't breathing. Toby put his hand to Walt's throat. Still a faint beat there.

Toby set his gun on the stoop and opened Walt's mouth. His breathing passage was clear. He lifted Walt's chin to tilt his head back, pinched his nose, placed his mouth over Walt's mouth, and blew breath into his lungs. Walt's chest rose. Toby sucked in air and blew a second breath into Walt. He raised up and crossed the palms of his hands on Walt's chest. He pushed down, counting the compressions. "One, two, three, four." He picked up the pace, aiming for two compressions per second.

At thirty compressions, Toby stopped and blew two more breaths into Walt's mouth. He returned to the chest. Thirty compressions. Two more breaths. Again.

On the fourth or fifth cycle, the pit bull crawled out from under the house. Toby thought about grabbing his gun, but he didn't want to break the rhythm of the compressions unless the dog charged. Eighteen, nineteen, twenty, twenty-one.

The dog sat on its haunches and stared at Toby.

At the count of thirty, Toby put his mouth over Walt's mouth and blew. Once. Twice. Then back to the chest. One, two, three, four. The pit bull sat still and watched.

Toby forgot about the dog. Thirty and two. Again. Thirty and two. Again. And again. And again. And again.

Chapter Nineteen

THE BOYFRIEND

March 4, 1967, Saturday morning

WALT BALLARD WAS in surgery when Cole arrived at Dolley Madison at four A.M. A short, pudgy emergency room doctor with a sallow face pitted with acne scars said Walt had lost almost 40% of his blood volume and had gone into hypovolemic shock. If he survived, he would probably lose his leg.

Cole went out to the parking lot and climbed in his patrol car. It was unseasonably warm and sultry. He wiped his face and neck with a kerchief. He looked at the pink predawn crescent glowing on the horizon and tried to figure out what the hell was going on. His instincts told him all the crimes were related. The pace of the violence alarmed him, and he sensed there was more to come.

Toby and Frank were still gathering evidence at Walt's house. Frank's forensics team was stretched thin. Analyzing the evidence about the attack on Walt and about the corpse Chase had found on Bobcat's summit yesterday required time, but another act of violence might come at any moment. Cole needed to act now.

He rubbed his eyes and sighed. He had only one lead about any of the crimes: the identity of the man Betty Lou had met at Kelly's Place. Cole doubted Elwood Critzer murdered Betty Lou, and he couldn't imagine he was involved in the other crimes, but for now he was Cole's only suspect.

Cole started the car and drove north out of Jeetersburg. By the time he passed through Fox Run, the sun was up. Deep in the hollow, a couple miles short of Whippoorwill Hollow Dam, he turned onto a red clay driveway and drove up a steep slope to the top of a little knoll. At the crown, in a grove of giant oaks with trunks as big around as fifty-gallon barrels, sat an old farmhouse whose paint had worn away to expose rotting planks.

Cole parked in the shade next to an old green Hudson pickup and climbed out of the car slowly, pressing his hand against his lower back. Chickens scattered in all directions as he limped around the house to the front porch. The screen door squeaked open and Sadie Critzer, a short, stringy woman in her late sixties with a weathered, dried-prune face and iron-colored hair pressed tight to her skull, came out on the porch. She was barefooted and a faded brown dress hung on her frail figure like a feed sack.

"Good morning, ma'am."

"Reckon so. Right smart hot for this time a year, though. Ony six thirty and I done sweat a bucketful."

"Yes, ma'am. It's mighty hot. Is Elwood home?"

"Done milkin by now. Cleanin up." She jerked her thumb toward the back of the house. "Barn's down the hill. You see him you tell him to get his ass up here to mend the chicken wire or the chickens'll be in Fox Run by sundown." She went inside and the screen door slapped shut behind her.

Cole walked around the house and stopped under a big oak. A footpath descended a steep slope to a red barn. Downhill climbs were hardest on his back. By the time he reached the barn door, it had tightened up. He leaned over. His back relaxed. He straightened up and it tightened.

He adjusted his back brace and looked the barn over. With new timbers and a fresh coat of paint, it was in much better shape than the house. He opened a tall, wide door and stepped inside. Fluorescent lights ran the length of the ceiling. Stainless steel drums with black tubing stood against the wall. The floor was broom-finished concrete.

Elwood Critzer stood on the other side of the barn in front of huge sliding double doors that had been rolled open. He was a tall, heavyset man with a double chin and a bald head rimmed with gray. He wore rubber boots, bib overalls, a long-sleeve undershirt, and a red ball cap. He was hosing down the concrete, flushing cow dung out the back. He looked Cole's way, froze for a moment, and then went about his business.

Cole waited. When Elwood finished, he turned off the water and dropped the hose. He faced Cole and jammed his hands in his pockets. "I wondered when you'd come around."

"Sounds like I don't need to tell you why I'm here. Anywhere we can sit and talk? My back don't take kindly to long stand-ups."

Elwood picked up two wooden stools and placed them in front of the double doors. He sat down and Cole joined him.

The morning sun behind the barn cast a long shadow over a pasture that dropped down to Black Snake's Creek. Over a hundred head of Holsteins grazed along its banks, their bells tinkling.

Elwood thrust a pack of Domino cigarettes at Cole, who declined. Elwood lit one and smoked silently. Cole waited him out.

A rooster crowed. The faint sound of a tractor laboring over rough terrain farther down the creek came to them on the back of a hot breeze.

Elwood finished his cigarette and flicked it out the door, where it died in a puddle of hose water and barn muck. He leaned forward, his arms propped on his knees, his hands clasped together. "You won't believe it, I s'pose, but I didn't chase after her. She come on to me. Little girl grabbed hold of this old mule and rode him hard, like he was a young stallion."

"You met up with her at Kelly's Place?"

Elwood nodded.

"What were you doing there?"

"Drinkin."

"Thought you were a teetotaler."

"I am." He took off his ball cap. "At least, I was." He dropped it on the floor and mussed up his gray fringe with calloused, knotty hands. "I hauled some cattle to market that afternoon, three old cows, dried up, not worth the feed. Sixteen, seventeen years old. I raised em from calves." He ran his hand over his bald head and rubbed the back of his neck. "When the ole boy at the intake shed herded em into the holdin pen for the slaughterhouse, I cried. Scared me. I couldn't look the ole boy in the eye. Grabbed my check and drove off fast as I could." Elwood shook his head back and forth slowly. "How old are you?" he asked Cole.

"Sixty-two."

"You gettin up there. Maybe you can understand." Elwood looked down at the floor and spat between his feet. Cole watched the saliva sparkle and then sink into the concrete. "I'll be seventy July nine. Most of what I care about is gone from here. Our girls grew up and moved away long time ago. Gave us four grandkids. We never see em. They don't call. They don't write." He looked down at his hands. "Used to be I couldn't keep my hands off Sadie." He rubbed his arthritic fingers. "Way it is now, she's cold as a winter wind. We ain't touched in years." He let out a long breath. "Ain't nothin left for me now but the cattle. That's why I cried that day, I reckon."

Cole understood. To a lesser degree and in a different way, he was living it. It took him a few moments to shake off Elwood's comments and return to the subject of the murder. "So you met Betty Lou at Kelly's Place?"

Elwood nodded. "Kelly's Place got a billboard on the state road comin away from the market. Has a pretty woman on it, blonde, big smile. A barmaid, I reckon. I turned the truck around and drove downtown to the address on that billboard. Went up to the bar like a regular drunk. Ordered straight whiskey. Drank it down. Ordered another one. Knocked that one down. Kelly McNiel tended the bar. She told me I had to slow down or I'd be sick. I heeded her warning and drank real slow like she said. Seemed to bring my dobber up a little. But not much." He took in a breath, held it for a moment, let it out. "Until little girl come in there."

"That's the second time you've described Betty Lou as little, but she wasn't little."

"It ain't a description. It's a name. It's what she told me to call her. Little Girl." He looked out at the mountains on the horizon. "And I sure as hell did whatever she wanted, I'll tell you that damned much for certain."

Cole took his notebook out of his shirt pocket and jotted down the pet name. "What happened when she came into Kelly's Place that night?"

"I noticed her when she come in, like every good ole boy in there. She ate her supper by herself in one of them booths. When she finished her meal, she walked over to the bar real slow, showin off what she had, and sat down on the stool beside me and asked me to buy her a drink. I figured she was fixin to fleece an old fool. I said, 'What do I get for it?' She pressed her titties up against my arm. 'You won't be sorry,' she said. I figured she'd milk me dry and move on down the bar to the next dumb farmer with more money than good sense, so I told her, 'You don't fool me none, missy.' She smiled and said, 'How's about I buy the drinks? All you want.' She ordered us a round and rubbed herself up against me. Half the men in that place come up to her and tried to peel her away from this ugly old fool. Young stallions. Good lookers. Big-shouldered boys." A wistful smile crossed Elwood's face. "She told every damned one of em she was with me. Bout eleven o'clock when I was so drunk and stirred up I like to busted open, she said, 'Let's go have us some fun.' She pulled me off the stool and on out to her car. Took me to the Robert E. Lee Motor Court over by Beacon Hill." He shook his head. "Little Girl sure-God knew how to pleasure a man, tricks I'd never heard of, much less tried out. My head was spinnin and I was plum wore out when she drove me back to my truck."

"What did Sadie do when you got home?"

"Nothin. She never said a word. Didn't seem to care."

"So you did it again the next night?"

"You bet your ass I did, and most every Friday and Saturday night after that till her husband shot her."

Cole paused. Elwood's assumption that Leland killed Betty Lou sounded sincere. He didn't seem shrewd enough to plan an offhand remark to cover his guilt, but he'd apparently learned a lot of new tricks since New Year's Eve. Cole ignored the comment for the time being. "You always met her at Kelly's Place?"

"She wouldn't go no place else with me. I tried to get her to meet me at the motel. 'Let's leave out the drinkin at the bar,' I said. 'Ain't you worried evibody can see you comin on to me out in the open? What if your husband finds out?' She said she hoped he did. It would serve him right."

"Did she say what she meant by that?"

"I asked her, but she wouldn't talk no more about it."

Cole remembered that Betty Lou's mother died on Christmas. It seemed curious she would be partying so soon after her death. "Did she mention that her mother passed on a few days earlier?"

Elwood nodded. "She said she wanted to have a high ole time cause her momma had just died."

"Trying to get over it, you figure?"

"It was the other way around, more like a celebration. She said she hated her momma. Said the old bitch deserved what she got."

Something about that didn't fit with a detail that chewed around the edges of Cole's memory, but he couldn't get a grip on it. He gave it up for now. "Were you with her the night before she was killed?"

Elwood's eyes clouded over. He nodded somberly. "We met at Kelly's Place and went to the Robert E. Lee, like always."

"What time did you check in?"

"Bout eleven, but you won't find my name on the register. She always made me sign as Mr. and Mrs. Clarence Emley. Clarence was her daddy's name."

"Why did she want you to use his name?"

"I don't know. She wouldn't say."

"What time did you leave the motel?"

"Bout three. She drove me back to my truck at Kelly's Place and let me off."

"Where did you go from there?"

"Home."

"What time did you get back here?"

"Four."

"Will Sadie vouch for the time you got home?"

Elwood shrugged. "She was awake when I crawled in bed."

"Does she know about Betty Lou?"

"She ain't stupid. She's bound to know I been runnin with a woman, but she never asked me anything about it. "

Cole looked over his notes. "Anything else you can tell me about your time with Betty Lou?"

Elwood picked his ball cap up off the floor and put it on. "When we was in bed, she called me Papa Bear. Only it didn't seem like she was talkin to me when she said it. I had the feelin she was thinkin about some other man."

Cole looked out at the field. A goldfinch darted across the pasture and lit on top of a fencepost by the creek. It fluttered its wings to hold its spot against a light breeze.

Bessie Tilden said the man who took the nude photograph of Betty Lou had signed a note to her as Papa Bear. Now, many years later she called Elwood Papa Bear, told him to call her Little Girl, and made him sign in at the Robert E. Lee with her father's name. Elwood was old enough to be her father. It didn't take much imagination to speculate that Betty Lou was using Elwood as a substitute for her daddy. Cole wondered how many other affairs she had with men old enough to be her father.

He put his notepad and pencil in his shirt pocket. "A little while ago you let on you thought Leland Mundy killed Betty Lou," he said to Elwood. "As things stand now, it's an open question who killed her."

Elwood looked surprised. Then awareness dawned in his face. "Well, you're a damned fool if you think I killed her. Hell, Little Girl lit up this ole boy's night like a bolt of lightning. I'd sell my soul to the devil if he'd give her back to me for one more roll-around. And if the sumbitch who killed her ain't her dead husband, you find him and give me five minutes with him and you won't need to waste no time on a judge and jury."

The passion in Elwood's denial was convincing. What's more, he'd never been much of a liar, but then again, he'd never gotten drunk as a polecat and chased a loose woman with his tongue hanging out. Thirty-eight years in law enforcement had taught Cole that human nature often defied reasonable expectations.

Cole put his hands on his knees and pushed his way to a standing position. "I'm afraid I'll need more than your word that you got home at four A.M. the night Betty Lou was murdered. I have to ask Sadie about it."

Elwood nodded. "I understand."

"You wait here."

Cole limped to the barn door and went outside. The sun bore down hard and sweat beaded on Cole's brow and ran into his eyes and stung them as he climbed the hill. At the top, he stopped under the big oak tree and leaned over, relieving his pain, but when he straightened up, it returned.

He walked around to the front of the house. Sadie sat at the top of the porch steps, her elbows propped on her knees, her hands cupping her face.

"You find him?"

"Yes, ma'am."

"You tell him to come up here and mend the chicken wire?"

"No, ma'am. I'm afraid I forgot."

She gave him a disgusted look.

He took off his hat and wiped sweat off his brow. He squinted at the sun, considering an appropriate way to ask her about Elwood's infidelity. He decided there was no kind way to get into it, so he went straight at it. "I s'pose you know Elwood's been running around with a woman."

"Course I know. I ain't a idjit. What kinda slop he dip his wick in? I heard tell they sell it for fifty cents in them shanties down by the railroad tracks in Tinker's Mill. That where he went to get it?" She pulled her dress down over her knees and gathered it under her legs, her face scrunched up in a frown.

"No, ma'am. Elwood says he went to Kelly's Place. Says he met a woman there Saturday night, February eighteen. Claims he came home Sunday morning at four A.M. Do you happen to remember that night, ma'am?"

"Course I member it cause it was the last time he done it. Rutted around like a billy goat evy Friday and Saturday night and then shut it all down sudden-like. Ain't done it since."

"Did he come home at four in the morning like he says?"

"You tell me who gave it to him, I'll tell you what time he got home."

"I'm sorry, ma'am. I don't trade information."

She stared intently at Cole. "You say he went to Kelly's Place?"

"Yes, ma'am."

Her eyes widened, cornflower blue eyes he hadn't noticed before, eyes that he guessed were once bright and shining, even fetching, and all the wind seemed to go out of her. "He's the one they been talkin about."

"Pardon, ma'am?"

"I thought he took up with some old whore," she said with a tremor in her voice. "An old man sowin wild seed one last time afore he gave it up. My daddy did it when he got old. Crawled back to Momma when he found his senses. I figured that's all it was." A tear slipped out of the corner of her eye. "But it wasn't some old whore." She faltered and swallowed hard. "Betty Lou Mundy," she whispered. She covered her eyes with her hands and wept.

Cole gave her some time. Then he said gently, "Excuse me, ma'am, but did Elwood come home at four A.M. that morning, like he says?"

She dried her eyes with the hem of her dress. She drew herself together and cleared her voice. "He come home at four, smellin of liquor, a woman's bathwater, and sex." She fought back new tears. "Betty Lou's sex."

"Are you sure it was four A.M., ma'am?"

She nodded. "He come home at four. Got up at six. Milked the herd. Stayed down at the barn till the sun was high." She wrapped her arms around her trembling shoulders.

"Thank you, ma'am." Cole started around the house, then stopped, and looked back at her. She stared off into the distance, her eyes full. "I'm sorry, ma'am."

She looked at him. "What you sorry for? Ain't none of it your fault."

Cole looked away and then at her. "I'm sorry just the same, ma'am."

She ran her arm across her nose, got up, and walked slowly to the screen door, her head down. She stopped there and looked at Cole, her eyes shining, then went inside the house.

He sighed heavily, limped around the house, and forced his aching back to descend the hill again.

Elwood had put the stools away. He leaned against one side of the open rolling doors, his hands in the pockets of his bib overalls, looking out at the pasture. Cole walked across the concrete and stood beside him.

Most of the Holsteins had crossed the creek to the opposite slope. One of them stood in the stream, drinking. She lifted her head and looked up at the barn, water drooling from her jaws.

"Sadie backed you up."

Elwood didn't say anything for a while. Then, without looking at Cole he said in a gritty voice, "You tell her it was Betty Lou I took up with?"

"I didn't tell her, but she figured it out. Like you said, she's not stupid."

Elwood looked down at the toes of his boots. "What did she have to say about it?"

"She cried."

Elwood shot Cole a surprised look. His face flushed. He stared at Cole hollow-eyed, his lips quivering. Then he looked out at the field and clenched his jaw.

They stood silently side by side for a good while, Cole's iliac crest throbbing. The cow standing in the creek stretched out her neck and let out a long, low moan. A cow on the slope answered. And then a third.

"I reckon you heard about my wife a while back," Cole said.

"I heard, and I'm mighty sorry for it."

"Thank you. I appreciate that." Cole took a deep breath and let it out. He propped his hands on his hips and arched his back. "I realize it's none of my business and you didn't ask for my advice, but if I was you, I'd go up to the house and talk to my wife."

"It's too late for that."

"It's not too late as long as she's still here."

Elwood glanced at Cole and looked back out at the field.

"Thank you for your help," Cole said.

He left the barn, climbed the hill, and walked around the house to his car. He climbed into it slowly, groaning as he dragged his trailing leg inside. He gripped the steering wheel tightly. When the pain subsided, he mopped his face with a kerchief, and thought about Bessie Tilden's boyfriend theory. Elwood didn't murder Betty Lou, but an earlier boyfriend might have killed her. Cole recalled his conversation with Kelly McNiel about rumors of Betty Lou engaging in affairs carried out with discretion behind closed doors.

Normally, Cole would have dismissed the rumors as unreliable gossip, but at the moment, they stood alone in an otherwise barren field of information.

Cole started the car and headed down the driveway to Whip-poorwill Hollow Road.

Chapter Twenty

THE PREACHER

March 4, 1967, Saturday noon

AT NOON, Cole arrived at Grace Church and parked in front of the wrought iron fence that separated the churchyard from the cemetery. He looked across the rows of headstones that ran to the foot of Feather Mountain. On the far side of the cemetery, Reverend Willis Chatham moved among the graves, his big shoulders swaying back and forth as he walked, leaned over, bent down.

Cole got out of the car. The sun beat down scorching hot, the mercury pushing the hundred degree mark, the warmest March day in Cole's memory. Sweat soaked his shirt as he went through the cemetery gate and walked past the tombstones, keeping his eyes away from Carrie's grave in the southernmost corner.

The preacher looked up at Cole and tossed his gardening gloves in a wheelbarrow filled with plastic pots and dead flowers, his shirt also drenched.

Cole nodded to him. "Preacher."

"Sheriff."

The preacher wiped sweat from his face with a kerchief and

swept his hand through his unruly mane of coarse black hair. "How are you?" he said, his violet eyes searching Cole's face.

"Fine, thank you." Cole moved on quickly so the preacher wouldn't ask him about Carrie. "I'm told you have information about Betty Lou Mundy."

The preacher paused. "Who told you that?"

"I dropped by Gertie Wilson's shop this morning. I asked her about gossip she's been passing along that Betty Lou was unfaithful to Leland. She didn't want to admit to spreading rumors, so she threw you to the wolves. She claims she heard Leland and Betty Lou came to you for marital counseling."

The preacher smiled. "Gertie knows everything that goes on in Selk County, and quite a few things that don't." His smile drifted away and he took a deep breath. "Let's sit in the shade." He led Cole back across the cemetery and through the gate. A line of picnic tables sat along the fence under pine trees. The preacher sat down at the table nearest the gate. Cole sat across from him.

"It's interesting you came by here today," the preacher said. "I've been worried about whether I should talk to you. My bishop says the priest-penitent privilege prohibits revealing parishioners' confidences even after their deaths." The preacher shook his head. "He's long on book learning, but short on common sense. The way I see it, Betty Lou and Leland would want me to tell you what I know. I had decided I'd talk to you, but I hadn't built up the courage to defy the bishop's orders yet. I guess the Good Lord sent you to me to give me a shove."

"The Good Lord and Gertie Wilson."

The preacher smiled. "He works in mysterious ways."

"So I've heard." Cole took his notepad and pencil out of his shirt pocket. "When did you meet with the Mundys?"

"Betty Lou came to see me five years ago. She had an affair and Leland found out about it. He had left her. She was racked with guilt and self-loathing."

"Who was the man?"

"She didn't name him, but from our conversations I gathered he was an older man, in his sixties. Married, educated, well-off."

"Why did she take up with a man so much older than she was?"

"She said she had craved the attention of older men since she was a little girl."

"Why?"

The preacher folded his hands on top of the table and looked down at them. "Betty Lou's childhood was horrific. Her father died when she was seven years old, and her mother turned to prostitution." A look of revulsion came across the preacher's face. "When Betty Lou was ten years old, one of her mother's customers molested her. She had a hard time talking about it, but as best I could tell, this man assaulted her on a regular basis for several years until she ran away from home."

Anger welled up inside Cole. This had occurred when he was a young deputy sheriff. He couldn't shake the feeling he should have known about it and put a stop to it.

"Betty Lou couldn't afford a psychiatrist," the preacher continued, "and I'm not a competent substitute, but I read everything I could find about child molestation and talked to church members across the state who are experts. Betty Lou's father was good to her and prevented Hazel from mistreating her. When he died, Hazel was free to abuse Betty Lou as she pleased. Two of the psychiatrists I talked to thought the little girl inside Betty Lou pursued older men in search of the affection and security her father gave her." The preacher wiped sweat from his face with his hand and dried it on his pants leg. "They said molestation as a young child often translates into a highly sexualized adulthood. I'm not smart enough to know if they're right, but it was obvious to me Betty Lou's sexual attraction to older men was a powerful compulsion, like an addiction."

"How did Leland fit into that picture?"

"She said Leland was the only man her age who treated her with kindness and respect. She fell in love with him and married him, hoping to put the misery of her childhood behind her, but shortly after their marriage her compulsion overwhelmed her and she had an affair with an older man."

"Shortly after their marriage," Cole repeated.

The preacher nodded.

Leland and Betty Lou had been married about twenty years when she was killed. Bessie Tilden had guessed that the nude photograph of Betty Lou took place about fifteen years ago, but her memory was imprecise and she said it could have been longer ago than that, so the timing of this first affair might fit.

"Betty Lou said Leland never knew about that affair," the preacher said. "Apparently it ended badly, with some sort of catastrophe. She wouldn't give me the details, but she said the tragedy helped her to resist her urges after that. She claimed she was faithful to Leland until the affair of five years ago."

"Why did Leland stay with her after that affair?"

"I reached out to him, and he met with me and Betty Lou. She told him everything. He was angry and hurt, like you'd expect, but it was clear to me that he loved her. When she told him about her childhood, he cried. Eventually he forgave her and rose above his jealousy. He was one of the strongest men I ever met." The preacher rubbed his eyes wearily and put his palms on his thighs. "Their marriage seemed stable until last summer. Leland came to see me and said Betty Lou had taken up with another man. He suspected it was the same man she'd turned to five years ago. I tried to reach out to her, but she refused to meet with me. Then she showed up at the front door of the parsonage at nightfall on Christmas. She was in a bad way. Sobbing. Drunk."

"Why was she so upset?"

The preacher looked at Cole wearily. "She said she believed Leland had been seeing her sister, Reba."

"What made her suspect that?"

"She said something about a perfume she smelled on him. I knew she was right about the affair. Leland had confessed to me that he slept with Reba when Betty Lou began seeing the man last summer, but he told me about it in confidence so I didn't tell her what he said. She didn't need my confirmation, though. She was certain of it. She was angry and hurt, but she didn't blame Reba for it. She blamed her mother. She said Hazel ruined both their lives by selling them to men for sex, and that she and Reba couldn't maintain a normal relationship with a man or lead a normal life because of it. She was so upset that I was afraid she might harm herself. I tried to persuade her to spend the night with Irene and me at the parsonage, but she wouldn't hear of it. I asked her to let me call Leland and have him join us. She refused that, too, and told me I couldn't tell Leland she knew about him and Reba. I begged her to stay and let me help her, but she said that no one could help her. She finally ran out to her car and drove away."

Cole looked out at the cemetery, thinking. As best he could recall, Betty Lou's mother, Hazel, died that same night. "What time did she leave?"

"About eight o'clock. I wish I could have convinced her to allow me to call Leland. Despite his affair with Reba, he loved Betty Lou and wanted to save the marriage." A look of abject defeat came across the preacher's face. "During the weeks before her murder, he met with me every Sunday, searching for guidance and strength. I didn't have much to offer him, and I never told him that Betty Lou knew about him and Reba because of the bishop's almighty priest-penitent privilege. I wish now I'd told him everything. It might have made a difference. I failed him. I failed them both."

"You did everything you could do," Cole said.

The preacher shook his head. "Leland's jealousy and frustration overwhelmed him, and he killed her and turned the gun on himself. I was their only chance of overcoming their problems, and I failed them."

"It's not clear that Leland killed her."

The preacher looked up. "Is there a chance someone else murdered her?"

"Some of the evidence points away from him. Is there anything you can tell me that might shed light on her murder?"

The preacher thought for a moment. "Nothing substantive. Only an opinion. I saw Leland the Sunday before the murder. He didn't act as though he could have killed Betty Lou. In fact, he was miserable because he still loved her."

Cole stood and extended his hand. "Thank you, Preacher. You've been a big help."

The preacher stood and they shook. The preacher's violet eyes bored in on Cole. Cole turned and walked away without giving him a chance to ask about Carrie.

When Cole reached his car, he glanced in the direction of Carrie's grave, then climbed in awkwardly, his back stiff. He sat behind the wheel and watched the preacher walk back through the cemetery.

The preacher couldn't give him the name of Betty Lou's boyfriend of last summer, but someone must know who he is. If Betty Lou found Elwood at Kelly's Place, she might have picked up her previous boyfriend there, too. It was worth another talk with Kelly McNiel.

Chapter Twenty-One

A SENSE OF URGENCY

March 4, 1967, Saturday afternoon

THAT AFTERNOON, Kelly McNiel stood behind her bar across from Archie Snyder, who was on his regular stool at the end nearest the back door. His gray combover clung to his head like spider webbing, covering less of his freckled scalp than showed through, his heavy-lidded watery eyes bloodshot, his nose purple-veined and cankered. Kelly slid a glass of red wine to him, his second of the afternoon. Archie grasped it with a pale claw and downed it in several deep gulps. He set the empty glass on the bar, pulled the corners of his thin lips down into the folds of his jowls, and belched. "Water," he croaked.

Kelly drew a tumbler of water over ice. "Same routine every time you come in," she said as she set the water in front of him. "Two glasses of wine with a water chaser."

"Secret to my good looks and winning personality."

"What's on for today?"

"Hot date for the early-bird supper." He cradled the tumbler of water in both tremulous hands, drank it down in one long turn, set it on the bar, and belched again.

"Who's the lucky girl?"

"Tilly Goodstone."

"You're moving in fast. Fred's only been dead a few weeks."

"When you're ninety-four, it pays to drop the landing gear early. The runway is mighty short."

Archie claimed to be an ace World War I fighter pilot, but Kelly didn't believe him. He would have been over forty at the start of the Great War, as he called it, and he was known for spinning tall tales, most of which featured himself as an epic hero, but she didn't call his bluff. She figured when you live to be as old as Archie, you're entitled to a few fantasies. "How old is Tilly?"

"Eighty-two."

"Robbing the cradle again."

Archie's pile of wrinkles scrunched into a frown. "I hope she's not too young to understand my sense of urgency." He drew in a long breath and let it out nervously. "You'd better pour me another glass of wine."

She poured the wine. As she set the glass down, Cole Grundy walked in the back door. She'd been thinking about Cole since they'd met in her office yesterday. She felt a strange tightness in the pit of her stomach when she saw him. His eyes settled on her and the tightness became a knot as he walked over to the bar.

"You have a few minutes?" he asked.

"Sure," she said, in as casual a tone as she could manage.

She called a waitress over to tend to Archie and led Cole to a booth in the back corner.

Cole took off his hat and set it on the table. He looked worse than he had yesterday, his face more pallid, the bags under his eyes bigger and darker.

"I spoke with Elwood Critzer this morning. He was with his wife when Betty Lou was murdered. I've tracked down Gertie's rumors as far as I can trace them and turned up no names. I'm back to square one. I thought maybe there's a chance we missed something yesterday. Are you sure Betty Lou never met another man here?"

For some unknown reason, his question about the murder set her on edge. She fell silent, trying to figure out why. She'd hoped his visit was not about police business, she supposed, but that made little sense, given he was the county sheriff.

"Kelly?"

"Yes. Well, we canvassed the entire staff. No one saw her with anyone other than Elwood. We searched our records going back two years. You have the only receipts we found."

Cole tapped the brim of his hat, his face a portrait of dejection. When a faint spark flickered in his sad brown eyes, her stomach fluttered.

"What about the parking lot?"

Another swell of disappointment put her off. "What?"

"The night Betty Lou was murdered she drove Elwood to a motel and brought him back at three A.M. to his truck parked in your lot. It's possible someone waited in his car out there and followed her home from here. Did any of your help see a car in the lot late that night?"

Her disappointment turned to irritation. "We close at two," she said sharply. Realizing her aggravation was irrational, she reined herself in and forced herself to answer in a reasonable voice. "We lock up and leave here by two thirty. Even if we stayed late that night, we wouldn't have considered a car parked in the lot at three as remarkable. Heavy drinkers sometimes leave their cars in the lot overnight and take a cab home. It's a frequent occurrence on Saturday nights."

Cole seemed sensitive to her earlier sharp tone. "I'm sorry to cause you more trouble, but would you mind asking your staff if any of them saw a car out there in the lot that night?"

"It's no trouble. I'll talk to them and let you know what I find out."

"Thanks for your help. Like I said, I'm sorry to bother you, but I don't have much to go on in this case." He grabbed his hat and started to get up.

She put her hand over his. "Wait. Don't go."

He looked at her curiously.

Faced with his departure, her thoughts flashed back over her meeting with him yesterday and her conversation with Rachel the night before, and she suddenly understood her feelings. It took her breath way. She drew her hand back and blushed. "I'm sorry," she said softly.

There was an awkward silence between them while he stared at her, looking mystified. It gave her time to calm her emotions and decide what she wanted. As with her business dealings and everything she'd done since Charley walked out on her, she resolved to go after it. "Can you stay for supper?"

"What?"

"Stay and have supper with me. We haven't talked in ten years. Let's catch up."

His confusion seemed to mount. "I . . . I don't have time." He stood. "I'm late for a meeting at headquarters."

"It's Saturday afternoon. Don't you ever take an evening off?"

"I . . . We're working hard." He seemed flustered. "I don't have time."

"How long since you talked to anyone about something other than one of your cases?"

He gripped his hat tightly in both hands. His face flushed.

"Take a break, Cole. Have supper with me. I'll tell you what I've been doing for the last decade. I haven't murdered anyone recently so it'll be a change of pace from your daily routine." She smiled.

"I . . . I can't do that. I have a meeting."

"Come by later tonight, after your meeting."

"I can't do that either. I have . . ." His voice trailed off. "I just can't." He lingered for a moment, looking as perplexed as she had felt until a few moments ago. "I'm sorry. I have to go." He bolted across the room. He stopped at the door and looked back at her, an abashed expression on his face. Then he pushed the door open and he was gone.

Running scared, she thought. Still faithful to Carrie. Kelly's eyes filled up. She sat in the booth until she cooled down. That was stupid, she told herself. He's set in his ways, dedicated to his memory of Carrie. Besides, it's too late. We're too old for such foolishness. She resolved to purge her feelings for Cole from her mind.

She went behind the bar and poured herself a glass of wine.

The back door swung open. Her head turned to it quickly, but it wasn't Cole reconsidering her invitation as she found herself hoping, despite her resolve of less than a minute ago. Short, stumpy Tilly Goodstone filled the bottom half of the doorway, squinting into the restaurant through the thick lenses of her purple horn-rimmed glasses.

Archie sucked in his breath.

Tilly limped into the room, leaning on a cane.

Archie climbed down off his barstool. Hunchbacked by age, he teetered over to Tilly and grasped her elbow.

She looked up at him, frowning sternly. "Archibald! What's this urgent business you called me about?"

"It's a personal matter of great importance. I'll tell you all about it over a glass of wine."

Kelly watched Archie guide the unsuspecting Tilly to a booth by the windows.

Chapter Twenty-Two

REBA'S ALIBI

March 6, 1967, Monday morning

MONDAY MORNING, Cole sat at his desk at headquarters, feeling stupid. His reaction to Kelly's invitation had bothered him all weekend. He'd acted as though socializing with her constituted cheating on Carrie, which was ridiculous. She'd merely invited him to supper, for pity's sake. He told himself he would apologize for brushing her off so brusquely, but when she called that morning to report that no one on her staff remembered seeing a car parked in the lot the night of Betty Lou's murder, the apology caught in his throat. After an uncomfortable silence, he mumbled a thank you and hung up.

Embarrassed yet again, he considered calling her back to apologize. He picked up the phone, but his hand hung in the air. After a few moments, he placed the receiver back in its cradle and stared at it until he realized why he was flustered. He was attracted to Kelly, but he couldn't pursue a relationship with her. When Carrie passed on, she took his heart with her. There was nothing left to give to someone else. It wasn't fair to Kelly to pretend he could forget

Carrie. And it wasn't fair to Carrie. He wouldn't apologize to Kelly. He wouldn't approach her again. He would put her out of his mind.

He burrowed into his work and spent the rest of the morning catching up on the status of the investigations. Frank Woolsey updated him about the assault on Walt Ballard. Walt was alive, but still unconscious and in critical condition. Frank's team was in the process of analyzing a bloody shirtsleeve, a set of tire tracks, and boot prints found at Walt's place Saturday morning, and Frank had taken custody of the bullets Walt's surgeons withdrew from his thigh and shoulder.

Frank's work on the crime scenes on Bobcat Mountain and at Bessie Tilden's place had borne fruit. The bullets fired at Cole were .30-06 longs, as Frank had said. The shell casing Chase found at the big white pine had housed one of the bullets. Frank had lifted a partial fingerprint from it.

Shirley West estimated the time of death of the corpse on the summit as falling within a forty-eight-hour period around Betty Lou's murder. Frank recovered four prints from the wine bottle Chase discovered on the summit, and they matched the corpse's fingerprints.

The partial print on the shell was different from the corpse's fingerprints, and neither of them matched any prints on file with the county. Frank sent them to the Virginia State Police Central Criminal Records Exchange Friday afternoon, requesting an expedited statewide check.

A couple hours after Frank left Cole's office, Mabel came in to report that the Records Exchange had gotten a hit. She handed Cole a manila folder containing a mugshot of a horse-faced young man with stringy blond hair.

Thurman Durwood Bowie
Inmate 38686, Richmond Penitentiary
Birth date: 01/03/43
Height: 6' 1"
Weight: 158 lbs.

Hair: blond

Eyes: brown

Intake: 06/12/62

Release: 06/22/66

Last known address: Box 440, Dealeton Rd., Dealeton, Va.

Thurman's rap sheet was impressive for a twenty-four-year-old man. Tried for murder and acquitted; convicted of assault with a deadly weapon, burglary, and robbery; a string of criminal misdemeanors.

"I called Buck County Sheriff Feedlow," Mabel said. "He said a woman from Dealeton named Rosabelle Sally Steeger reported Bowie missing two weeks ago."

"What's her connection to him?"

"She says they're engaged to be married. Chase wants to go to Buck County to talk to her."

"Tell him to go ahead."

"I did. He's on his way."

Mabel handed Cole the Mundy case file. "Rachel McNiel called this morning. She represents Reba Emley. She offered to bring her in for questioning. I knew you'd want to jump on it fast, so I set it up for one o'clock, here in your office. You've got one hour to prepare."

"Let's review the file together. I want you in the meeting with me."

COLE AND MABEL sat side by side at the conference table across from Rachel and Reba.

The unseasonable scorching weather continued. Headquarters wasn't air conditioned, so Mabel had set an oscillating floor fan beside the table and opened the office windows.

Rachel had arrived first and told them Reba had been at Walt Ballard's bedside since the shooting. Cole was surprised. Reba was the one who filed for divorce.

While her client chain-smoked and stared off into the distance, Rachel laid out Reba's history with Leland and Betty Lou. Dressed in a black suit jacket over a long-sleeved white blouse, sweat beading on her brow, black curls sticking to her forehead, Rachel impressed Cole with her advocacy. The little girl he had known years ago had come a long way.

Too buttoned-up by their almighty lawyer rules, most criminal defense attorneys held their cards close to the vest, but Rachel knew better. In this meeting she followed the "open kimono" strategy Cole remembered as a trademark of her deceased mentor, Burton Jaffee. She showed Cole everything, knowing some of it didn't look so good for Reba, but figuring full disclosure would enhance her credibility.

Nothing Rachel presented was surprising until she placed a handgun on the conference table and said Reba shot Betty Lou with it twenty years ago. Cole looked at the gun closely. A miniature revolver. Ancient and in poor condition. He wasn't convinced it could still fire a round.

Still, Reba's attempt to murder Betty Lou troubled Cole. She'd had a powerful motive to kill her back then, and that same motive could have driven her to murder her sister in February. Reba was in love with Leland and Betty Lou stood between them.

When Rachel finished her presentation, Cole turned to Reba. "You said Leland left your trailer the morning of the murder at six thirty."

"That's right."

"What did you do after that?"

Reba looked at Rachel.

"Tell them," Rachel said.

"When Leland left, I thought about everything he'd said and I knew he'd never come back. Betty Lou ruined my life and broke Leland's heart, but she had Leland and I had nobody. It wasn't right." She nodded toward the pistol lying on the table. "I got that gun out of my dresser drawer and went out to my car. I was halfway to Fox Run when I heard about Betty Lou and Leland on the radio." She gave Cole a hard look. "I would have killed her if someone hadn't beat me to it."

Cole searched her face. He saw no signs of deception, but the timeline of her story was uncorroborated. If both Leland and Reba left her trailer earlier than she claimed, she could have followed him to his house and arrived in time to kill Betty Lou.

Apparently, Mabel had the same thought. "Can you prove you didn't leave your trailer until sometime after six that morning?" she asked.

"We have a witness," Rachel said. "Floyd Spivey was watching Reba's trailer that night."

Cole felt a jolt of surprise.

"Why was this man watching her trailer?" Mabel said.

"Sheriff Grundy knows the reason."

Cole said, "I take it Floyd's been up to his old tricks."

"I'm told it's an addiction," Rachel said.

Cole knew all about Floyd Spivey. His rusted-out Airstream squatted like a broken-down dwarf blimp directly across the road from Reba's trailer in Hukstep's Trailer Park. A snaggle-toothed, scraggly-haired man in his fifties, so short and skinny he could hide behind a fence post, Floyd was a peeper.

Six months ago, Reba caught him looking in her bathroom window as she stood naked in front of the mirror applying her makeup. "It's the third time he did it," she'd told Cole last fall. "I saw him at the window when I stepped out of the shower the first two times, but he only got a glimpse before he ducked down. I didn't turn him in cause I felt sorry for him. Probly the only time in his life he got a good look at a naked woman without paying for it. So I said what the hell and let it go, but this time he got too good a look for too long. Gave me the creeps."

Cole had walked across the trailer park road and knocked on Floyd's door. Floyd turned pale as a head of cauliflower, broke down, and admitted everything. Cole marched him across the road to Reba's trailer. She stood in the doorway while Floyd shifted from one foot to the other, sweating bullets, his head bowed, clutching a Southern States ball cap.

"Go on and tell her," Cole said.

"I'm s-s-s-sorry, m-m-m-missy. I w-w-w-won't do it n-n-no more. S-s-s-swear to God!"

"Good enough for you, Reba?"

She hesitated.

"I'll take him in if you want."

Cole watched Reba's anger drain off. "I won't file charges, but he damn straight better not do it again."

Cole marched Floyd back to his trailer. "You got off easy this time, Floyd. If there's a next time, I'll run you in and Judge Blackwell will lock you up for a couple months." He tapped Floyd on his sunken chest. "No more peeping."

"I p-p-p-promise. I w-w-won't d-d-d-do it n-n-no more."

Apparently, Floyd had broken his promise.

"When Reba told me about the peeping," Rachel said, "I sent my law clerk out to talk to Floyd on the off chance he might have seen Leland or Reba leave her trailer. He denied watching them at first, but when my clerk pressed him, he broke down and admitted he'd been peeping again."

"He was at my bedroom window while me and Leland was . . . together," Reba said, blushing.

"He saw Leland drive away from Reba's trailer at six thirty," Rachel said. "He saw Reba leave at nine." Rachel withdrew a document from her briefcase and handed it to Cole.

"Affidavit of Floyd R. Spivey." Cole scanned it. He didn't doubt its veracity. Floyd's peeping was a grave embarrassment to him for which he expected to be jailed. He wouldn't lie about it.

Cole handed the affidavit to Mabel. She looked it over, grinning.

Floyd's statement swept both Leland and Reba off the table as suspects. Cole's thoughts fell back to Betty Lou's boyfriends.

"Leland told you Betty Lou cheated on him," Cole said to Reba. "Do you have any idea who the man was?"

"No."

Cole thought about Saturday's interviews. "Have you ever heard her refer to anyone as Papa Bear?"

"Betty Lou called Daddy Papa Bear. Momma did, too, but that was forty years ago. How do you know about it?"

"Betty Lou was seeing a man just before she was murdered," Cole said. "Twenty years older than she was. She called him Papa Bear. She told him to call her Little Girl. Do you know why she would do that?"

Reba looked perplexed. "Betty Lou said Daddy called her Little Girl and, like I said, she called him Papa Bear. He died when I was two, so Betty Lou was seven when he passed. I don't know why she'd use those nicknames with some man she took up with lately."

"What was your father like?" Mabel asked.

"I don't remember him, but Betty Lou worshiped him. Said he was kind and gentle and always took up for her when Momma treated her bad."

"What did your mother say about him?"

"Momma hated him for dying without leaving us a penny."

"What did he die of?" Cole asked.

"Heart failure."

"How old was he?"

"In his sixties."

"So he was a lot older than your mother," Mabel said.

"Thirty years older."

"How did they meet?"

"I don't know. She never said."

"Why did she marry a man so much older?"

"She said he told her he was rich. He was old and sick, so she figured he wouldn't last long, and she thought he'd leave her a fortune when he died, but if he ever had any money, he lost it all somehow. When he passed on, all we got was that old shack in

Saddleback Cove and the little clump of piss-poor land it sits on. Momma said if she'd known he was dirt poor she never would've polished his knob."

Mabel frowned.

"Her words," Reba said. "Not mine."

"How did Betty Lou get along with your mother?" Cole asked.

"She hated her, same as me."

That seemed to pique Mabel's interest. "Did they make amends before your mother's death?"

"No way. Momma could never make up for what she did to me and Betty Lou."

"That brings us to the last subject we want to talk to you about," Rachel said. She looked at Reba. "Are you okay with this? I won't tell them if you don't want me to."

"I already agreed to it. Let's get it over with."

Rachel then told Cole and Mabel that a man wearing a leather mask paid Hazel to molest Reba repeatedly for two years, starting when she was ten years old.

When Rachel finished, Mabel left the room. Another wave of guilt came over Cole for not having found out and stopped it.

Mabel returned with a box of tissues. Rachel took one. So did Mabel. Reba did not. Her eyes were dry and angry.

Mabel picked up her pen. "How old are you?" she asked Reba.

"Forty-two."

"What's your birth date?"

"March third."

"The last time he raped you. How long was it after your twelfth birthday?"

"About a month, maybe two."

"So the last time would have been in April or May, 1937."

Reba thought for a moment and then nodded.

"You say he was bleeding after you shot him. Do you know precisely where the wound was located on his body?"

"I aimed for the middle of his gut, but my fist clenched when I squeezed the trigger. When he stood beside the bed, it looked to me like I shot him in the side."

"Which side?"

Reba thought about it. "Left side."

Cole knew what Mabel was thinking. "Did he bleed a lot?" Cole asked.

"He bled some, but not enough to die from it, I'm sorry to say."

Cole and Mabel fell silent.

"Is there any chance you can find the man, Sheriff?" Rachel asked.

"There's always a chance."

Reba gave Cole a hard look and then averted her eyes.

He had the feeling she hadn't told them everything.

Chapter Twenty-Three

THE FIANCÉ

March 6, 1967, Monday noon

AFTER MABEL GAVE Chase Dooley the go-ahead to track down Rosabelle Steeger, the woman who reported Thurman Bowie missing, Chase headed west to Dealeton, a town in Buck County. In the past, the region's two main industries were coal mining and rock products, but the coal mines shut down in the thirties and the quarries petered out ten years ago. By 1967, most of Buck County's residents were unemployed and dirt poor.

Chase stopped at Buck County Sheriff Hubert Feedlow's office at noon to ask him to go along.

"Hell, no," Feedlow said.

Tall, lean, and lazy, his feet propped on his desk and his jaw pooched out by a huge chaw of Redman Chewing Tobacco, he spat into a Styrofoam cup. "Bowie was murdered in Selk County. It ain't my problem. You wanna talk to Rosabelle, you're welcome to go out there by yourself. Ain't no trouble finding her place. It's the stinkin shithole sits at the end of Dealeton Road."

So Chase drove out to the Steeger place alone. Feedlow's

description was dead-on. Dealeton was a hole-in-the-road just inside the Virginia-West Virginia state line. Three miles south of it, fifty feet past a yellow End State Maintenance sign, Chase parked beside a rusty mailbox, "St g r" the only letters still showing through the corrosion.

A tarpaper shack slouched in a ragged yard. A plastic sheet spanned a large hole in the roof above the front door. Cardboard covered one window; another window was cracked. A pig's snout, twitching and grunting, poked through the planks of a wooden pen beside the house. An outhouse stood in the far corner of the yard at the foot of a steep mountain that cast a dark shadow over the property.

When Chase got out of his truck, a short young man with long mousy hair and a handlebar moustache threw open the front door shouting, "Y'all won't take me alive!" He pointed a pistol at Chase and fired three quick rounds that kicked up clods of dirt at the base of the mailbox and sprayed over Chase's boots.

Two more shots ripped through an oak sapling beside the mailbox while Chase rounded his truck to take cover. By the time he drew his service revolver and peeked over the hood, the man was no longer in the doorway.

A few seconds later, the man jumped out from behind the outhouse and fired a round that whizzed by Chase's head. Chase returned fire and the man dove behind the outhouse.

Another thirty seconds passed before he burst into the open and charged up the mountain. He was only fifty yards away and Chase had a clear shot at his back, but he held his fire. The man scrambled up the slope and disappeared in the trees.

Chase let out a long breath. "What the hell?" he muttered.

A short, chubby woman clutching a coal-black puppy under her arm appeared in the doorway. Her purple housecoat exposed a slip that stretched taut over her distended belly. "Y'all might as well give it up," she shouted. "Don't matter how many y'all come round here, Sonny won't never go."

She stepped out on the stoop and stomped across the yard toward Chase. The puppy wriggled to free himself but she held him tight, scowling darkly.

Chase holstered his gun and came around the truck.

The woman marched up to Chase and stood too close to him, the toes of her filthy house slippers touching the tips of his boots, her belly pressing against his belt buckle. She squinted up at him through thick glasses that magnified her crossed green eyes. A wave of body odor hit him as he looked down at her tangled, ratty hair, pimpled button nose, and buck teeth. He had to swallow hard to fight off an urge to gag.

"Sonny'd kill hisself fore he'd go with y'all!" she shouted. Her breath smelled like sour milk. "You might as well get back in your truck and go on away from here."

"I don't know what you're talking about, ma'am."

"I ain't no ma'am. I'm Rosabelle, and y'all done caused me more'n enough trouble. Evy time y'all come around, Sonny runs off for a month a Sundays and I have to do all his chores." She pointed toward the pigpen. "Who you reckon's gonna slop at hog tonight? Sure as hell won't be Sonny now that you done run him off again."

"Who is Sonny?"

"Well, shit! He's my brother, as if you don't know."

"The man who fired at me?"

Rosabelle paused, looking confused. "Ain't you the army?"

"My name's Chase Dooley. I'm a deputy sheriff from Selk County."

She jabbed her stubby finger at Chase's truck. "That's a army truck if ever I saw one."

Chase glanced at his truck, awareness of a misunderstanding creeping over him. Sheriff Grundy had granted his request to paint his patrol truck army green when he signed on as a deputy fresh off his discharge. Neither of them thought the distinctive color would cause a problem, and it hadn't up to that point. "I'm not with the army, ma'am." Chase pointed at the county logo on the truck's door.

"I'm a Selk County deputy sheriff. I didn't come out here to see your brother. I came to see you about your missing persons report on Thurman Bowie."

She scowled. "Well, I'll be damned. Sonny done run off for nothin." The puppy wriggled and whined. She stepped back from Chase and set it on the ground. It waddled over to the mailbox and cocked its leg on the post.

"Why did your brother shoot at me?"

"Sonny run off from the army last year. They come after him four or five times now. He don't want to go back so he shoots at em and runs off evy time they come around. He dug a pit somewhere up on top the mountain. Covered it with branches and leaves and such. He crawls in it evy time them army men come. They climbed all over the mountain last time they was here, but they couldn't find him. He thought you was one a them when he saw your truck." She sighed and rubbed her belly. "Trouble is, he'll hole up in that pit for a month to make sure he won't get caught, and I'll be stuck here with no help now that Thurman run off."

"Sheriff Feedlow tells me you reported Thurman missing, Tuesday, February twenty-six," Chase said, trying to get back on track.

"Lotta good it did me. Sheriff Feedlow won't even go lookin for him. Said it was a waste a time cause Thurman probly disappeared on purpose to get away from me." She looked at the puppy, trotting off toward the pigpen, his tail wagging. "The sheriff's bout as useless as Tater." She looked up at Chase with a spark of hope in her eyes. "Wait a minute. Did y'all find Thurman over there in Selk County?"

Chase hesitated, not sure how to approach the subject of Bowie's death or how Rosabelle would react to it. He noticed two wooden lawn chairs under a persimmon tree near the house. "Can we sit over there and talk for a few minutes?"

"I s'pose."

She walked across the yard. Chase followed. Chase helped Rosabelle sit down on the more sturdy-looking of the two and he sat down carefully next to her. They were downwind of the pigpen and the scent of slop soured the air.

"How long have you known Thurman?" Chase asked.

"Since he come home from the big house last summer. His momma lives up a road here. She threw him out after he run his daddy off. That's when he moved in with me and Sonny. Him and Sonny got on pretty good, so he let him stay. Pretty soon, Thurman and me got on real good, too." She sniggered and rubbed her swollen belly.

"When are you due?"

"Next month. Thurman and me's s'posed to get married fore the baby comes. That's why I been chasin after him. We're runnin outa time."

"When was the last time you saw him?"

"Saturday, bout three weeks ago. We'd spent Friday night drinkin and such. He'd come home with a bottle so we could celebrate bout his new job."

"What kind of job?"

"A contract job, spot work. Thurman don't like regular work. He hires out his services for a fee. Some man came along to the firin range and hired him to shoot at big game on a huntin trip." She smiled, her buck teeth gleaming yellow in the sunlight. "He's a helluva shot. Evibody says so."

"What kind of rifle does he have?"

"Thirty-aught-six. Good for long shots. He zeroed it in so he can hit a dime at three hunnerd yards."

"Did he say who hired him?"

"Said his name was Ray. Thurman didn't know his last name."

"Did you meet the man?"

"Naw, but I saw him that Saturday when he come by to pick up Thurman to go do the shootin job."

"What did he look like?"

"I didn't get a good look at him. Parked out there by the road. Didn't get out of his truck. Gray hair and a gray beard is all I saw."

"What kind of truck did he drive?"

"Black Dodge pickup. Couple years old."

"What time on Saturday did he come to get Thurman?"

"Bout noon. Thurman said he'd be back here in four or five days, but he ain't never showed up." She scrunched her face into a frown, the buck teeth sliding over her lower lip. "What's all these questions about? Did y'all find Thurman or what?" Rosabelle looked at Chase with a hopeful expression.

Chase looked around at the house and the yard. Some of the foster homes he'd grown up in were as rough as this one. Most of his foster mothers were cut from the same cloth as Rosabelle, considered by the general public to be white trash, worthless, no-account, with no prospects and no hope of rising out of the squalor of poverty. Some were cruel and Chase had suffered at their hands; others were kind and treated him with care. Rosabelle probably ranked somewhere in between. He knew her type well. Despite her rough appearance, her heart wasn't made of stone. She had feelings, just like expectant mothers with good breeding. The life of a young woman like Rosabelle was a parade of heartbreaking setbacks and disappointments, he knew, so she probably saw this one coming, but that didn't make it any easier to tell her.

"I'm afraid I've got some bad news, ma'am."

She put a trembling hand to her lips and her eyes brimmed with tears.

He spoke in soft tones. She put her hands over her belly and broke down. He put his arm around her and drew her to him. She buried her face in his shoulder and sobbed.

Chapter Twenty-Four

THE NAKED CORPSE

March 6, 1967, Monday afternoon

COLE AND MABEL sat at Cole's desk after Rachel and Reba left his office. Cole wiped the sweat off his face with a kerchief. "I'd give my badge to catch the man with the leather mask."

Mabel dabbed her own flushed brow with a tissue. "Reba gave us a slim lead, you know."

"The wound."

She nodded. "Thirty years ago the state didn't require a doctor to report a gunshot wound to the authorities, but if we're lucky, the man went to Dolley Madison. They keep records going back decades. Down in some dank basement archive there may be a cardboard box containing the name of a patient the hospital treated for a small-caliber gunshot wound between April one and May thirty, 1937."

"See what you can find."

"Will do." She looked over her notes. "One thing Reba said puzzles me. She claimed Betty Lou hated their mother."

"That's consistent with what I've learned. Betty Lou told

Elwood Critzer she was glad Hazel died, and Reverend Chatham says she blamed her mother for ruining her life."

Mabel looked perplexed. She went to the file cabinets, withdrew a file, and placed it on Cole's desk. It was labeled "Emley, Hazel."

"Read this while I type up my notes of the meeting with Reba." Mabel left the room.

Since Hazel Emley died of natural causes, the sheriff's office conducted no investigation of her death and the file contained only three documents: notes from dispatch about the discovery of Hazel's body, Deputy Karson Deford's report about his response to dispatch's call, and a copy of the death certificate.

The notes from dispatch indicated that Hazel's neighbor, Jerry Caldwell, reported the discovery of her body at 11:15 P.M., December 25, 1966. The dispatcher sent Karson Deford to Hazel's home at 43 Blackberry Road in Saddleback Cove and called the rescue squad and the medical examiner, Randy Hotchkiss.

Karson Deford was in his midforties, six foot five, lean, with a long, thin face, fierce black eyes, and a complexion the color of pecan shells. He was the only black man on the force. Five years ago, he resigned from his twenty-year position as a Virginia state trooper and accepted Cole's offer of a job as a county deputy to be closer to home after his wife suffered a spinal injury that rendered her a paraplegic. He was a good officer, calm under fire, quiet, but forceful.

Cole turned to Karson's report about Hazel Emley's death. "Arrived at 43 Blackberry Rd at 11:45 P.M. Jerry Caldwell and Elizabeth Louise Mundy, Hazel Emley's daughter, met me at the door." Cole paused. That was the detail about Hazel's death he hadn't been able to recall. Betty Lou's presence at her mother's house had seemed insignificant when he scanned Karson's report in December and he had forgotten it, but it took on new meaning in light of Betty Lou's comments to Elwood. If she hated her mother, what was she doing at her house on Christmas night? Mabel's photographic memory had recalled the detail and noticed the inconsistency.

"The residence has two rooms," Karson's report continued, "a combined sitting area/kitchen and a small bedroom. Hazel Emley lay on her back on the bed in the bedroom with a blanket pulled up to her chin. She was naked. Her clothes lay on the floor at the foot of the bed. She had no pulse. Her eyes were open and glazed over. Her body was cold. Mr. Caldwell told me she was not breathing and had no pulse when he arrived a half hour earlier. I radioed dispatch to notify the rescue squad to return to the hospital."

"I then spoke to Mrs. Mundy and Mr. Caldwell. Mrs. Mundy said she arrived at the house to check on her mother's condition about 10:30 P.M. She found Mrs. Emley in her bed unconscious and unresponsive."

Cole put his hand to his chin, thinking. Reverend Chatham said Betty Lou had learned Leland had an affair with Reba that day and she blamed Hazel for it because she sold them to molesters, poisoning their relationships with men. Betty Lou "found" Hazel's corpse only a few hours after her meeting with the preacher. The timing begged the question: Did Betty Lou harm her mother?

Cole returned to the report. "Mrs. Emley's house does not have a telephone, so Mrs. Mundy drove to the residence of the nearest neighbor, Mr. Caldwell, and Mr. Caldwell called our office. Mrs. Mundy drove back to her mother's house with Mr. Caldwell following in his truck."

"Mrs. Mundy said her mother was seventy years old, a lifelong smoker with a history of respiratory problems, and in poor physical condition. She said Mrs. Emley suffered from a severe cough that had grown much worse during the last month."

Cole reread those sentences. Betty Lou's comments implied she had been a concerned daughter, monitoring her mother's health.

Cole read on. "Dr. Hotchkiss arrived at 12:45 A.M. At 1:00 A.M. I helped him place the corpse in a body bag. We carried it to his van, and he left the premises."

"I released Mr. Caldwell and Mrs. Mundy at 1:15 A.M. I went

through the residence after their departure and found nothing to indicate foul play. I locked the door and left the scene at 1:40 A.M."

"By all appearances, Mrs. Emley was an elderly woman in poor health who died in her sleep. Pending Dr. Hotchkiss's determination, I recommend no further action."

Cole reviewed the report a second time, then buzzed Mabel and told her to ask Karson to come to Cole's office.

Cole turned to the last document in the file, the death certificate, a one-page form. Randy Hotchkiss had checked its boxes and filled in its blanks. His practice throughout his tenure as the local medical examiner had been to supplement the form with a memo to the sheriff's office summarizing his observations from his external inspection of the corpse, but there was no memo from Randy in Hazel's file.

On the death certificate, Randy had provided uncharacteristically sparse information. For cause of death, he entered "Pneumonia." He left blank the spaces calling for the date of the onset of the disease and any other underlying diseases, injuries, or significant medical conditions that contributed to the death. Under "Autopsy?" Randy marked "No."

Cole stared at the death certificate with a growing sense of unease.

The document listed Holbeck and Hollingsworth Funeral Home as the undertaker. Cole telephoned George Hollingsworth.

"When did Randy deliver the corpse to you?" Cole asked.

A rustle of papers came across the phone line. "Says here we took possession at nine A.M. on December twenty-six."

Cole was surprised. Randy had released the corpse less than eight hours after he took custody of it. Normally, he would have reviewed a decedent's medical records to corroborate his determination of the cause of death before he transferred the body to the undertaker. Having been indigent, Hazel probably couldn't afford a family doctor's care, but the emergency room at Dolley Madison or one of the free clinics would have treated her from time to time.

Randy couldn't possibly have talked to them and researched her medical history in the short time he retained custody of the corpse.

"Who paid for the burial?" Cole asked George.

"Her only surviving relatives were Reba Emley and Betty Lou Mundy. They both refused to take responsibility. The state paid for a pauper's burial at Grace Church Cemetery."

Betty Lou's concerned-daughter act apparently fell away the day after her mother's death, Cole thought.

Karson Deford appeared in Cole's doorway. Cole thanked George for his help and hung up the phone. Karson folded his tall lanky frame in the chair across the desk from Cole. "I just reviewed your report about Hazel Emley," Cole said. "I have a few questions. Did Betty Lou Mundy seem distressed that night?"

"She wasn't in tears, but she seemed upset."

"She told you she dropped by at ten thirty to check on Hazel. Seems late for a call on an elderly woman."

"She said she'd been at a party. Came by the house afterward."

That didn't make sense to Cole. Given the preacher's description of Betty Lou's agitated state of mind, she would have been in no mood to go to a party.

"Your report says you didn't see any evidence of foul play. Did you see anything at all irregular?"

"There wasn't much furniture in that old shack, but it was all in the right place. Nothing damaged or overturned. No signs of a struggle. The only thing I found curious was the old lady didn't have a stitch of clothing on her. The temperature was in the twenties, and that place had cracks in the wall big enough to stick a finger through. No covers on the bed except for a natty old army blanket. I asked Doc Hotchkiss about it. He told me it wasn't unusual for an elderly woman in Mrs. Emley's condition to go to bed naked in the cold. He said she looked like she hadn't eaten in days and that malnutrition and the cold weather probably brought on hypothermia, which would have made her feel so warm she took off her clothes to cool down."

This seemed farfetched to Cole. "Was Randy sober that night?"

"He didn't seem drunk, but I smelled whiskey on him."

"Anything unusual about his behavior?"

"He was mighty anxious to put her corpse in a bag and carry it out to his van. He didn't spend more than five minutes with the body."

Another possible reason for Randy's hasty disposition of the corpse, much more troubling than mere drunkenness, took seed in Cole's mind. "How about Betty Lou? Was she sober?"

"She was a little tipsy. I chalked it up to the party she went to."

"Was there any contact between Randy and Betty Lou?"

"After we loaded the body in his van, he came back inside the house and spoke to her."

"What did he say?"

"He kept his voice low so I didn't hear it, but at the time, I figured he gave her his condolences."

"Did she say anything to him?"

"No."

"Did she tell Randy about Hazel's respiratory problems?"

"She didn't say anything to him."

"Did you tell him Betty Lou said Hazel had breathing problems?"

"No."

Cole leaned back in his chair and rubbed the back of his neck.

"Did I miss something on this one, boss?"

"No. You did a good job, as always." Cole thanked Karson for his help and he left the office.

Cole looked at the death certificate again. No one told Randy about Hazel's respiratory condition, he spent five minutes with the body, and he didn't research her medical history. And yet he entered pneumonia on the certificate as the cause of death.

Cole stared out the windows. The sun had set behind Beacon Hill, tinting cumulus clouds with maroon and amber streaks.

He buzzed Mabel and asked her to come into his office. He

handed her the file and asked her to review it. She sat across from him and looked it over. When she finished, he told her the additional information he'd learned from George Hollingsworth and Karson. "What do you think?"

She looked vexed, her eyebrows pulled together in a straight black line. "We'll need Wiley to file a petition to exhume the body." Wiley Rea was the commonwealth's attorney.

"Get Shirley West on the phone," Cole said. "She'll have to write up a report for Wiley, explaining the reason we need to dig up Hazel and perform an autopsy three months after her burial. Call Rachel, too, and ask her if Reba will consent to the exhumation."

She nodded and left Cole's office.

Cole looked at the death certificate again. At minimum, Randy had done a piss-poor job of examining Hazel's corpse, but Cole was afraid he had done much worse.

Chapter Twenty-Five

THE ENEMY FOR LIFE

March 6, 1967, Monday afternoon

AFTER LEAVING Rosabelle Steeger's house, Chase went back to Sheriff Feedlow's office, and Feedlow gave him directions to Cantrell's Shooting Range where Rosabelle had said Bowie met the man named Ray who hired him to hunt big game. Chase arrived at the range midafternoon. The vehicles in its gravel lot spanned the economic spectrum. He parked his patrol truck between a gleaming black 1967 Ford F-250 with a Confederate flag tied to its radio aerial and a 1947 army surplus Jeep with a missing passenger door and a bashed-in front bumper.

At the edge of the parking lot, two long, low structures with lacquered pine pillars and canted corrugated tin roofs stretched across the base of two horseshoe-shaped earthen berms enclosing flat fields of mown grass. Between the structures, a check-in and monitoring shack on an elevated concrete platform overlooked the stations and the ranges. Life-sized silhouettes were stapled to posts at various distances up to 200 yards in the handgun range and 500 yards in the rifle range. Plywood walls divided each structure into firing stations with shoulder-high hitching posts for bracing shots from a standing position and tables with anchored stools for seated shots.

The extraordinary heat wave had broken that afternoon and the temperature had dropped into the fifties. Cottony clouds floated in a pale blue sky. A mild breeze cooled Chase's brow as he climbed out of his truck and headed toward the monitoring shack.

A nonstop cacophony of gunfire filled the air, rapid-fire pops and staccato booms. Two shooters occupied stations on the handgun range, a middle-aged man in a business suit and a short young woman with long blond hair, both wearing earmuffs and using two-handed grips and wide stances. A dozen men of various ages and body styles, mostly dressed in hunting gear, stood in the stations on the rifle range. A young man in the station closest to the check-in shack looked to be in his early twenties. Tall and wiry, he wore a straw hat with the brim rolled up on the sides and a long pheasant feather curling from its red band. He sat on a stool, braced a scoped rifle on the table, and squeezed off a shot. A hole pitted the center of a silhouetted figure's head posted beside a 300-yard marker. The young man looked over at Chase. A cocky smile came across his face and he winked.

Chase nodded to him and climbed the concrete steps to the check-in shack and stepped inside. Behind a counter that cut the room in half, metal filing cabinets were shoved up against the back wall. A short, fat old man with a blind milky eye stood behind the counter wearing bib overalls and a Smith & Wesson ball cap. He pored over a sheet attached to a clipboard.

Sheriff Feedlow had warned Chase about old man Pinkerton Cantrell, the owner-operator of the range. "Pinky looks like a hayseed, but don't underestimate him. He turned a big pile a dirt and an open-air cowshed into a small fortune when most people in this county don't have two dimes to rub together. Trouble is he's a pain in the ass and he holds grudges. You rile him, you've made an enemy for life."

Chase approached the counter cautiously. "Afternoon, sir."

Cantrell squinted at Chase's uniform with his good eye and grimaced, exposing a gap where his upper front teeth should have been. "Only state troopers and Buck County law men shoot for free. You ain't neither. You want to shoot, you pay the full fee." The missing teeth caused a heavy lisp.

"I'm not looking for a free turn on your range. I'm looking for information about a man I have reason to believe was here on Friday, February seventeen. He might have been here with Thurman Bowie."

"Bowie? You looking for Bowie?"

"No, sir. Bowie was murdered three weeks ago."

"Murdered?" Cantrell's good eye widened and the milky one narrowed. He took off his cap, set it on the counter, and scratched a full head of thick, wiry gray hair, causing it to stick out in all directions. "How was he killed?"

"Gunshots. One to the head, one to the chest."

"Execution style," Cantrell said. "I ain't surprised. Bowie beat up on anybody and everybody. It stands to reason he'd bully the wrong man sooner or later."

"Did you know him well?"

"I didn't have much choice. He bought a volume discount package. Came here most every day. He was the best shooter in the county. Nobody else was close, except maybe that Gilchrist boy out there in station one, and he's only in the running because his .35 Remington Carbine is a better rifle than Bowie's weapon."

"What did Bowie shoot?"

"A Brown Precision thirty-aught-six bolt-action with a walnut stock and black recoil pad. Bowie outfitted it with a Leupold scope. It's a good weapon but not as accurate as Gilchrist's Remington. Even so, standing or sitting, Bowie could put every shot within a two-inch ring on a five-hundred-yard target. On his best day, Gilchrist couldn't do half that good. Bowie wasn't worth a damn for much of anything else, but when it came to long-range rifle shots, they don't come any better."

The question of Bowie's presence on Bobcat's summit was even more puzzling now. He had stood behind a tripod three hundred yards from Betty Lou Mundy's house within a forty-eight-hour window around the time of her murder, and yet he wasn't her murderer. What the hell was he doing up there?

"Who killed Bowie?" Cantrell asked, bringing Chase out of his thoughts.

"I don't know. The man I'm looking for may know something about it. He may have been with Bowie the last time he was here. I don't know his last name, but his given name is Ray."

Cantrell's eyes hardened. "Tall, thin bastard, about sixty-five years old."

"You remember him?"

"Hard to forget the biggest asshole come through that door this year."

"You remember his last name?"

"Middleditch," Cantrell said, curling his lip. "He signed in, paid his fee, went to the window there, and looked out at the rifle range. Had bo-nocs hanging round his neck. Must have stood there five minutes looking at the shooters and checking the targets. I finally said, 'You paid to shoot, not to look. Take a station or get off the range.'

"He looked like he wanted to give me some lip, but he swallowed whatever smart-ass remark he had in mind and asked me the name of the man in station five. Thurman Bowie, I told him. Then he asked me what kind of man Bowie was. I told him I ran a shooting range, not a gossip parlor. He told me I should watch my mouth or somebody might knock the rest of my teeth out."

Cantrell reached under the counter and placed a pistol on top of it. "You run a shooting range you never know what kind of shithead will come along. I keep this here Luger P08 under the counter for such occasions. Lightweight, easy to handle, semiautomatic. Handy enough to get the drop on some shiftless prick thinks he's big enough to push me around, like this here Middleditch piss-ant. I pulled it out of the drawer and pointed it at his chest. Told him he had five seconds to get out of the shack and twenty seconds to get off the property. He looked mad as a bull with a beehive up his ass, but he backed out the door and got in his truck and drove off. Ain't seen him since."

Chase suppressed a smile. Sheriff Feedlow's warning about Cantrell hit the mark. You rile him, you've made an enemy for life. "What kind of truck did he drive?"

"1965 Dodge-100 light duty pickup, black."

"I don't suppose you got the plate number."

Cantrell gave Chase a smug look, turned to the filing cabinets, pulled out a drawer, flipped through folders, extracted a piece of paper, and handed the page to Chase. Scrawled across the top in ink was "February 17, 1967." Below that were three columns with headings: "Name, DL No., Plate No."

Halfway down the page Chase found Ray Middleditch. Under the driver's license column, Cantrell had written "S.C. 100264309."

"S.C. stands for South Carolina?"

"That's right. He showed me a South Carolina driver's license. Said he'd moved to Virginia couple months ago and hadn't had time to get a Virginia license. The truck had a Virginia plate on it, though."

Chase looked at the plate number: 684–651. He wrote the driver's license and plate numbers on his notepad. "Anything else you can tell me about Middleditch?"

"He was toting a Winchester thirty-thirty, lever action, old. He didn't take good care of it. Barrel hadn't been blued in a good while. Dulled down bad. Walnut stock had a satin finish but it was mostly worn off. He had a handgun, too. He didn't show it to me, but in my business, you develop an eye for concealed weapons. Whatever he was carrying, it was big enough to swell his coat pocket."

Chase made more notes. "Anything else?"

Cantrell put his hand to his chin, closed his milky eye, and looked up at the ceiling with his good one. He leveled his one-eyed gaze on Chase. "He'd dealt with trouble before. He's experienced."

"What makes you say that?"

"When I pulled the Luger on him, he was mighty pissed. A hothead who's never stared down the barrel of a gun might have let his temper get the best of him. An amateur would have gone for that gun in his pocket or tried to cock his thirty-thirty, and I would have dropped him in his tracks. Middleditch knew better. He made the smart move and backed down. He knew what he was doing. He'd been in tough spots before." Cantrell picked up the signup sheet for February 17, filed it away, and put the Luger back under the counter. "Middleditch is either a career criminal, or he's a lawman." A half smile, half sneer twisted Cantrell's mouth. "Or he's both."

Chase gave Cantrell a long look and then touched the brim of his hat. "Thank you, Mr. Cantrell. You've been a big help."

He went out the door and walked down the steps. The young man Cantrell referred to as the Gilchrist boy stood in station one behind a shoulder-high hitching post, his rifle braced on it. He fired his Remington. The butt of the rifle kicked his shoulder but he barely moved. Smoke curled from the end of the barrel. The black silhouette posted at 300 yards sported a bullet hole in its head, dead center, and yet Cantrell called Bowie a better marksman than Gilchrist.

Gilchrist looked over at Chase. His pheasant feather quivered in the breeze. A self-satisfied smile came across his face.

Chapter Twenty-Six

THE DRUNKEN DOCTOR

March 6, 1967, Monday night

THAT NIGHT, Cole and Mabel went out to Fox Run in Cole's patrol car. They parked across the road from Randy's house, a yellow two-story home with a wide front porch and a green tin roof. The house was dark except for a soft light that glowed in a row of little square windows across the top of the front door. Cole knew that when Randy drank himself into a stupor and passed out at the kitchen table, which was most every night, kitchen light spilled down the hallway to cast a faint glow in the little windows.

"You gonna be okay, Cole?" Mabel asked. At the end of the day, when he decided to question Randy about Hazel Emley's death, she'd suggested that she come along. "He was your close friend until he took to the bottle. You're conflicted. You shouldn't do this alone."

Cole agreed. He and Randy had been close friends, but he didn't believe Hazel Emley died of pneumonia. He thought Betty Lou killed her mother and Randy covered it up, but Mabel suspected Randy of much worse.

"He's old enough to be one of Betty Lou's Papa Bears," she had said. "He started drinking heavily about five years ago. His wife left him shortly afterwards. Betty Lou told Reverend Chatham she had an affair with an older, well-off, married man about five years back. He has a dark blue Cadillac, and Bessie Tilden saw a big car like that the night of the murder. His Cadillac has big wide tires, like the tire track left near the gate at the Mundy place. The morning of the murder, he fell on Betty Lou's dead body, sobbing. Chase thought he was drunk, but he could have been overcome with guilt and grief."

Cole believed Randy could have been one of Betty Lou's lovers, but he didn't think he was capable of murder. The evidence against him on that count was circumstantial and thin, raising questions, but it fell far short of proving guilt.

Cole thought he could extract the truth from Randy because of their long friendship, but as he and Mabel sat in front of Randy's house, he wasn't so sure. Cole's friend drowned in a sea of vodka years earlier. The man he had become was a stranger.

Cole broke open his gun and checked that it was loaded.

"You think you'll need that?" Mabel asked.

"I hope not." Cole holstered it and got out of the car.

A purple night sky framed the house. The barren branches of the big oaks in the front yard swayed in a cold wind, the temperature having fallen into the forties. Cole's back ached as he and Mabel crossed Randy's brick walkway and climbed the porch steps. At the front door, Cole peered through the row of little windows. The entry hall and parlor were dark. As he'd assumed, the light in the kitchen was on.

He pounded on the door. "Randy?"

No response.

"Maybe he's not home."

"He's home."

Cole tried the door. It was unlocked, as usual. Randy had stopped caring enough to lock it years ago. They walked through the entry hall and down the hallway and stood in the kitchen doorway.

Across the room, Randy sat slumped over the kitchen table, his head resting on his left arm, his right arm stretched toward an empty fifth of vodka and an overturned bottle of orange juice. The juice had pooled around his arms and puddled at his feet. His tweed jacket lay in a heap on the floor, the coattail sopping up the juice. Wind blew through an open window by the table, carrying the stench of rancid orange juice and alcohol across the room.

"Oh," Mabel gasped, covering her nose with her hand.

Dried-out orange juice stains splotched the speckled linoleum floor. The sink overflowed with dirty dishes and glassware. Fragments of burned toast and crumbs covered the stove top. The refrigerator door stood open, its interior light burned out.

Cole crossed the room and closed it.

Mabel stayed at the doorway. "How can he live like this?"

"Too drunk to care."

He searched the cabinets for clean linen but found none. A dirty dish towel lay on the floor. He picked it up, moved a pile of dishes from the sink to the countertop, ran hot water on the rag, wrung it out, and carried it over to Randy.

Mabel walked across the room and stood beside Cole. "I didn't know he was this far gone."

"Alcoholism is a progressive disease. It'll kill him in the end."

Cole took Randy by the shoulders and pulled him up to a sitting position. His body seemed stiff, his head unnaturally cocked to one side, dried orange juice crusted in his scraggly hair and beard.

Mabel's eyes widened. She grabbed Cole's arm. "Look, Cole."

Randy's right sleeve was rolled up to his bicep. An auburn line ran from a puncture mark at the crook of his elbow down his arm to a crusted pool of blood on the table. Beside it lay a syringe.

Cole's chest tightened. He put his hand to Randy's throat. His flesh was cold, and there was no pulse. Cole dropped the towel and stepped back from the table. Mabel stepped back with him, clutching his arm so tightly her nails bit into his flesh through his uniform. They stared at Randy, speechless. Then Mabel said, "We'd better call Shirley West."

"The telephone's in the parlor."

Mabel lingered for a moment, then let go of Cole, and went down the hall toward the parlor.

Cole took in Randy's appearance, his matted hair and tangled beard, his sagging shoulders and pot belly, his gray, fleshy face bloated by liquor fat. He'd tried hard to drink himself to death, but apparently vodka worked too slowly for him.

The cold wind that belled the curtain died down. It fell back to the window, its hem dragging across a medicine vial by the empty vodka bottle. Cole leaned over and looked at its label. Blue letters against a white background: "Succinylcholine."

Chapter Twenty-Seven

SHIRLEY'S TEARS

March 6, 1967, Monday night

AT TEN P.M., Shirley West joined Cole in Randy Hotchkiss's kitchen. Cole watched her look over Randy's corpse. In her midforties, average height, chunky figure, she wore a shapeless, wrinkled gray dress and no makeup. Her short, stiff brown hair looked as though she'd cut it herself with a pair of dull scissors. On her best day, she looked bedraggled, but that night she looked worse—grief-stricken, devastated.

Cole was surprised. Shirley was the consummate professional. Unmarried with no children and no close friends other than lab workers and law enforcement personnel, her job was her life. In fifteen years of working with her, Cole had seen her maintain a stoic attitude throughout the most graphic, heartbreaking crime scenes but that night she wept openly.

Cole put his hand on her shoulder.

She wiped tears from her face. "When the Virginia Chief Medical Examiner appointed me the assistant in charge of the Western District Office, I was thirty-one. He passed over several older men who did everything they could to undermine my authority. Almost everyone treated me like an amateur. The local medical examiners were the worst of the lot. Randy was the only one who supported me. He never once questioned my direction and spoke up for me every chance he got. Firing him broke my heart."

"You made the right decision. He wasn't fit to do the job."

"I know, but it's a shame. Just a few years ago, he was a fine doctor. A careful medical examiner. A good man. What the hell happened to him?"

"Betty Lou Mundy happened to him."

Shirley looked surprised and troubled. "What do you mean?"

Cole told her about his suspicion that Randy was Betty Lou's lover, that Betty Lou killed Hazel Emley, and that Randy covered it up. Cole had sent Mabel home to take care of her kids before Shirley arrived, so she wasn't there to explain her reasons for believing Randy might also be Betty Lou's murderer. Cole laid out the circumstantial evidence supporting her theory. "The evidence is weak. I'd hoped to learn enough from Randy to rule him out as her murderer. His suicide leaves us without answers to a passel of questions."

Shirley gazed at Randy morosely. "What a tragedy. Such a waste of talent." She stared at Randy for a long time. Then she seemed to remember her professional responsibilities. She walked around to Randy's right side and looked at the syringe on the table and the puncture mark in his arm. A perplexed frown came across her face. She looked at the vial beside the bottle of vodka. She stepped closer to it and peered at it, then straightened up and looked at Cole. "Something's wrong here."

Cole looked at Randy, the syringe, and the vial. "What do you mean?"

"The wound from the injection is in Randy's right arm. If he gave himself the shot, he used his left hand to do it. Randy was right-handed, and he had severe right hand dominance. Using his left hand to inject a drug into his right arm would have been unnatural and awkward for him."

Shirley was right, Cole thought. Randy had rarely used his left hand to do anything. "He was drunk. Could that explain it?"

"Intoxication would have made it more difficult for him to accomplish the injection with his left hand." Shirley pointed to the vial. "Besides, Randy would never have chosen to kill himself with succinylcholine."

"Why?"

"Succinylcholine is a skeletal muscle relaxant. An overdose paralyzes you within thirty to sixty seconds after the injection. You're trapped inside your body, immobile and helpless, while the drug shuts down your lungs. You suffocate slowly, your breath growing shorter and shorter until you can't breathe at all, and you don't lose any brain function while this goes on. You know exactly what's happening to you right up to the moment of death. No one would choose to die that way, least of all a doctor, who knew what the drug would do to him."

Cole stared at Randy, digesting the implications of Shirley's reasoning. "Are you saying someone poisoned Randy with that drug?"

"That's a more logical explanation than suicide for what we've found here. It may not be the only explanation. I'll reserve judgment until I perform an autopsy." Shirley withdrew a pair of plastic gloves from her bag, put them on, picked up the vial of succinylcholine and held it up to the overhead light. "Randy had no use for succinylcholine in his medical practice. He was an internist. Succinylcholine's an anesthetic that enables intubation."

"What's intubation?"

"An anesthesiologist gives a patient succinylcholine so he can slide a tube down his throat to help him breathe during surgery. In small doses, it paralyzes the throat and the patient feels no pain when the doctor inserts the breathing tube. But in large doses, it's lethal. As an internist, Randy wouldn't have kept a supply on hand."

"Where did he get it, then?"

"He had privileges at Dolley Madison. He could have gotten it there, I suppose, but there's still no way in hell he would have killed himself with it. There are a hundred easier ways to die, and as a doctor, Randy knew them all."

"I'll get Frank and the forensics team out of bed again," Cole said wearily.

Shirley set the vial on the table. "Tell them to scour the whole house for signs of an intruder."

Cole thought about murder by injection of a lethal drug. "We're looking for a doctor, a nurse, or someone in the medical field. The run-of-the-mill murderer wouldn't know about such a drug, much less have access to it."

Shirley started to say something and then seemed to reconsider.

"One thing we know for sure," Cole said. "If Randy didn't kill himself, we're looking for one hellacious cruel son of a bitch."

Chapter Twenty-Eight

THE HEALING TIME

March 7, 1967, Tuesday morning

RAY AWOKE in bed shortly after dawn. He rolled over and looked out the bedroom window. Behind the apple orchard at the rear of the property, a red sun rose into cardinal, gold, and russet clouds. Crimson dust motes floated in a shaft of light pouring in the window.

He had slept fully dressed under an old musty quilt for nearly seventy-two hours. His clothing and the sheets beneath him were wet with his perspiration. He had hoped to sweat out the poison of infection, and it seemed to have worked. He felt much better.

He stroked the bandage that covered his forearm. The drunken doctor had lanced the wound, sterilized and dressed it, and had given him a tetanus shot, antibiotics, and an injection of morphine. Afterwards, Ray rummaged through the doctor's cache of drugs and stole enough amoxicillin, morphine, and gauze to treat the wound himself from there on. Since then, he had changed the bandage twice and given himself periodic shots of morphine, the last twelve hours ago.

The morphine had worn off and his arm hurt again, but not as badly as the day before. He was on the mend, but he needed at least another day's rest to regain the strength to eliminate the last target, the softest of the five.

He ran his hand over his brow and sighed. He'd be relieved to finish up. This project had very nearly become his white whale. If he hadn't realized at the last minute that he could make the doctor help him, he would have perished.

He sat up on the edge of the bed. He held his head in his hands and waited for the dizziness to pass. He needed another shot of morphine. He'd have to cut himself off from it soon, though. One more shot, maybe two. That would be his limit. He could take out his last target even if he was in the midst of withdrawal, but when he turned to Cole, he would need all his faculties. No weaknesses. No distractions.

The lightheadedness subsided. He stood and walked carefully out of the bedroom, down the stairs, and through the hallway to the kitchen where he'd stored the drugs.

Chapter Twenty-Nine

THE AUTOPSY

March 8, 1967, Wednesday afternoon

COLE STOOD at the door of the Western District's autopsy laboratory, a large room with stainless steel counters and sinks, white tile walls, recessed fluorescent lighting, and a gray linoleum floor. Three stainless steel gurneys stood parallel to one another in the center of the room. Shirley West, dressed in a blue smock, mask, and cap, leaned over the middle gurney where Hazel Emley's cadaver lay naked, her chest and belly fileted and hollowed out, her breastbone still in place, bleach-white, with rib bones fanning out from it like bedsprings.

The commonwealth's attorney had filed a petition for an expedited exhumation Monday night and Judge Blackwell granted the application first thing Tuesday morning, primarily because Rachel McNiel consented to the exhumation and autopsy on behalf of Reba. The body was exhumed late Tuesday and transported to the autopsy room in Roanoke overnight. Shirley began the autopsy Wednesday morning. Cole arrived at her laboratory that afternoon.

He ran his eyes over the length of Hazel's body sprawled on the gurney. Stringy gray hair, long, thin face, eyes closed, blue lips parted slightly, bony arms at her sides, a patch of gray pubic hair, mottled cellulite along stick-thin thighs, knobby, bunioned feet. George Hollingsworth had done a good job with the corpse, Cole thought. Hazel had been in the ground for three months and Cole saw little sign of decay.

Cole cleared his throat to get Shirley's attention. She looked up at him, a scalpel in her hand poised over the corpse. She set it on a tray at the head of the gurney and crossed the lab to a small office with a half window looking out on the autopsy room, gesturing for Cole to follow. They went inside.

Shirley stripped off her surgical gloves and took off her cap and mask and tossed them in a bin by the door. She sat down behind a gray metal desk by the window.

Cole sat down across from her. "Mabel said you wanted to talk to me right away."

"I haven't finished the autopsy, but given the pace of homicides in your county, I figured you'd want to discuss my tentative conclusions as soon as possible." She paused. "Conclusions is too strong a word. Educated guesses would be more accurate."

Shirley straightened a pile of documents and handwritten notes on her desk and folded her hands on top of it. "I think someone killed Hazel with succinylcholine, but I can't prove it. Results from the blood and tissue samples won't be ready for a few days, but they won't support my guesswork. We won't find succinylcholine in her system. It disappears within minutes of injection, breaking down into metabolites that normally exist in the body. It's a poison that can't be traced. The perfect murder weapon."

"If you can't trace it, how do you know someone murdered Hazel with it?"

"I don't know. I'm guessing, and I wouldn't venture such a guess if Randy hadn't died from an injection of succinylcholine. I found visceral congestion, severe pulmonary edema, and petechial hemorrhage of the lungs in Hazel's corpse. All the same conditions were present in Randy's corpse and are consistent with a succinyl-choline injection, but they could have natural causes as well. Certain metabolites are present in both corpses at higher than normal levels, but that could also occur for health-related reasons. Beyond that, all I've got to support my guesswork is circumstantial evidence, suspicious minor injuries on Hazel's corpse that may indicate a forcible injection." Shirley handed Cole three photographs.

He looked them over. The first depicted a fist-sized purplish bruise in the center of Hazel's back. The other two were close-ups of her right forearm, showing an inch-wide bruise about three inches above the wrist.

"The elderly tend to bruise easily," Shirley said, "and the discoloration lingers, so these injuries could have been inflicted within minutes of her death or hours earlier. I'm betting on minutes before." Shirley handed Cole another photograph. It was a close-up of Hazel's buttocks, her cheeks gray and cratered with cellulite. Shirley pointed to a spot in the center of the right buttock. "Look closely there."

Cole held the photo up to the light and squinted at it. The wound was almost invisible, a small dot the size of a pinhead. "What is it?"

"The entry point of a hypodermic needle. I think someone held Hazel facedown, placed his knee on her back, grabbed her right arm as she tried to fight him off, and plunged a syringe into her hip."

"You think Randy did this?"

"He's the most logical suspect. His external examination of the corpse was cursory to nonexistent; he ruled the cause of death as pneumonia in the absence of any evidence; and he released the body to the undertaker in record time. It's possible he conspired with Betty Lou to murder Hazel with a drug he hoped would be untraceable and then rushed the body to the funeral home to make sure no one had a chance to discover what they'd done. The problem with that theory is I can't establish where Randy would have gotten the succinylcholine he used to kill Hazel."

"You said the other night he had privileges at Dolley Madison."

"He had access to the succinylcholine at Dolley Madison, but the succinylcholine we found in his home beside his corpse didn't come from the hospital. The label on the vial says it was manufactured by Sandoz, a Swiss company. The succinylcholine Dolley Madison has in stock was manufactured by Pfizer."

"Could he have bought the drug directly from Sandoz?"

"Drug manufacturers typically don't sell directly to doctors. Randy could have purchased it from a wholesaler, but I don't think he did. I talked to his partner, Ralph Packer. He says he orders all the drugs for their office and he's never ordered succinylcholine. He talked to their wholesaler to see if Randy had purchased any drugs on his own. The wholesaler hadn't taken an order from Randy in more than a year."

"So where did Randy get it?"

"One possibility would be a veterinarian. Vets sometimes use it to euthanize livestock and household pets."

"Why would Randy go to a vet, rather than a hospital or his wholesaler?"

"If he was trying to cover his tracks, an obscure source makes sense."

Cole thought about that. He didn't believe Randy was capable of murder, but if he fell under Betty Lou's spell, maybe he lost his bearings. "I'll have one of my men canvass the veterinarians."

Cole looked through the window at Hazel's cadaver. He stared at the soles of her feet splayed at a forty-five-degree angle, blue-gray, withered. A cold anger came over him. That old lady sold her daughters to men who raped them. He couldn't help but feel she deserved the hard death succinylcholine inflicted on her.

"Are you all right, Cole?"

"I'm fine."

When he put his hands on the desk and pushed himself up to stand, his back clenched and his knees buckled. A groan escaped his lips. Shirley jumped up and grabbed him by the arm to hold him up.

He leaned forward on the desk, breathing hard.

"Cole?"

"Spinal stenosis. It comes and goes."

"Maybe you should take some time off. Give your back a rest."

"No need. I'm fine now." He walked out of the office and through the autopsy room, pain shooting down his legs with every step.

Chapter Thirty

THE VETERINARIAN

March 9, 1967, Thursday morning

DEPUTY KARSON DEFORD took on the assignment of determining where Randy Hotchkiss purchased succinylcholine. Neither of the first two veterinarians he visited used the drug to treat animals. The third, Dr. Creasy Ashburn, was a different story.

Ashburn's Animal Hospital was in a little brick building next to a Dairy Freeze on Wellington Street in Jeetersburg. On Thursday morning, Karson stepped into a small room that smelled faintly of cat urine. A black leather sofa and a matching chair sat in front of a fiberboard desk on a green wall-to-wall shag carpet. A little white-haired old woman sat in the leather chair holding an aged, bony Chihuahua in her lap. When Karson entered the room, the Chihuahua snarled at him.

A pimply-faced teenage girl with collar-length black hair sat behind the fiberboard desk, chewing and popping gum. When she looked up at Karson, her eyes widened and her jaw froze midchew.

"I'm looking for Dr. Ashburn," Karson said to her.

The girl swallowed hard. "Well . . . what exactly you want

him for?"

The Chihuahua jumped to its feet in the old lady's lap, barking furiously. He tried to lunge at Karson, but the old lady held him in check. She shrugged and smiled sweetly. "Ain't nothing I can do," she said, raising her voice to be heard. "He don't like coloreds."

Karson gave her a cold look and turned to the teenage girl. "I'm here on official business," he said, also raising his voice. "Is Dr. Ashburn in?"

The girl shouted back at him. "We don't normally serve . . . I mean y'all don't never come here!"

"Y'all," Karson repeated silently in his head. He had been down this road so many times he knew every bend and twist in it, but it never failed to raise his temperature.

"I'm not a customer," he shouted. He pointed to the badge on his chest. "I'm here on official business. Is Dr. Ashburn in?"

The Chihuahua's racket reached an ear-splitting decibel; spittle was flying from his toothless jaws and his rheumy eyes were wild with rage. Karson glared at him. Here for a rabies shot, no doubt. The old lady continued to smile fondly at the dog and made no attempt to calm him.

Karson looked at the girl. She stared at him vapidly, her mouth hanging open, a wad of gum lodged between her bottom teeth and lip.

"How old are you?" he shouted.

"Fourteen," she shouted back.

"You have a work permit?"

"No."

"You've got five seconds to tell me where Ashburn is before I strip you of your job and write him up for unlawful employment of a minor."

Her eyes widened. "Well, jeez Louise! Jest keep your drawers on!" She jumped up and hustled through a door behind her desk.

The Chihuahua continued to bark at Karson, his fierce blind stare aimed slightly to the left of him.

"He's from Mexico," the smiling old lady said loudly. "That's why he don't like coloreds." Karson had no interest in asking what in the hell she meant by that.

She looked down at the crazed Chihuahua lovingly. "My late husband drove him all the way back from Tijuana for my fifty-fifth wedding anniversary present."

"How thoughtful of him." Karson stepped back to dodge foam spraying from the dog's writhing mouth.

The old lady's smile widened. "His name is Jesus," she said, using the Anglicized pronunciation.

Karson gave her a tight smile. "That would have been my first guess."

DR. CREASY ASHBURN'S office was in a rear corner of the building next to an operating room. It was a ten-foot-square windowless box with a Virginia Polytechnic Institute diploma and framed photographs of American bulldogs hanging on the wall behind the desk. The same hideous cat-piss-scented, lime-green carpet that polluted the lobby graced the floor.

Ashburn, a short, balding man in his fifties with a flap of wavy brown hair that he raked over his bald spot every thirty seconds and a plastic face that twitched and crinkled into contortions as he talked, leaned back in a swivel chair with his size-twelve boots propped on his desk. Karson sat across from him.

"We kinda got off on the wrong foot here," Ashburn said. He pulled on the lapels of his white lab coat. "I apologize for Libby. She's my neighbor's kid. I let her sit at the desk in the lobby to give her something to do, you know, as a favor to my neighbor. I know she's underage, but it's legal, see, cause she's a volunteer. I don't pay her, which is a good thing because she's dumb as the wad of Juicy Fruit she never stops chewing." He held his hands up in the air. "I would never hire a minor. Never have, never will. Swear on my mother's—"

"I don't care about the girl. I'm investigating a case involving succinylcholine. Do you stock that drug?"

Ashburn raked his hair and scrunched his eyes down to little slits. "Why do you want to know?"

"Answer my question. Do you have a supply of that drug?"

"I'm not the only one," Ashburn said defensively. "Lots of veterinarians use it. It's a muscle relaxant for surgery, and sometimes we euthanize an animal with it."

"Who manufactures your succinylcholine?"

"Used to be Pfizer, but a salesman came through here last fall and offered us a good price to switch over to a company in Switzerland."

"Sandoz?"

Ashburn flinched. "How do you know the name?"

"Did Dr. Randall Hotchkiss ever buy succinylcholine from you?"

"There's nothing wrong with buying drugs from a company in Switzerland, is there?"

"Answer my question. Did Dr. Hotchkiss buy succinylcholine from you?"

Ashburn's eye twitched. "No. Far as I know, Doc Hotchkiss never owned a pet."

"You're sure no one in your outfit gave him that drug?"

"Yeah, I'm sure." Ashburn pulled at his ear and raked his hair. "Listen, the reason these drug questions make me kinda nervous is I got in trouble long time ago when I didn't do anything wrong."

"What kind of trouble?"

"Cole knows all about it."

"I don't know about it and I'm the one sitting here. Answer my question."

Ashburn looked like he might cry. "Well, I had a girl working for me long time ago." He flinched again. "Now, she was over eighteen, so don't get your dander up."

"Just tell me what happened."

"Well," he whined, "she started selling my painkillers to high school kids. I didn't know anything about it till I caught her on the way out the door one night with codeine and hydrocodone in her purse." Ashburn held up his hands again. "I called the law right away. Cole arrested her. Judge Blackwell sent her up the river for a year." Ashburn dropped his hands into his lap and grimaced. "Thing is, see, *The Daily Record* ran articles about it for a week. The bad publicity cost me a passel of customers. After that mess, I put my drugs under lock and key. Nobody has access to them except me."

"You're sure you've never given or sold succinylcholine to anyone."

"I'm sure." Then he flinched for the third time in the meeting, and his mouth, both eyes, and one of his cheeks twitched violently. "Well, there's Percy, but that's a different situation."

"Who's Percy?"

"Percy McDibble. He's an old boy lives over in Tinker's Mill. We're partners in a dog breeding business. American bulldogs." He pointed at the photographs behind him.

"Did you sell succinylcholine to him?"

Ashburn spread his hands out like an umpire giving a call of safe to a base runner. "It's all legal and aboveboard. I supply him with drugs for the business: vaccinations, antibiotics, and the like."

"So you supply him with succinylcholine?"

"Well . . ." Ashburn looked uncomfortable.

"If I have to tell you to answer my question one more time, I'll throw the book at you for little Miss Juicy Fruit. It's illegal to employ her without a permit whether or not she's paid."

"It is?" Ashburn whimpered.

"This is your last chance, Mr. Ashburn. Did you give succinylcholine to this man, McDibble?"

Ashburn held up his hands. "All right, all right." He let out a long breath. "One of Percy's dams had cancer a couple years ago. I couldn't save her. I gave him ketamine and succinylcholine to put her down. He had enough left over to euthanize a dog for a friend. I have to charge fifty dollars to cover the cost of pet euthanasia, but Percy did it for his friend for free. There's nothing illegal about it." He hesitated. "Far as I know, at least." He took a deep breath. "Thing you need to understand is Percy has a soft heart."

"What's that have to do with succinylcholine?"

"Well," Ashburn said, raking his hair with a trembling hand. "People who can't pay my fee started going to Percy a few years back. He asked me for more ketamine and succinylcholine, and I sold it to him."

"How much did you sell him?"

Ashburn swiped his hand across his mouth. "He's got enough on hand to put down a dozen dogs."

"All of the succinylcholine you sold him was manufactured by Sandoz?"

Ashburn shrugged. "Yeah." He crunched his face into a pile of wrinkles. "It's because Sandoz is a foreign company, isn't it? That's what's got the law on my tail. Swear to God I had no idea it was illegal to buy drugs from a foreign outfit. I thought they were on the up and up."

"Where is McDibble's dog breeding operation?"

"Tinker's Mill, on the corner of Horsehead and that dirt road that goes up to the top of Bald Eagle Mountain."

Karson stood.

Ashburn looked up at Karson fearfully, as though he expected him to slap the cuffs on him. His eyes filled with tears. "I didn't know it was illegal. You've got to believe me."

Karson suppressed a smile. Finding the source of succinylcholine almost made up for Jesus and the Juicy Fruit girl. Almost, but not quite.

"Thank you for your help, Mr. Ashburn." Karson stepped over to the door and looked back at Ashburn. "I'll come back next Wednesday. You have until then to get a work permit covering the young lady." His smile widened as he walked out the door.

Chapter Thirty-One

THE PROVOCATION

March 9, 1967, Thursday morning

THAT SAME MORNING, Cole sat at his desk looking at his outline of a theory about the murders of Hazel Emley and Betty Lou Mundy. Betty Lou and Randy became lovers five years ago. Leland found out she was having an affair with someone and left her. She went to Reverend Chatham for counseling; she and Leland reconciled; and she broke off the affair with Randy. He began to drink heavily when she rejected him, and his wife left him, either because of his excessive drinking, because she found out about Betty Lou, or both.

After Randy somehow convinced Betty Lou to take up with him again last summer, Reba ran into Leland at Carter's Tavern and he gave in to temptation. When Betty Lou discovered the affair between Leland and Reba, she blamed her mother for poisoning all their future relationships with men. The affair drove her over the edge and she enticed Randy to help her kill her mother. Randy gave Hazel an overdose of succinylcholine and rushed her body to the undertaker to make certain the murder would not be discovered. He and Betty Lou then had a falling out for some unknown reason. Randy followed her home from Kelly's Place February 19 and tried to convince her to take him back. They argued at her front gate. She pulled the Baby Browning on him. They struggled for control of it, and he shot her, either accidently or in anger.

Cole leaned back into his lumbar pillow and looked over the outline again. It all made sense except for the timeline. Betty Lou left the preacher's house on Christmas night only a few hours before Hazel's death. The preacher had the impression she'd discovered Leland's affair with Reba that day. If that was the case, she would have decided to kill Hazel and convinced Randy to help her only that night, but Randy would have needed at least a day's advance notice to acquire succinylcholine from an unconventional source.

Cole was puzzling over that problem when Frank Woolsey showed up at his office door. "Finished working with that photograph of Betty Lou you gave me," he said, his waxed moustache twitching. "Let's talk at the table. I need to spread out my work."

Cole carried his lumbar pillow over to the chair at the head of the conference table and sat down. Frank sat to his left and placed before them the original photograph and several enlargements.

"Rupert Dilbey figured out the photograph was taken with a Kodak Flash Bantam camera," he said, "a popular model in the forties. The photographer used Kodak 828 film. There are only six photo shops still operating in southwestern Virginia that were in business fifteen years ago, and we checked with all of them. None of them keep sales records that far back, but a few of them still employ people who were working back then. I spoke to all of them. No one remembered a particular sale of that kind of camera or developing the photo of Betty Lou."

"So we've hit a wall," Cole said.

"Yep, so I fell back to trying to identify the house where the photograph was taken. This is the clearest enlargement Rupert could manage." Frank pushed an eighteen-by-twelve-inch photo across the table and handed Cole a magnifying glass. "You can see the headboard has a reddish-brown stain. The bedpost is hexagonal with a sphere at the top, about the size of a baseball. The enlargement blurs the images behind Betty Lou, but you can make out a pale blue wall with a big crack in the plaster that starts out at the corner near the ceiling and runs along a jagged slant toward a door."

Cole used the glass to follow the path of the blurred crack and held the magnifying glass over the door. It was closed, its wood stained dark. Hanging on a hook on the back of the door was a bulky garment.

"I'm guessing that's a closet door," Frank said. "Looks like a winter coat hanging on a hook on the outside of it."

Cole squinted at the photograph. The enlarged image was grainy, but the garment hanging on the door was discernible, a winter coat, jet-black in color, heavy fur, long enough to come down to midcalf on a tall person. The coat looked familiar to Cole. While he stared at it, a memory of that coat flashed across his mind's eye and a tingle went up his spine.

"If we knew where to look for that bedroom," Frank said, "we might be able to make a match. Of course, by now the bed may be long gone, the wall repainted, the crack repaired."

Cole set the magnifying glass on the table, stunned. The pieces of the puzzle of Betty Lou's murder all came together in a matter of a few seconds. It was as if Cole had been wandering around in a dark room and he suddenly found a light switch and turned it on. "I've been played for a fool," he said.

"What?"

Cole stood and went to the file cabinets. He found the old musty folder he was looking for in a bottom drawer. He opened it, checked the date of death, and read Randy Hotchkiss's report.

"What are you looking at?" Frank said.

Cole went back to the table, put the photograph of Betty Lou Mundy in the evidence pouch, grabbed his hat, and headed for the door.

"Where are you going?" Frank said.

"Down the right path, for a change." Cole headed out to his patrol car.

AN HOUR LATER, Cole stood on Bessie Tilden's front porch looking through the screen door. Bessie sat hunched over the piano, her hands crab-walking across the keys, her foot tapping the pedals off rhythm. She played in fits and starts, the tune slowing, dying out, beginning again, then faltering. Cole barely recognized the song, a disjointed, slowed-down rendition of "Alexander's Ragtime Band." He waited until he was certain she'd finished. Then he knocked.

She didn't seem to hear him. Her hands lay idle on the keys. She looked up at the array of family photographs on the wall above the piano and sighed.

Cole rapped on the screen door a second time. "Excuse me, ma'am. It's me, Cole Grundy."

She wiped her eyes, got up off the bench with difficulty, and hobbled to the door. She frowned at Cole. "I don't want to talk about Leland."

She'd aged considerably in the few days since he'd seen her. Her face sagged more and she stood more humpbacked. Tear tracks had cut rivulets through the heavy coat of rouge on her cheeks. She wore a loose-fitting purple blouse with green ruffles and bright yellow slacks with huge red roses over the thighs. He had always thought she had eccentric taste in clothing. Now he wondered if she was trying to create a false sense of gaiety, or if her loud outfits might even represent the outward vestiges of a growing madness.

Dreading the conversation to come, he took a moment to harden his resolve, and then said, "You lied to me, ma'am."

She bowed her head, her chin quivering.

He opened the screen door and stepped inside. He guided her to the sofa and helped her sit down.

He sat in the rocker and withdrew the evidence pouch from his pocket. He opened it and spilled the photograph on the coffee table.

She glanced at it and winced.

"Tell me again how you found this picture, ma'am."

She balled the leg of her slacks in her fist and looked out the window. Her lips parted and then closed. She swallowed. "I . . . I found it . . ." She drew in a deep breath and seemed to gather what little strength she could manage. "It was on the kitchen table. Inside his *Field and Stream* magazine." She looked at Cole vacantly. "He loved to hunt and fish, you know."

"Leland?"

She appeared to be lost for a moment and then seemed to regain her presence of mind. "Yes, of course. Leland."

"Where was Betty Lou when you found the picture?"

She hesitated, and then put her hand to her eyes. "I think she . . . Someone came to the door, I think." She dropped her hand to her lap. "Yes. Someone knocked on the door and she went into the living room to answer it."

"Who was at the door?"

"I don't remember. A delivery man, I think."

"Last time you told me she went into the living room to answer the telephone."

She looked down at her fist and kneaded her slacks. "Maybe it was the telephone. I don't remember. It was a long time ago and I was upset . . . It . . . it was such a shock when . . ." She ran her hand across her brow. "Must we talk about this?"

Cole blew out a short heavy breath, wishing there was a less painful path to the truth. He picked up the photograph and held it up to her face.

She turned away.

"Look at it, ma'am."

"No, please."

"Look at it," he said sharply.

Her head turned slowly and her tortured eyes settled on the

photo. "See the bedpost in this photo, ma'am. It's reddish-brown with a sphere on top. Do you know anyone who owns a bed with a post like that?"

Bessie turned her head away and closed her eyes. A tear bumped its way down the crevices of her cheek.

Cole set the photograph on the table. "You didn't see any head-lights out by the gate the night of the murder, did you?"

She let go of her slacks and clasped her fists together in her lap. "There was a big dark car—"

"No, ma'am. I believed you when I was here before, but I know better now. There were no headlights. There was no car. You made that up. You lied to me."

She didn't look up.

"Based on your word, I thought a man I knew killed Betty Lou, but he didn't kill her. He didn't have anything to do with her murder."

She looked down at her hands and said nothing.

Cole stood and went over to the piano. He took one of the framed photographs off the wall, came back to the sitting area, set the frame on the coffee table, and sat down in the rocker.

"That's a pretty picture of you in front of Monticello, ma'am. When was it taken?"

"Nineteen thirty or thereabouts," she said weakly.

"That's a handsome skunk-fur coat you're wearing in that picture. Where'd you get that coat?"

"Milton gave it to me back in the twenties."

Cole was quiet for a while and then said, "That morning you found me on Leland's porch, the morning of the murder, you wore that same skunk-fur coat. Do you remember that, ma'am?"

She didn't respond.

Cole pressed on. "Those skunk-fur coats were popular when I was a little boy, but they fell out of favor long ago. You've got the only one left I know of."

She donned a wan smile. "It's torn at the seams and worn and frayed, but I can't bring myself to throw it out. It brings back so many fond memories." A faraway look came across her face. "We were so happy back then."

Cole leaned forward, his forearms on his thighs, his hands clasped together. "This photograph of Betty Lou," he said. "There's a coat hanging on a closet door behind her. You can't see it too good with the naked eye, but we put a magnifying lens on it. It's a big old black fur coat, ma'am. It looks an awful lot like that skunk-fur coat Milton gave you back in the twenties, the one you wore the morning of the murder when you found me on Leland's porch."

She clasped her hands in her lap, looked down at them, and sat very still.

A tractor droned faintly in the distance and then grew louder. Cole looked out the window and watched it roll down the hill, a blond teenage boy wearing a denim jacket and jeans, jouncing along on its seat. The tractor passed the house and the sound of its engine faded away below the Mundy property.

Cole gave Bessie a few moments to come to terms with the fact that he knew what she'd done and then said, "How'd you get your hands on Betty Lou's gun, ma'am?"

She didn't reply for a long time. Then she said in a voice so soft it was almost inaudible, "I took it out of her purse."

"When was this, ma'am?"

"That last night, a Saturday night." She took a tissue out of her pants pocket and dabbed her eyes.

"Before Leland came home?"

She nodded.

"Where did you meet her?"

"She came over here on Saturday nights those last few weeks, crying and drunk, smelling like a distillery. Said she had to talk to someone or she couldn't go on. She claimed Leland had been cheating on her with her sister." Bessie shook her head and scowled. "The nerve! Accusing Leland of being unfaithful after what she did with . . ." Bessie trembled, then went still, and stared off into space.

"What happened that last night when she came over here, ma'am?"

Bessie wiped her eyes with the tissue. "She sat at my kitchen table, crying and carrying on about her sister and Leland. Her purse lay open on the table with a little gun inside it. I didn't hear anything she said after I saw it. I couldn't take my eyes off of it." She paused for a long time. Then she said, "I'd been careful for twenty years not to come anywhere near a gun. I couldn't even trust myself around my kitchen knives when Betty Lou was here, but that night, that little gun lay right there within arm's length, and before I knew what I'd done, I reached out and took hold of it and hid it in my lap under the table while she sat right there, too drunk to notice."

"But you didn't shoot her at that time."

"No, I didn't." She looked at Cole and then down at the floor. "I didn't want you to find her body in my kitchen." She wept softly.

He gave her a little time before he asked, "What happened that morning when she came home?"

There was a long pause while Bessie stared at the tissue in her lap, squeezing it with both hands, her knees pressed together. "She usually came home from her carrying-on around five. I waited up for her, watching from my window. When I saw her headlights pull into the driveway, I went outside and walked along the road to their gate. She parked under the carport, like always. When she got out of her car and walked around toward her front door, I called out to her, 'Come out to the road. I'm hurt. I need your help.'" Bessie shook her head back and forth slowly. "When she came through the gate, I pointed the gun at her and pulled the trigger. It made a little snap-bean noise." She swiped her hand across her brow. "After so many years of thinking about it, it was over in only a few seconds." She wept feebly again.

Cole watched her cry, feeling bad for her. When she stopped crying, he said, "Did you wipe your fingerprints off the gun, ma'am?"

Another long silence and then, "I didn't want to get caught. I wasn't worried about the punishment. I'm old and broken down and I don't have much time left anyway." She looked at Cole, her face flushed. "It's the shame I didn't want to face. The shame of people finding out she stole Milton from me." She let out a long breath. "I wiped the gun off with my coat sleeve and dropped it on the ground beside her and came back here and called your office."

Cole could see in his mind's eye what happened after that. Leland came home after Betty Lou was murdered, like he told Cole. He found her corpse in the yard. Probably grieved over her. Embraced her so that her blood got on his shirt. Saw the gun lying beside her. Maybe he picked it up thoughtlessly because he was in shock or maybe the idea of killing himself sprang to mind when he saw it. For whatever reason, he pocketed her little gun and went to the porch and sat there until Cole came along and drew him out of his trance. His misery got the best of him and he put the gun to his head.

Cole looked at Bessie, her shoulders slumped, her fists balled around the tissue. A heartbroken old woman who deserved pity, but the law wouldn't look upon her in that light. Her actions were damning. Premeditation, lying in wait, elaborate efforts to conceal her guilt. First degree murder, an open and shut case.

"I need to look around the house, ma'am. You wait here."

He got up and walked through the kitchen and down a hallway to the master bedroom. A four-poster bed with a canopy stood against the wall.

He found a smaller second bedroom across the hall. He went inside and stood beside a double bed. Its arched headboard was reddish-brown. Its bedposts were hexagonal, crowned by a sphere the size of a baseball. A crack in the plaster on a pale blue wall ran in a jagged line from an upper corner to a dark-stained door, faded with age, with a hook on it. On the hook Bessie's skunk-fur coat hung just as it did in the photograph twenty years ago.

Cole looked down at the floor and sighed. The sheriff's office file about Milton Tilden's death reflected that he died on July 16, 1947, at the age of sixty-four. Randy Hotchkiss's report said Bessie found him in bed at eleven o'clock in the morning after returning from grocery shopping. The cause of death was a massive coronary arrest. The file shed no additional light on the circumstances surrounding his passing.

Cole considered those circumstances. He wondered if Milton suffered a heart attack while making love to Betty Lou. He wondered if Bessie came home from grocery shopping to find Milton's corpse in the bed in the spare bedroom instead of the master. He wondered if Milton was dressed in his bedclothes or naked. He wondered how much time had passed after Milton's death before Bessie found the photograph of Betty Lou in Milton's *Field and Stream* or in his *True Detective* or in some random hiding place, a locked desk drawer, a box in the attic, or a bedside table drawer in that spare bedroom.

Cole went out to the living room.

Bessie sat on the sofa, staring into the distance.

"I'm afraid we've got to go into town now, ma'am."

She looked at Cole. "What will they do with me?"

Cole couldn't look her in the eye and tell her the truth. She was an old lady with a mountain of provocation. Judge Blackwell would likely be lenient, but she couldn't escape serving time in prison, and even a short sentence would be the same for her as the death penalty.

"I don't know, ma'am."

She gave him a pleading look. "I resisted temptation for twenty years. That ought to count for something, don't you think?"

Twenty years was a long time to live next door to a woman who'd slept with a man you'd loved all your life. A woman whose nude photograph your husband took with your Kodak camera in your spare bedroom fresh off a lovemaking fest, a photograph you hid from everyone while you pored over it every day for two decades.

"I hope it counts for something, ma'am."

He took her arm and helped her stand.

She looked up at him, a perplexed expression on her face. "You want to know the worst part of it all, Cole?"

"What's that, ma'am?"

"It still hurts."

"Some types of pain never go away," he said with sand in his voice.

He guided her out the door and closed it behind them.

Chapter Thirty-Two

THE TRAILER PARK

March 9, 1967, Thursday noon

WHILE COLE WAS DRIVING Bessie Tilden to headquarters, Ray Middleditch headed over to Hukstep's Trailer Park to scout Reba Emley's trailer for the contract's last hit.

He was looking forward to getting this cursed project behind him. Back in December when he considered his approach to the first hit on Hazel Emley, his plan was to smother her with a bed pillow to make it look like she died of natural causes, as Boss requested. Homicide by suffocation wasn't the perfect crime. A good medical examiner could find signs of foul play—pale lips and nose, minor hemorrhaging under the flesh of the face, flecks of blood in the lungs—but Ray thought it was his best alternative until he saw a newspaper article about a lethal drug that disappeared from the victim's corpse almost immediately after death. Because the drug was untraceable, poisoning by an overdose appeared to be the perfect crime. A minimal amount of medical research informed him where he could purchase it without raising suspicion and how to administer a fatal injection.

On Christmas night he parked his truck down the road from the old lady's shack and knocked on the door, pretending to be an out-of-town john, horny for a woman his own age. From the looks of the old hag, she hadn't plied her trade for years and she was skeptical of his offer, but a wad of cash warmed her up. When she took off her clothes to do the deed, he held her down and plunged the needle in her hip. She struggled against his restraint for a short while and then went limp. Her breathing gradually slowed and then stopped. The drug worked as advertised, a quick trip to hell, less than five minutes from injection to the devil's furnace.

He was searching for a bed gown to dress her up so she looked like she died in her sleep when a car drove up outside. There was no back way out, so Ray drew his gun and hid in the bedroom closet. Betty Lou Mundy stormed into the bedroom, drunk and crying. When she saw the old lady lying naked face down on the bed, she apparently thought she was asleep. She grabbed her by the shoulders, shook her, and shouted angrily at her. Ray was considering killing Betty Lou then and there, but within seconds, another car arrived and Doc Hotchkiss staggered in, also drunk.

He seemed alarmed when he saw Betty Lou roughing up the old lady. He pulled her away from the corpse and leaned over it. He ran his hand over bruises on the old lady's back and arm and then put his fingers to her throat. He straightened up and looked at Betty Lou fearfully. "You've killed her," he said.

Betty Lou denied it, but he didn't believe her. Ray gleaned from their back-and-forth that they'd had an affair, she'd broken it off, and Hotchkiss had followed her there to beg her to take him back. He was certain she'd murdered the old lady because she'd told him in the past that she hated her and wanted her to die. "I'm Papa Bear," he pleaded over and over again. "I'll protect you. Call the sheriff's office. They'll call me to take care of the body, and I'll fix it so no one will ever know what you did."

She refused at first, but Hotchkiss finally convinced her the sheriff's office would think she killed the old lady, whether or not she had, unless he shielded her from suspicion. He rolled the old lady over on her back and placed a blanket over her, and they left the shack together.

Ray scoured the place to make sure he'd left no sign of his presence and then fled.

That first chaotic hit had set the tone for the whole project. Some random killer got to Betty Lou only hours before Ray could take down Leland, nullifying weeks of preparation and prompting him to eliminate Bowie, which dropped in Cole Grundy's lap a bonus corpse and a crime scene that could lead to Ray.

Then came Ballard and his pit bull. If Ray hadn't remembered Hotchkiss from the night at Hazel's shack, he would have died from the mauling. Then, of course, after he forced Hotchkiss to treat his wounds, he had no choice but to kill him, handing Cole another corpse. He staged it as a suicide with the poisonous drug, hoping Cole wouldn't investigate, but transmissions Ray intercepted over the scanner told him his ruse was unsuccessful. To make matters worse, he'd learned that morning from a communication between Toby Vess and dispatch that Ballard was still alive, unconscious in the intensive care unit at Dolley Madison, his prognosis uncertain.

A bad result, but curable. Security in hospitals was lax, and there was no radio talk about posting a guard on Ballard's door. If Ballard didn't expire on his own, Ray could pay a quick visit to the hospital and finish him off without much risk.

But first he had to deal with Reba. Eight miles from Fox Run in Saddleback Cove, Ray turned off Whiskey Road into Hukstep's Trailer Park. Thirty-four trailers were spaced closely together along both sides of a horseshoe-shaped dirt road with access to Whiskey Road.

Ray drove toward the first bend in the road where Reba's trailer sat on the outside of the horseshoe. A white-haired old woman wearing a winter coat came out of the shabby gray trailer next door. Ray slowed to watch her. A middle-aged man wearing a felt hat and an overcoat steadied her walker as she struggled across a concrete pathway toward a black Lincoln. The man looked at Ray's truck, the lenses of his glasses glinting in the sun. Ray waved to him, playing the role of a friendly neighbor, and the man waved back.

Ray eased the truck forward and stopped in front of Reba's little trailer. Its two-toned aluminum glistened in the sunlight, the bottom half pale green, the top white. Three windows faced the road. Kitchen, living room, and bedroom windows, he guessed. The front yard provided no cover for an approach. No trees, no shrubs.

He urged the truck along to the next trailer, a new double-wide. A carport over the driveway sported two large stickers facing the road, one with a Confederate flag, the other with red letters on a blue background: NRA.

Ray drove to the top of the horseshoe, pulled off the road short of a telephone pole, and looked up at the floodlight mounted on it. Old man Hukstep had staked three telephone poles topped with floodlights along the dirt road, two about fifty feet inside the access points to Whiskey Road and a third at the top of the horseshoe. At night, the floodlights would illuminate every inch of the dirt road, leaving Ray no place inside the park to hide his truck.

He looked back at Reba's trailer. It was no more than fifty feet from the pole at the top of the horseshoe. In the dark of night, the trailer would be well within the wash of its floodlight. He ran his hand through his thinning hair and sighed. Floodlights, no cover, and a gun enthusiast living next door.

He looked around. The telephone pole stood in a patch of weeds between two trailers. A path ran from the pole into a pine forest that bordered the back yards of the trailers on the outside of the horseshoe. No vehicles were parked in the driveways of the trailers on either side of the pole or near those on the other side of the road. He saw no one around and no movement in the trailer windows.

He got out of the truck, crossed the path from the pole into the trees, and then picked his way through the woods around the backside of the park until he came up behind Reba's little lot. Her trailer sat fifty feet from the forest's edge. The backyard was as barren of cover as the front except for a car shed, open in front and closed in on the other three sides. The trailer had four windows along the back, the one on the end smaller than the others; a bathroom window, he guessed.

He stared at the windows pensively. He could set up on the edge of the woods and fire at Reba when she walked past a window, he supposed, but he didn't like it. The windows were small. She'd be a moving target. He'd get one shot. If he missed, he'd have to run.

He looked at the shed. In the dark late at night, he could walk from the trees to the shed and from there to the trailer without being seen. The trailer was narrow. If he stood just outside her bedroom window, her bed would by necessity lay within ten feet of his gun, but the bedroom window looked a little too high to give him a level shot from the ground. He would need a boost.

He looked around the yard. His eyes fell on a metal folding chair just inside the open end of the shed.

The trailers on each side of Reba's looked vacant for now. He had seen the old lady leave her trailer, and the NRA member's carport had been empty. He should be able to approach the shed without being seen.

Ray crossed the yard and stepped inside the shed. The chair leaned against the wall under a window. It was covered with dust and spider webs. He cleaned it off with his kerchief and lifted it. Not too heavy to carry to the trailer with his good arm. He unfolded it and stepped up on it carefully. It held his weight. He put it back where he found it and returned to the woods.

Back in the truck, he sat behind the wheel and ran his hand over the bandage on his arm. It didn't hurt. His arthritic knee was another story. Even the short walk over flat terrain had inflamed it, and it throbbed.

He withdrew the Cutty Sark from the glove compartment. Two big swallows. Then two more. He leaned back in the seat and relaxed to give the whiskey time to do its job.

Despite the floodlights, this hit ought to be easy enough. He had done his research on Reba in November. She worked as a secretary for a State Farm agent in Jeetersburg, and she was always home by eight on weeknights. Lights out by midnight. She would be asleep when he approached. She would never know what hit her. The only issue that worried him was that he didn't want to park his truck under the floodlights.

The whiskey kicked in and the pain eased.

He put the bottle back in the glove compartment, started the truck, drove around the horseshoe to the other access point, and pulled out onto Whiskey Road. A quarter mile from the park, he found a copse of cedar trees beside the road with a clear space behind them. He eased the truck into a shallow ditch, accelerated gently out of it, and drove around behind the cedars. The cedars were thick. In that spot his truck would not be visible from the road.

He looked around. The pine forest ran from there to Reba's trailer at the southern end of the trailer park. He didn't look forward to the hike, but his approach would be concealed.

He sat behind the wheel and gathered his thoughts. He would park his truck there tonight after midnight and kill Reba. If Ballard hadn't died by tomorrow, he'd go to Dolley Madison and finish him off. Then he would turn his attention to Cole.

He pulled the truck onto Whiskey Road and headed toward the rented house. He was almost done with this cursed project, thank God.

Chapter Thirty-Three

THE OLD JOLLEY PLACE

March 9, 1967, Thursday afternoon

CHASE DOOLEY SPENT two days trying to track down Ray Middleditch. The South Carolina DMV sent Chase a copy of his driver's license. It was issued to him on April 6, 1966. South Carolina could find no record of a prior license under that name. The photograph on the license presented a pasty face with lots of mileage on it, droopy eyes with puffed blue bags underneath, an uneven gray beard, and thinning silver hair.

Date of birth: January 18, 1902. Height: 6′ 2″; Weight: 190 lbs.; Address: 2193 Dave Lyle Blvd, Rock Hill, South Carolina.

The York County, South Carolina, sheriff's office told Chase no residential homes or apartments were located on the 2100 block of Dave Lyle Boulevard. It was lined with commercial businesses. The address 2193 didn't exist. The closest street number to it was 2197, a Sears, Roebuck store. The sheriff could find no record of a Ray Middleditch ever living anywhere along that street or at any location in Rock Hill or York County.

Running the Virginia license plate number, Chase located a car dealership in Lynchburg, Virginia, that sold a black 1965 Dodge 100 pickup truck to a Ray Allen Middleditch on November 13 of last year. A salesman at Beech Motor Company told Chase that Middleditch paid $1100 cash for the truck and refused to give a mailing address until the manager explained that state law required the dealership to provide the DMV with a buyer's current address, and that without it, he couldn't allow him to drive the truck off the lot. Middleditch only then gave up his address: P.O. Box 39, Tinker's Mill, Virginia.

THURSDAY AFTERNOON, about an hour after Ray Middleditch had finished scouting Reba Emley's trailer, Chase drove out to Tinker's Mill, a small town in the northeast corner of the county with ten houses, an Esso station, a Baptist church, a country store, and a little white cinderblock post office, all clustered around Horsehead Road.

Chase found Clayton Fiddler sitting on a stool in the post office, sorting mail into boxes on the wall. A short, fat pig farmer with black hair, Clayton became Tinker's Mill's part-time postmaster three years ago to supplement his income when falling pork prices put the squeeze on him. He told Chase that Middleditch rented a post office box on December 1.

"Told me he moved here from South Carolina. Retired from a real estate outfit down there. Comes in once or twice a month to get his mail, which ain't nothin but circulars and the like. He don't get personal mail, and he don't never say much. Keeps to himself."

"Where does he live?"

"Rents the old Jolley place from Sam."

"I don't know the Jolley place."

Clayton said Sam Jolley inherited a house and some land from his mother when she passed on last year. It was in bad shape and Sam hadn't been able to rent it out until Middleditch came along.

Chase drove a short way down Horsehead Road to the Esso

station Sam Jolley owned and operated. Chase found Sam under a Chevy convertible with the transmission strewn all over the floor. A big, bald-headed, barrel-chested man in his fifties with a dark complexion and a beer belly, Sam rolled out from under the Chevy and wiped his hands on a rag. He led Chase into the gas station's little retail shop and sat on a stool behind the cash register eating a Baby Ruth and drinking an orange Nehi while he answered Chase's questions about Middleditch.

"He stopped here for an oil change couple days after Thanksgivin. Said he was lookin for a place to stay. I told him about Momma's house. He went up there and looked her over. Said it fit his needs cause all the furniture and dishes and such were still there, so he could move right in. He offered me six months' rent in cash up front. I jumped on him like a tomcat on a rat."

Chase followed Sam's directions to the end of Horsehead Road and turned right onto an unnamed dirt road that climbed Bald Eagle Mountain. There were only three houses along that road, and the first two were abandoned. The third, on a flat shelf of land about a hundred feet from the summit, was the old Jolley place.

Chase pulled off the road in front of the house.

A black Dodge 100 with Virginia plates bearing the number Chase had traced was in a gravel driveway to the right of a dilapidated two-story frame house set back about twenty feet from the road. Most of its white paint had worn off and its felt roof tiles were curled and peeling, but it fit the needs of a man wishing to go unnoticed. No one had a reason to drive past it since no one lived beyond it and the road dead-ended on top of Bald Eagle.

Ten windows faced the road, five stretching across the length of an upstairs balcony; five downstairs, three to the left of the front door, two to the right. The front yard was barren of trees and shrubs save a few small cedar bushes under the windows. No one could approach from the front without being seen from inside; another advantage to a man trying to lay low.

Chase saw no movement in the windows and the house was quiet, but the truck's presence implied that Middleditch was there.

Chase got out of his truck. Before he took a step toward the house, he heard an explosion and felt a blow to his right collarbone, as though someone had hit him as hard as he could with the end of a steel bar, cracking the bone and plunging the bar deep into his flesh. The blow threw Chase back against his truck. He slid down it to a sitting position on the running board and looked at his shoulder. Blood oozed from a hole in his shirt the size of a quarter. He flattened his hand over the hole and tried to hold back the flow of blood. Another explosion. Something above Chase cracked and splinters of plate glass showered the brim of his hat and fell on his thighs.

Blood seeped through Chase's hand. He pressed harder and stared at the house. The pain kicked in and he suddenly understood. He was under fire. He needed to take cover.

When a third shot rang out, Chase saw the muzzle flash in a downstairs window. A thump sounded to the left of his head, and a wisp of smoke lilted up from a hole in the truck's door. Chase tried to stand, but he was too weak. He fell off the running board and rolled under the truck. His right arm didn't work, so he used his left to pull himself behind the front wheel. He extended his left hand across his body, awkwardly drew his gun, and looked out from under the truck at the window where he had seen the muzzle flash. The front door opened and an old man jig-jogged across the yard toward the Dodge pickup, limping badly. Chase's left hand shook as he pointed the gun, but he couldn't bring his right hand up to brace it. He'd never fired a gun with his left hand, but he let fly anyway. His bullet shattered an upstairs window fifteen feet above the man's head.

The man climbed in the truck. Chase braced his left hand against the front tire and fired again. The pickup's tailgate bucked and fell down. Its engine roared. It spun around in the gravel and sped across the yard, the man's thinning gray hair and gray beard visible in the door window. Chase fired three shots in rapid succession. None of them hit the man or the pickup.

The Dodge plunged down into a ditch. Its front end reared up in the air and fell back down hard. Its tires spun and then gained purchase on the dirt road. Chase fired another round and missed everything. The pickup sped down the hill and disappeared in a trail of dust.

Chase lay his head on the ground, breathing hard, gravel and grit pressing against his cheek. He lifted his head and looked at his chest. Blood mixed with white powder-dust had spread across the front of his shirt. He had to crawl out, get to the radio, call for help. He grasped the front tire with his left hand, but he didn't have the strength to pull himself out from under the truck. He took several deep breaths and tried again, but it was no good. His breath came in short bursts. The ground whirled beneath him. I'll die here, he thought.

He extended his hand out into the sun, palm up, a smear of crimson glistening in the light. Not much chance anyone will come by and see it, but it's all I can do, he told himself. Stay awake. Don't give up.

He tried hard to hang on, but his strength slowly slipped away; the light faded and went black.

Chapter Thirty-Four

THE DOG BREEDER

March 9, 1967, Thursday afternoon

PERCY MCDIBBLE LIVED with his mother in Tinker's Mill on the corner of Horsehead Road and the dirt road that climbed Bald Eagle Mountain. A plain man in his fifties, tall and wide with narrow shoulders, a bald pate rimmed by a fringe of black hair, a long nose, and jug ears the size of cabbage leaves, Percy knew he wasn't much to look at. That was half the reason he never married. The other half was Momma. After Percy's father was killed in a hunting accident when he was a toddler, Momma had sacrificed everything for him, so when she got old and had no one to take care of her, Percy stayed by her side.

He didn't regret his decision. His only concern about his life choice had been financial. He couldn't make ends meet with his meager paycheck from Bootsie's Country Store and Momma's Social Security check, and he slid deeper into debt every month until Creasy Ashburn came up with the idea of partnering with him in a dog breeding business. The breeding stock fell in Creasy's lap for free when the county pound asked him to take in five American bulldog dams that belonged to a breeder the state sent to the big house for murdering his wife and her boyfriend. "I'll supply the dams and the working capital," Creasy had said. "You take care of the dogs, and we'll split the profits fifty-fifty."

So Percy converted Momma's garage into a kennel. He built five stalls separated by chain-link fencing and lined the opposite wall with feed bins, storage cabinets, a sink, and a counter. He cut a dog door in the wall of each stall and enclosed half Momma's back-yard in chain link so the dams could go outside when they pleased.

When Creasy said the breeders were bulldogs, Percy assumed they were the short, stubby flat-faced dogs he'd seen on television, which turned out to be English bulldogs. Creasy's dams were American bulldogs, a different breed altogether, tall with broad chests, rangy and athletic, seventy to ninety pounds, short-haired with smooth coats, white with patches of fawn. Beautiful, graceful creatures. They formed an immediate bond with Percy, and he fell in love with them.

The kennel didn't turn out to be a gold mine, but it generated enough profit to solve Percy's cash flow problems. Best of all, Percy liked almost everything about dog breeding: caring for the dogs, birthing the pups, placing them in good homes for a reasonable price, even cleaning up the kennel.

The one and only exception was the put-downs. The put-downs broke his heart.

Thursday afternoon just before Chase Dooley approached the old Jolley place, Percy spread a blanket on the counter in the kennel and laid a dog on it gently. Henry was a dusty brown short-haired mutt, a mongrel so mixed that none of the traits of any breed came through. Rainey Meechum and her mother, Lee Anne, had brought him to Percy a half hour ago. Percy was headed across the backyard when Lee Anne pulled her rattletrap Nash eggbeater into the gravel turnaround behind the kennel and Rainey, a skinny blonde-haired thirteen-year-old, got out of the car. She ran over to Percy carrying the little mutt in her arms, crying so hard she couldn't catch her breath. Lee Anne came up behind her. A single mother saddled with taking care of three kids and two low-paying jobs, she looked worn out. "Thank God you're home," she said.

They'd just returned from Creasy's office. He said Henry had incurable lung cancer, he was in great pain, and it was past time to put him down. Lee Anne didn't have the fifty dollars Creasy charged to euthanize a dog, and she'd heard Percy would put Henry out of his misery for much less.

Percy blamed himself for people bringing dogs to him for put-downs. When one of his dams had developed a brain tumor and lost her mind, Percy asked Creasy, "When do you know it's time to let a dog go?"

"There's three tests. The animal is in great pain and will never feel better; she doesn't know who she is; or she can't eat or do her business. A dog who meets any one of those tests should be euthanized."

Creasy gave Percy the drugs, ketamine and succinylcholine. "Make sure you give her the ketamine first. Then wait a little while before you give her succinylcholine. She won't suffer that way." Percy carried Belle out to her favorite spot in the dog pen under the shade of a maple tree, gave her the shots, and held her in his arms until she passed.

Shortly after that, when Rollo Brady's cocker spaniel went blind and stopped eating, Rollo didn't have the money to pay Creasy to put her down. "Would you do it for me?" he asked Percy. "Only other way is my shotgun, and I'll never be the same if I have to shoot her."

Percy put Maisy down. He figured it was bad enough Rollo lost his best friend. Making him pay seemed just flat cruel, so he refused to take a penny.

Rollo had a big mouth. Word got around. People showed up at Percy's door, and he didn't have the heart to turn them away.

So Rainey and Lee Anne Meechum brought Henry to Percy that afternoon. A quick look at Henry left Percy with no doubt he met all three tests. He told Rainey it was time to let Henry go to heaven. She was a brave, smart kid. She hugged Henry, kissed him goodbye, handed him to Percy, and ran around the kennel to the car, sobbing.

Lee Anne stared after her, wiping tears from her eyes. "We gave him to her on her first birthday, back before Rudy left me."

Henry's head lolled over Percy's arm as he breathed in short heavy gusts. Percy couldn't stand to see him suffer. He hurried toward the kennel.

"How much?" Lee Anne called after him.

"No charge," he said over his shoulder.

She came running up behind him as he opened the kennel door. "What about . . . the body?"

"I'll take care of everything if you want me to."

"Oh, God, I . . . Thank you." She kissed him on the cheek and then hurried back to her car.

Now, standing over Henry at the counter, Percy rubbed the spot on his cheek where Lee Anne had kissed him. He heaved a sigh and withdrew the vials of ketamine and succinylcholine from a cabinet over the sink. He set them on the counter and opened the drawer where he stored the needles.

He was unwrapping the package to extract a clean needle when Henry took a deep breath, held it, then let out a long slow breath, and went still. Percy set the needle down and put his hands on the dog's flank. No movement. No trembling. Percy held his hand at Henry's muzzle. No wind. His eyes were open, but glassed over. Percy rummaged around in a cabinet and found the stethoscope. He put it to Henry's chest. Nothing.

Percy placed his palms on the counter and sighed. "Goodbye, Henry."

He closed Henry's eyes and walked over to a large floor-to-ceiling cabinet whose four shelves held pine boxes that he had made by hand. He withdrew a smaller one and carried it to the counter. He put Henry's blanket in the box. He laid Henry on top of it and wrapped it around him.

While he tucked Henry in, he heard a car drive into the gravel turnaround. All the dams in the dog run kicked up a big ruckus. Percy turned to see a tall, thin man with a wide-brimmed hat standing in the doorway, the late afternoon sunlight behind him. When the man stepped into the kennel out of the glare, Percy could see him clearly, a colored man wearing the tan uniform of the sheriff's office.

Percy had never met Karson Deford, but he'd heard about him. People cut Sheriff Grundy to shreds when he hired him. "Boy claims his wife got sick so he quit his state trooper job," Rollo scoffed. "How much you wanna bet the state fired him? Cole Grundy's the only sheriff in Virginia dumb enough to hire a colored boy who can't even hold down a job with the no-account state police." Five years later, the trash talk continued, especially among diehards like Rollo.

"Afternoon," Deford said to Percy. "Are you Mr. McDibble?"

Percy nodded. "You lookin to buy a pup?"

"No, sir." Deford crossed the room and extended his hand. "Karson Deford."

They shook.

Deford looked past Percy at the pine box on the counter.

"Neighbor's dog," Percy said. "Lung cancer."

"That's too bad." He stepped around Percy. He looked at Henry and touched him gently. Then he picked up one of the vials on the counter. "Succinylcholine," he said. "You got this drug from Ashburn Animal Hospital, right?"

Percy nodded.

"You ever sell succinylcholine to anyone?"

Percy's gut clenched. "Creasy told me not to sell it," he said.

Deford half smiled. "But you sold it anyway."

Damn, Percy thought. He had made one mistake since he started the kennel, and he knew at the time it would come back to bite him. So be it. Might as well fess up to it. Like Momma says, you tell one lie, you'll have to tell a hundred to cover it up.

"I sold ketamine and succinylcholine to a man to put his dogs down," Percy said. "Creasy told me not to sell the drugs to anyone, but I felt sorry for him."

"What's the man's name?"

"Ray Middleditch."

That seemed to throw Deford off track. "Middleditch," he repeated, frowning. "You ever sell succinylcholine to Dr. Hotchkiss?"

Percy shook his head.

Deford looked down at the floor. He seemed to take a few moments to get Doc Hotchkiss off his mind. Then he said, "When did you sell succinylcholine to this man Middleditch?"

"A week or so before Christmas. He showed up about noon on a cold day when I was workin on the baseboard heaters, tryin to get more heat in here for the dogs."

"You'd never met him before?"

"I seen him at Bootsie's Store a couple times. He lives up a road here a ways."

"Did he say why he wanted to buy the drugs?"

"He said he heard I put down dogs for people. Said he had two German shepherds. Raised em up from pups. Fourteen years old. They come down with cancer about the same time. One had a tumor wrapped around his spine. The other'n had cancer in his belly. Said they couldn't walk. Couldn't eat. Fished out two hunnerd-dollar bills. Said he needed to buy the drugs so he could put em down."

"And you sold the drugs to him?"

"Not at first. I told him I wasn't allowed to sell em. Asked him to bring his dogs in. Said I'd put em down at no charge. But he said he couldn't do it that way. Said he owed it to his dogs to be the one who put em down. He begged me. I felt bad for him. So I gave him the drugs. He stuffed the two hunnerds in my shirt pocket and took the drugs on off with him."

"How much succinylcholine did you give him?"

"He said both dogs was well over a hunnerd pounds. Said he

wanted three bottles of each drug cause he didn't want to come up short, botch up the put-downs, and make his dogs suffer more. It was way more'n he needed, but he was real worried about makin sure it would do the job, so I didn't fight him on it."

"You know where the man lives?"

"He rents the old Jolley place up on Bald Eagle."

Deford asked for directions, then hurried out to his patrol car and drove off.

Percy was relieved. Most lawmen would have busted him for selling the drugs. This Deford seemed a more decent sort. Hell, on his way out, he went so far as to thank Percy for his help. Even Rollo would have to admit that was mighty white of him.

Percy turned back to Henry. He nailed the lid on the coffin, retrieved a big smooth river rock from Momma's flower bed, and carried it and the pine box out to his old yellow GMC pickup, where he put them in the truck bed beside the shovel.

He got in his truck and started the climb up to the plot of land he had chosen for his dog cemetery on top of Bald Eagle, a pretty spot under a big oak tree with a view of the hollow. He had placed a big smooth river rock over each of seven graves under the old oak. Henry would be number eight.

The sunset colored the clouds butterscotch, strawberry, and peach. Half-dead honeysuckle vines clung to falling-down barbed wire fencing along both sides of the road. Halfway up Bald Eagle a hawk floated on the wind, hunting prey in the neglected pasture of an abandoned farm. Twilight brought a cold breeze in the truck window. Percy rolled it up and twisted the dial on the heater. It kicked in with its usual racket, sounding like BBs banging around inside a tin can, and the cab slowly warmed up.

When he rounded the turn to the old Jolley place near the summit, he came up on a patrol car parked behind an olive-green county truck. He slowed down and stopped. Deputy Karson Deford was down on one knee beside the truck, holding a man's bloody hand. The rest of the man seemed to be under the truck.

Percy parked in the Jolley driveway and shuffled across the road as Deford pulled the man out from under the truck. Percy recognized him: Dooley, the foster boy who made good. He was in a bad way. A huge blood stain smeared with grit covered the front of his shirt. His body was limp; his eyes closed. Deford put his hand to Dooley's throat.

Percy stood over them, gawking.

Deford pressed his hand against Dooley's chest up near the shoulder. "Kneel down here," he said.

Percy knelt beside Dooley.

"Put your hand where mine is. Press down on the wound."

Percy didn't move, his mouth hanging open.

Deford took his hand and pressed it flat against Dooley's chest. The slick warmth of blood repelled Percy. He tried to pull his hand away, but Deford forced it over the wound. "Press hard right there." Percy made himself do it. The metallic scent, like the butchering room in Bootsie's Store, almost made him gag.

"Don't let up on the pressure. I'll be back in a minute."

"Wait! Don't leave me!"

Deford ran to his car and talked to someone on his radio. Only a minute passed, but it seemed like an hour before he returned to Percy's side. He ripped open a plastic wrapper and withdrew a big wad of red cloth.

"What's that?"

"Carlisle bandage. Keep pressing down on the wound."

"I never seen a bandage like that. Where'd you get it?"

"Korea."

Deford unraveled the ball of red cloth. In its center was a heavily gauzed cream-colored patch an inch thick. "Hold him up while I wrap this around him."

Percy lifted Dooley's head and torso off the ground. Deford placed the thick gauzed part of the bandage over the wound, unspooled the lengths of red cloth from both sides of the gauze, wound them twice around Dooley's back and chest, and tied them at his back, pulling hard on the ends to cinch it tightly.

"Stretch him out on the ground."

Percy eased Dooley down on his back.

Deford took off his jacket. "Take off your coat," he said.

Percy took off his coat.

Deford rolled his jacket and Percy's coat together, placed them under Dooley's feet, and ran back to his patrol car.

Percy stared at the blood on his hands and arms and on his shirt and pants. When Deford returned with a blanket, Percy saw that he was covered with blood, too. There was blood all over Dooley, and blood had sunk into the dust where Deford pulled him out from under the truck. Percy never would have believed a man's body contained as much blood as Dooley had lost. He couldn't imagine there was much left inside him. "He's going to die," Percy said.

Deford spread the blanket over Dooley and tucked it in at his sides and around his neck. He placed his hand on Dooley's throat. "He's not dead yet." Deford looked down the road. "Time's running out, though." He swiped sweat from his forehead, smearing blood on his face.

Percy looked at the fancy bandage. "All of you have them?"

"What?"

"That Carlisle bandage. All the county officers carry them?"

Deford shook his head. "I brought a few back from Korea after the war. Keep them in the trunk of my car. Thought they might come in handy for gunshot wounds."

"Looks like you thought right."

Deford put his hand to Dooley's throat again. "Don't die on me, son." He checked the bandage and then looked down the road. "Come on," he said under his breath.

"Who did this to him?" Percy asked.

"You know what kind of vehicle Middleditch drives?"

"Black Dodge pickup."

"A black pickup tore past me when I pulled out of your driveway. I almost went after him. Thank God I didn't."

Percy was stunned. "Middleditch seemed like a nice feller. Loved his dogs. Wanted them to go out the right way."

"My guess is Middleditch doesn't own a dog."

The truth gradually dawned on Percy. "I'll be damned."

Percy looked at Dooley. His chest rose and fell under the blanket. He was alive, if only barely.

Deford checked the bandage again. Percy studied the man. Cool. Professional. Smart. Doing his job right. If Dooley survived, Deford would be the reason.

Percy resolved to have a sit-down with Rollo. Set him straight about Deford. Tell him to shut down the trash talk. Or else he could find a new friend. Do his own goddamn put-downs.

Chapter Thirty-Five

THE SANCTUARY

March 9, 1967, Thursday afternoon and night

RAY RAN the stop sign at Horsehead Road and sped through Tinker's Mill, pounding the steering wheel with his fist and cursing. The speedometer crested eighty on the narrow straightaways out of Tinker's Mill, tires squealing on the turns. Halfway to Whippoorwill Hollow Road, he hit the brakes hard to turn onto a dirt road, slid into a ditch, and stalled out.

He turned the ignition key. The starter grinded. He pumped the accelerator, looking up and down the road. No one coming along, thank God, but he had to get out of sight. The starter coughed but wouldn't catch. "God damn you!"

The engine finally kicked over and sputtered. He floored the accelerator, holding the clutch down. Black smoke billowed from the exhaust pipe. The engine smoothed out and roared. He shifted into low gear and eased off the clutch. The rear wheels spun in the soft loam of the ditch, then gained traction and climbed out of the trough into a plowed field. He drove across it to the dirt road and sped along to the tree line of a poplar forest. He stopped a hundred feet inside the woods where the truck couldn't be seen from Horse-head Road.

He took deep breaths. The engine idled, the cab vibrating. The forest canopy arched over the dirt road, killing off the last remnants of daylight. He rolled down the window and a cold wind blew inside, bracing him.

Calm down, he told himself. You're all right. Dooley tracked down Ray Middleditch and found the house. That's all he knows. You expected as much. You planned for it. Take it in stride and move on.

He looked at the dark road ahead.

"Follow the plan," he said aloud.

He eased the truck forward. A quarter mile farther along, he emerged from the tree tunnel into the dying light. Blood of the Lamb Church stood in a little clearing, the cross atop its tall, narrow steeple catching a last ray of sunlight. He drove around to the rear of the building, parked at the back stoop, and tried the door. It was locked. He found the key in the same hiding place his father had used a half century ago, under a big rock beside a downspout at the corner of the building. He was glad. He would have hated to violate the old place by breaking in.

He unlocked the door and stepped into the little anteroom. It hadn't changed much, cream-colored beadboard walls and ceiling, dark-stained oak floors, the desk and cane chair along the wall, the daybed under the window now covered with a maize bedspread instead of the pale blue one he remembered. His father had set up the room to study and prepare his sermons. He had added the daybed to accommodate all-night sessions when the Holy Ghost would wring all the strength from his body and soul as he divined the Word of God. On those nights, his father would collapse on the bed in blissful exhaustion, sometimes sleeping straight through the next day. The preachers who succeeded Ray's father at Blood of the Lamb treasured the solitude and spiritual communion with God the little anteroom afforded them, and they had maintained it up to the present day.

Ray crossed the room to the door that entered the sanctuary from behind the pulpit, opened it, and stepped inside. Red carpet still covered the floor around the altar and ran up the aisles between the fifteen rows of pine pews that were striped with rainbow colors from the fading sunlight penetrating the stained glass windows.

He climbed the steps to the raised pulpit where his father had stood on Sunday mornings in 1915. He looked down at the offering table from which his father had dispensed communion, the altar where the sinners had knelt to be saved, and the front pew where he and his mother had sat dressed in their Sunday best.

The church was strong in his father's day, but the congregation dwindled after he moved on, its youth abandoning the faith, its aging faithful dying off. Now only a dozen survivors remained, all seventy or older. Ray had heard the bishop had given up on them. He had tacked Blood of the Lamb onto the Feather Mountain Circuit as the fourth and smallest church of Reverend Chatham's charge, its schedule of worship services squeezed out by the demands of the other congregations. Blood of the Lamb's parishioners only assembled on the second and fourth Sunday nights of the month now, and no one visited the church during the week. Sad for the church, but perfect for Ray's purposes.

He took a last look at the sanctuary and went back into the anteroom.

Luckily, just before Dooley showed up, he'd loaded the truck with almost everything he needed in preparation for leaving the county in a few days. He retrieved Bowie's .30-06, his Colt Python, and the drugs and bandages from the truck and carried them into the anteroom. When he'd set up everything the way he wanted, he sat down on the daybed with the Cutty Sark.

He took a swig, wincing as it burned its way down, and thought about his next move. The safest alternative was to cut and run, leaving Reba and Ballard, if he survived, alive, but if he did that, Boss wouldn't pay him the second thirty thousand.

Ray took another big swallow and set the bottle on the floor. He stretched out on the bed and draped his forearm over his brow. Staring at the beadboard ceiling, he weighed the risk of sticking it out to finish the job.

The law would be scouring the county tonight, but no one would think to look for him here. He would need to lay low, and now that the law knew what the truck looked like, he couldn't risk driving around in daylight tomorrow, but he still had time to finish the project. Sunday, when the church members would show up, was three days away. He could go after Reba tomorrow night and pay a visit to Ballard at the hospital the night after that.

Then he would run. He'd be across the state line by dawn on Sunday; in Cheraw by nightfall. He'd collect his thirty thousand from Boss and take a few months off. Buy a woman. Take her to the Outer Banks or one of the islands off the Carolina coast, someplace where he could lay out in the sun and drink whiskey. When he'd healed up to full strength, he'd go back to Cheraw, change his identity again, and return to Selk County to settle the score with Cole.

He sat up, lifted the bottle, and turned it up. Smooth as silk, like always. He swiped his hand across his mouth, got the ice sleeve out of the cooler, hitched up his pants, and wrapped it around his swollen knee.

He took the gauze bandage off his arm. The swelling had gone down. Ugly brown and purple stripes ran from his wrist to his elbow, but the lacerations looked clean and scabbed over. No pus. No brown blood. He poured disinfectant over the wound, gritting his teeth at the sting. He got a clean needle and gave himself another shot of morphine, his second since he'd vowed to cut himself off. "That's it," he muttered. "Last one." He wrapped his arm in clean gauze and tied it off.

He washed down two arthritis pills with whiskey, took a last big swallow, and stretched out on the bed. His eyes shifted up to the bed's bronze trellis. It looked the same as that first night he had found a different use for the bed than resting up after wrestling with the Lord's angels, a use his father never would have approved.

"Ain't you scared?" Franny Compton had whispered in his ear as he grinded away at her. "What if somebody catches us? What if your daddy walks in on us, nekkid as the day we was born, goin at it like a couple stray cats?"

"It's past midnight, Franny. No one ever comes to the church this late."

She bent her knees and tightened her legs around his waist. "You oughta know, I reckon, you bein the preacher's son and all."

"Trust me. I know." He arched his back, and his eyes fell on the bronze trellis just as he pushed inside her.

He smiled, remembering that night, the first of many late nights with different girls on the daybed. In his mind's eye, he ticked through them one after another in chronological succession until he came to the last. Not a girl, but a woman, and he not a teenage boy, but a man. His smile faded. He knew then he shouldn't have started down that track.

He sat up, put his palms over his eyes, and tried hard to extinguish her memory, but she wouldn't leave him. He grabbed the Cutty Sark and gulped down a quarter of the bottle. He leaned forward, gagging. When the nausea passed, he lifted the bottle again, guzzled too much too fast, gagged again, recovered, and repeated the cycle. When the bottle was empty, he dropped it on the floor and fell back on the bed. Her image receded into mist. His mind numbed. Night fell like a heavy curtain over his eyes.

He dreamed of a dark swamp with a thick fog hovering over its brackish waters. A huge serpent slithered through the mud at the shoreline. Cole Grundy stepped out of the miasma, his gun drawn. He pointed the gun at the serpent. The serpent coiled to strike. Cole fired just as the serpent lunged at him.

Ray lurched out of sleep, sat up on the edge of the daybed, and rubbed his eyes. Moonlight coming in the window fell across his bandaged arm. He stroked the gauze and thought about Cole. Killing him next fall would be the final act in the long drama between them. He would plan the hit carefully. Lie in wait at his house. Step out of the shadows. A close-in shot to the chest before he had a chance to draw his gun. A kill shot to the head while he was down.

Ray ran a trembling hand across his lips. Cole would be his last hit. He would be done then. There would be no reason to go on after that.

He looked at the vial of morphine sitting on the desk. He got out of bed and walked over to it.

Chapter Thirty-Six

THE FINGERPRINT

March 10, 1967, Friday morning

THE NEXT MORNING, Cole drove through downtown Jeetersburg on his way from Dolley Madison Hospital to headquarters. When he turned off Lee Street onto Lighthorse, he pulled to the curb beside the town square. A statue of a Confederate infantryman stood on one side of the square; General Robert E. Lee on the other. In between, neatly trimmed boxwoods bordered triangular wedges of mowed lawn. Pea-stone paths ran from the sidewalks into the square and encircled a fountain, a three-tiered stack of copper urns. Morning sunlight sifted through the shade trees to dapple a park bench that faced it.

Cole saw Carrie sitting on the bench on a pretty summer day as he walked over the pathway toward her. She looked up at him with a pixie grin, the sun streaking her red hair with golden highlights. He sat down beside her.

She wore a short, blousy dress with big red roses on a white background. Her legs were tan and freckled. He put his hand on her knee. She took his hand in both of hers, still grinning. "This is a treat, meeting you for lunch."

He set his lunch pail on the bench.

She laughed. "Lemme guess. Peanut butter and banana sandwiches."

He smiled. "You got me pegged."

The fountain trickled peacefully while Cole's heart drummed in his chest. He drew in a deep breath and let it out and reached into his shirt pocket. He took Carrie's hand and slipped the ring on her finger, a gold band with a garnet centerpiece, sparkling crimson in the sunlight, and two little diamonds, one on each side of the garnet.

She sucked in her breath and squeezed his hand, shaking all over. He didn't know what to say and he couldn't have spoken at that moment anyway, so he just held her hand and hoped the ring would say the words for him. After what seemed like an eternity, her hand relaxed and she ran her fingers over the ring, as though she needed to touch it to convince herself it was real.

She looked up at Cole, her brown eyes full, smiling through her tears. "I love you, Cole," she whispered. It took his breath away.

Forty years later, staring at the park bench, Cole's breath stopped again and tears beaded in his eyes. She loved him so much then. If only he could go back and start from that moment and live his time with her again. He wouldn't take her love for granted. He would keep her close and show her he loved her as much as she loved him.

He took in another deep breath and let it out long and slow. He had thought less about Carrie the last few days, immersing himself in the effort to solve the crimes, but that morning, she weighed heavy on his mind. Chase Dooley's brush with death was the reason, he thought.

He looked at the fountain, water spilling over the lip of each urn to trickle down to the pool at its base. When Chase came along ten years ago, they'd quickly bonded. There was no mystery about the reason. Chase didn't know who his father was. Cole's son had turned away from him when he was a little boy.

When Karson called to tell him Chase had been shot, Cole rushed to the hospital and sat in the waiting room all night thinking about loss and grief. He had lost Peter thirty years ago. Carrie three years ago. And that night he almost lost Chase.

"Your man Deford," the surgeon told Cole, "saved Dooley's life. Without the combat bandage he applied to the gunshot wound, he would have bled out before the rescue squad arrived."

Cole took a last look at the fountain and the park bench, started the car, and drove away from the town square.

THAT AFTERNOON he sat at the head of the conference table in his office at headquarters. Shirley West sat to his right; Karson Deford to his left.

"None of the veterinarians sold succinylcholine to Dr. Hotchkiss," Karson said. He told Cole about Ashburn's Animal Hospital and Percy McDibble. "Ashburn's succinylcholine is manufactured by Sandoz. He gave the drug to no one except McDibble, and McDibble only made one sale of the drug, three vials of it to Ray Middleditch one week before Hazel Emley died."

Cole looked at Shirley and frowned. "Could this man Middleditch have murdered Hazel Emley?"

"The timing of Middleditch's purchase fits, and we know Randy died from succinylcholine manufactured by Sandoz. Unless we think Ashburn or McDibble killed him, Middleditch is the only man who could have done it."

"Is Middleditch a doctor?" Cole asked Karson.

"He told Clayton Fiddler he was a retired real estate agent from South Carolina."

"I don't understand," Cole said. "I'd never heard of succinylcholine until we found the needle beside Randy's arm. How could a man with no medical training choose it as a murder weapon and kill someone with it?"

"I did some research on that question," Shirley said. "My guess is he heard news reports about it." She withdrew documents from her valise and placed them in front of Cole and Karson. "These are copies of newspaper articles about the Coppolino murder case. The press ran stories about it all through the fall of last year, leading up to a trial in December."

Cole thumbed through the articles. *The New York Times, Richmond Times-Dispatch, Jeetersburg Daily Record.* Articles starting in August and running through mid-December. Headlines: "The Perfect Crime," "Doctor Death," "The Untraceable Poison."

"This case made succinylcholine famous," Shirley said. "Carl Coppolino was an anesthesiologist in New Jersey. He had an affair with Marjorie Farber, a married woman. Her husband mysteriously died in his sleep. Then Coppolino's wife died in her sleep. Later, when Coppolino jilted Farber, she told the police he killed them both with succinylcholine. The court ordered exhumations. The medical examiner found injection punctures in both corpses, but he encountered the same problem I experienced with Hazel Emley's autopsy. If succinylcholine killed them, it disappeared by breaking down into metabolites that are normally present in the body. In the Coppolino trial, the medical examiner testified that he found abnormally high levels of these byproducts in the corpse of Farber's husband, but Coppolino's lawyer, F. Lee Bailey, forced the medical examiner to admit on cross-examination that he couldn't say with any degree of certainty that the high levels were caused by an injection of succinylcholine. The jury found Coppolino not guilty. He goes on trial for his wife's murder next month, but the state will face the same problem. There's no sign of succinylcholine in her corpse."

"So you think Middleditch knew about the drug because of this case?" Cole said.

"When the jury acquitted Coppolino, the press touted succinylcholine as the perfect poison. If Middleditch wanted to make Hazel's murder look like a death by natural causes, the publicity about the drug could have caught his eye and it would have been a simple matter for him to learn how to kill someone with it. Medical treatises list overdose amounts and manuals provide instruction on filling a syringe from a vial and administering an intramuscular injection."

Cole mulled over what Karson and Shirley had said and shifted his focus to the new murder suspect. "What do we know about Middleditch?" he asked Karson.

"Chase spent the last couple days tracking him down. I went over his notes this morning." Karson summarized Chase's information. "It's clear that Ray Middleditch is a false identity. The Social Security number he gave the South Carolina DMV belongs to a Texas resident born in 1871. I called the last known address for that Ray Middleditch this morning. His daughter said he died ten years ago, but Jolley, McDibble, and Fiddler all identified the man in the driver's license photograph as the Ray Middleditch they met."

"Let me see the photograph."

Karson handed Cole a copy of the license. A long, thin face, thinning gray hair, gray beard, tired eyes. Something about the man's face seemed familiar to Cole, but he couldn't place him.

Frank Woolsey and Mabel walked into the room. Both were pale. Mabel looked frightened. She walked over to the conference table and stood beside Cole. He looked up at her, then at Frank. "What's wrong?"

"We found tire tracks in the driveway at the Jolley place," Frank said. "The tire tread matches the tracks we found at Walt Ballard's house. Boot prints we found in both locations also match."

"So Middleditch shot Walt Ballard?"

Frank nodded. His green eyes darted around the room and then settled on Mabel. "You tell him," he said. He looked down at the floor.

Cole looked at Mabel. "What is it?"

"The bullets the surgeons recovered from Walt's shoulder and thigh were fired by the same gun . . ." She stopped and seemed to gather her emotions. "The same gun that shot Carrie."

A block of ice swelled up inside Cole's chest and he couldn't breathe.

Mabel put her hand on his shoulder.

Her touch brought him back. He took a breath. Then another. He looked down at the photograph of the man who had killed Carrie. The ice melted away as heat flooded his chest and blood rose into his face.

"That's not all," Frank said.

Cole looked up at him, his heart pounding.

"When I saw the driver's license photo, I thought I recognized him." Frank grimaced, looked down at the floor, and then at Cole. "It's my fault we didn't know earlier. I didn't search our personnel files for matches with the partial fingerprint on the shell casing Chase found, but when I saw that photo, I checked our records going back forty years. He's aged a lot and the beard makes him look different." Frank looked at Mabel and then back at Cole and swallowed. "Ray Middleditch is Jim Lloyd."

Cole's throat closed over. Mabel put her hand on his shoulder again, and again she brought him out of it. He breathed deeply and looked down at the photo.

"Who's Jim Lloyd?" Karson said.

"He was a deputy sheriff," Frank said. "Sheriff Musgrove hired him forty years ago, before he hired Cole. He was here when I came on board. He worked here until 1938."

"Why did he leave?" Karson asked.

"I fired him," Cole said.

Cole stared at the hollow eyes in the photo. An ancient hatred, long dormant, roared back with a vengeance. Cole had to look away from the photograph and keep breathing to keep from fainting. This can't be true, he told himself. Jim hated Cole more than any man alive, but he could not have killed Carrie under any set of circumstances. "You're wrong," Cole said to Frank. "You've made a mistake."

Frank shook his head. "There's no mistake. Jim Lloyd is Ray Middleditch. He shot at you from the white pine on Bobcat. He shot Walt and Chase. And he murdered Carrie."

Cole leaned forward, put his elbows on his knees, and covered his face with the palms of his hands. He rolled his memory reels back forty years, searching for an explanation. He could find none.

"Are you all right, Cole?" Mabel's voice. Strained. Tight.

Cole leaned back in his chair and looked around the room. All eyes were on him.

Shirley said, "Step back from this one, Cole. Let Toby handle it."

Cole clenched his jaw. "What's the status of the search?" he said, his voice low and guttural.

"We set up checkpoints on every road leaving the county," Karson said. "Unless he fled on foot, he's still here."

"Any leads on where he is?"

"Not yet."

Cole hadn't seen Jim in thirty years, but they were best friends at one time, and Cole knew him well. He was shrewd and careful. He would stay out of sight. He wouldn't make a mistake, but like all men, he had tendencies, preferences, patterns of behavior. Cole had the best chance of anyone in the county of analyzing Jim's predilections to discover where he would hide. He needed time to think. "You all go on with the search. Let me know of any developments."

They all looked at him with concern.

"I'll be all right," he said. "I want to be alone to review the case files, see if I can find something we missed, figure out where he might be hiding. You all go on and do your jobs. You can't find him sitting in my office."

Karson, the veteran, was the best at taking orders. He left the office first.

Frank's waxed moustache twitched. "I'm sorry I missed the

match on those fingerprints. It never occurred to me the murderer could be one of our own."

"You identified him before he got out of the county," Cole said. "That's what's important."

Frank shook his head back and forth, then walked out of the office.

Shirley got up from her chair slowly, walked to the door, and looked back at Cole. "Be careful, Cole. Don't do anything foolish." She gave him a hard look and left the office.

Mabel still stood beside him. "Why did you fire this man Lloyd?" she asked him.

"Poor performance."

"I see," she said in a tone of voice that told him she knew he was lying. "You sure you're all right?"

He nodded.

She put her hand on his shoulder again, squeezed it, went to the door, looked back for a moment, and then left him alone.

Cole looked at the driver's license photograph of Ray Middleditch. Now that he knew he was looking at Jim Lloyd, he could see remnants of the young man he had known buried under the ravages of age. Jim looked spent, worn down, miserable. He and Cole had a lot in common, he thought, just like thirty years ago.

Chapter Thirty-Seven

THE LAST HIT

March 10-11, 1967, Friday night-Saturday morning

THAT NIGHT, Jim Lloyd drove into Jeetersburg and ate a late supper at an all-night diner. At midnight, he drove out to Hukstep's Trailer Park, parked behind the copse of cedar trees along Whiskey Road, and headed into the woods on foot, a half moon's gray light piercing the pine canopy to speckle the forest floor.

He stopped fifty feet inside the trees and flexed his knee. He had taken arthritis medication before he left the church, and against his better judgment, given himself another shot of morphine, but his knee had already begun to swell and it hurt.

He rubbed it for a while and moved on, limping badly. About a hundred feet along, he stopped again to rest on a fallen pine. He swallowed two more arthritis pills dry and waited for them to kick in.

A fox farther up Saddleback Cove bayed at the moon. The sound of a vehicle moving along Whiskey Road traveled into the cove and faded away.

He walked on, each step grinding bone on bone. He stopped

twice more and took another pain pill before he came to the edge of the woods at Reba's backyard. Her trailer and those on both sides of it were dark. The floodlight painted the yard pale yellow except for slate-gray shadows cast by the shed and the trailer. Before his knee went bad, Jim would have run in a crouch to the shed and dashed from there to the trailer. He couldn't even manage a fast walk now.

He looked at his watch. Quarter to one. He withdrew his Colt Python from his side pocket and limped to the shed. Inside it, out of the light, he picked up the folding chair and carried it to the open end of the shed. He looked at the yard and the trailers. No movement. No sound.

He hobbled to the kitchen window and stood under it, listening. The park was quiet. He flattened his back against the wall and edged past the living room window to the bedroom window. He stopped and listened again. Nothing. He unfolded the chair and set it under the window.

He took a moment to concentrate. The bedroom was small and narrow. The bed would be no more than five feet from the window. Three quick shots while Reba slept. Three more if a man was sleeping with her. The silencer would suppress the reports, and if he was lucky, the muted gunfire along with the shattering window wouldn't wake the neighbors. If it did, the old lady in the gray trailer would pose no problem. The NRA member in the double-wide worried him, but it would take him at least thirty seconds to get out of bed, look out the window, and fetch a weapon. Even with Jim's bum knee, he could make it to the woods by then.

He drew in a breath, let it out, planted his right foot on the chair, and pushed up to a crouch under the window. He straightened up to peek over the sill. The moonlight fell across the bed, where Reba had the covers pulled up over her head. He gripped the Colt Python with both hands and took aim.

Something blunt and solid jammed hard against his crotch. He flinched.

"Don't move or I'll blow your balls off." A woman's voice, raspy with a lisp.

He looked down. Reba Emley's lipstick was glistening in the moonlight. She had a gun in her hand and was pressing the barrel into his crotch. "Drop your gun."

He considered making a move but assessed the odds of success as nil. Her gun was tight against his crotch.

"You got five seconds to drop it."

She had him dead to rights. He dropped the gun.

Reba picked up Jim's gun, put her pistol in her back pocket, and aimed the Colt Python at him. She looked like she knew how to handle it. Walt Ballard's service revolver was a Colt Python. He'd probably taught her what to do with it.

She took a step backwards. "Get down off that chair. Slow and easy."

When he bent his right leg to descend, it gave way, causing him to land hard on his left. A bolt of fire shot through his bad knee and he almost toppled over. He grabbed the back of the chair and fell into it.

Reba thrust the gun at him. "You stay back!"

He held his hands up in the air. "I fell," he said through clenched teeth. He groaned. "I've got a bad knee."

"One more false move, I'll blow you away."

"I couldn't help falling. I've got arthritis." He slowly lowered his hands and rubbed his knee.

She stood over him, watching warily, the gun trained on him. "Stand up."

He struggled to his feet.

"Move." She gestured at the corner of the trailer.

He limped to the corner and stopped.

"Go around to the front door."

He did as she said, stopping at the concrete stoop.

"Go on inside."

He climbed the steps, leading with his right leg, dragging his left along behind. He opened the door and stepped inside. She followed him in and jabbed him in the back with the barrel of the Python. He took a couple steps into the darkness. She flicked a light switch and he shielded his eyes from the glare.

"Get your hands up! Raise em high!"

He raised his hands, squinting until his eyes adjusted to the light. The room came into focus. He was in front of a little sitting area with a kitchen counter and stools to his right and a bedroom on his left. The bedroom door was open and the living room light fell across the bed. Pillows were arranged under the bedcovers in the shape of a body. Apparently she wasn't as dumb as he thought.

"Stand over there." She motioned to a spot in front of the bedroom door.

He stepped over to it.

"Turn around."

He faced her. She wore tight jeans, knee-high black leather boots, and a sable fur coat over a denim shirt. She stood with her feet wide apart, cradling the butt of the gun in the palm of her left hand, gripping the trigger guard with her right, her jaw clenched, a hard look in her blue eyes. "I been waitin for you since you shot Walt."

He was right. He'd badly underestimated her. "How did you know I would come for you?"

"I know why you killed the others. You want us all dead cause you think we know who you are. You're wrong. Only Betty Lou and Momma knew, but you couldn't be sure of that so you had to kill us all and I'm the only one left. I thought you'd come for me sooner. What took you so long?"

"Your boyfriend's dog tried to make a meal of me. Took me a while to heal up."

"Too bad he didn't kill you. Wish I'd killed you thirty years ago."

He searched her face for the meaning of her comment. "I don't understand."

"Bullshit. You understand good and well."

"I don't know what you're talking about."

She frowned, looking uncertain for the first time. "Take off your coat."

He took off his coat and draped it over the back of a chair.

"Take off your shirt."

"Why?"

"Do it!"

"All right. All right. Cool down."

He took off his shirt and dropped it on the chair.

"Keep your hands up. Raise em high!"

He did as she said.

Her eyes ran over his bare flesh, a fierce look on her face.

He looked down at his sagging chest and soft paunch, milk-white under the light, wondering what she found so interesting.

She seemed to focus on his midriff.

"Keep your hands up and turn sideways."

He turned. He stood that way for a long time with her peering at his side, her brow furrowed.

"Face the bedroom."

He turned his back to her. He heard her step closer to him. She was quiet for a short while and then said, "Turn around."

He faced her, his hands still over his head.

She stood only a foot from him, bending her knees, eye level with his stomach, squinting at it, the gun pointed at it. Her hands began to shake. "You're not the snake," she said, her voice quavering.

"What?"

"You're not him. There's no scar. You're not the snake."

Her hands shook more. Years of experience told him this moment was his best chance. He grabbed the gun barrel with his right hand and swung at her with his left. The left cross hit her jaw straight-on. The gun fired as he wrenched it out of her grasp. The silencer suppressed the explosion, but the bullet shattered the living room window. His blow to her face threw her into the wall. Her head bounced off the wood paneling and she knocked a lamp off a table, causing another loud crash. Stunned, but still standing, she reached for the gun in her back pocket. Jim hit her over the head with the butt of the Colt Python and she collapsed on the floor face-down. He leaned over her and took her gun out of her pocket. A little derringer of some sort. Old with rust spots. He jammed it in his pants pocket.

Reba rolled over on her back, groaning, her eye purple and swollen, her jaw jutting to one side, blood bathing her forehead and streaking her hair.

Shattering the window and crashing the lamp probably woke the NRA member. Jim had to kill her and get out. He grabbed his shirt and put it on. He picked up his coat and started to approach her for the kill shot when a high-pitched howl shattered the silence.

Jim looked up at the open door as a scrawny man with a twisted face and wild eyes charged him. Before he could react, the man's head bowled into his belly, knocking all the wind out of him. He tumbled backwards, lost his grip on the gun, and watched it fly out the window.

Jim fell into an easy chair, still in the man's grasp. It toppled over backwards and they rolled around on the floor. Still howling, the man clawed at Jim's eyes. Jim grabbed the man's pencil-thin wrists and struggled to his feet, pulling him up with him. He held the man upright and kneed him in the groin. The man fell silent, his mouth open midhowl, and sank to the floor like a balloon losing air, his hands clutching his crotch.

Jim staggered across the room, his knee grinding mercilessly. He picked up his coat and limped over to where Reba was lying on her back, holding her jaw, blood dribbling out of her mouth. He placed the derringer's barrel on the center of her forehead. Her eyes saucered. He pulled the trigger. The gun misfired. He tried to pull the trigger again, but the gun jammed. "God damn it!" He threw the gun across the room.

Headlights washed over the front windows. The hell with Reba. Get out now or perish. He put on his coat and hobbled to the front door and down the steps.

"You! Stop!" A shirtless teenage skinhead stood in the dirt road beside Reba's Impala, aiming a handgun at him. A pickup truck in front of the NRA member's trailer had its headlights pointed at Reba's place. An old man in pajamas and a cowboy hat stood next to the truck holding a rifle.

Jim ran to the corner of the trailer, pain stabbing his knee with every step. The boy fired the handgun. Pump, pump, pump. Muted reports. Two pinpricks in his shoulder blade, but he didn't go down. He grabbed his shoulder and looked at the kid. A small gun, black. A goddamn pellet gun!

He would have laughed, but the rifle boomed, blowing a hole in the aluminum siding just above his head. He rounded the trailer and headed to the shed, half running and half fast-walking, every step a knife slicing into his knee.

Pump. Pump. A pellet stung the back of his leg. He stopped and pointed his hand with two fingers extended at the skinhead teenager at the corner of the trailer. In the darkness, the ruse worked. The boy hit the ground and rolled under the trailer. The old man was nowhere to be seen.

Jim ran around the shed and into the forest. The rifle fired and a bullet rushed by his ear and cracked into a pine tree. He ran on into the woods, his knee an inflamed mass of ground meat, searing with pain. He ran on and on. Halfway to the truck, his knee gave way and he fell. He rolled under a clump of bushes and looked at the woods behind him, breathing hard. No one was there. They hadn't given chase yet. The old man looked too old to run after him and the stupid kid thought he had a gun.

Two full minutes passed while he lay under the bushes gasping for air. He had to get up and flee. They'd seen him go into the woods. They would come for him sooner or later.

He struggled to his feet and found a broken branch to serve as a makeshift cane so he could limp on toward his truck. When he was twenty feet from the road, he heard a siren in the distance. He stood in the woods and watched the flashing lights of a patrol car speed around a turn and head into the cove toward the trailer park. He caned to the truck and climbed in.

Another siren wailed. Flashing lights painted the night sky as he watched another patrol car round the turn and speed away. There would be more responders. He had to get out before they blocked Whiskey Road.

He started the truck and spun out. He was only a mile from Fox Run when he heard another siren approaching. They would recognize his truck in the glare of their headlights. He looked frantically for a place to pull off the road, but there was nowhere to hide. Red and blue lights washed over his windshield and a pair of headlights blinded him. He pulled off the shoulder, expecting the vehicle to block his path and its driver to jump out and level a gun on him. He'd lost the Colt Python. He couldn't even go down fighting. The hell with it. He would charge at his assailant. Force his hand. End it here.

The lights sped past him and a white van with blue markings disappeared around a turn. An ambulance. He laughed, a high nervous titter.

He slumped against the driver's door for a few moments, breathing hard, before he regained his composure. You can't relax, he told himself. It's only a matter of time until they block the end of Whiskey Road. He jammed the truck into gear and raced to the T intersection in Fox Run, turned left at Kirby's Store, and drove along Whippoorwill Hollow Road to the turnoff to Tinker's Mill. At the turnoff, he slowed to a reasonable speed. He was far enough away now. He was in the clear. He breathed easier. He had escaped. He would survive.

Chapter Thirty-Eight

THE LOVER

June, 1937

ON A CLOUDY DAY in June thirty years earlier, Cole sat in an unmarked county car under a big sycamore tree across the road from his house. He had rolled down the windows. It was hot and muggy, and the air was close. Thunder rumbled in the distance and he could smell the coming rain. He waited.

Shortly after noon, Carrie's black Chevrolet coupe rolled down the driveway and turned left onto Whippoorwill Hollow Road. Cole gave her time to get ahead of him, then started his car and pulled out onto the road.

There was no traffic on the country road in the middle of the day, so he was careful to keep his distance. Five miles north of their house, Carrie turned right and headed east on the road to Tinker's Mill. Cole was a quarter mile behind her on a long straightaway when she turned left onto a dirt road that cut a path through a poplar forest.

Cole took the turnoff and stopped just inside the woods to make sure she stayed well ahead of him. He knew there was no risk he would lose her. The road dead-ended in a clearing not too far ahead.

After a short wait, he drove into the forest and pulled off the road behind a clump of tangled vines, got out, and walked out to the edge of the trees. Blood of the Lamb Church sat in the clearing. The coupe was not parked in the churchyard, and he saw no movement in the church's windows. The air was still; the surroundings eerily quiet.

Staying inside the woods, he walked around toward the rear of the church. Lightning splintered the sky to the west. Rolling thunder sounded like distant kettle drums and a light mist began to fall.

The coupe was parked near the back stoop and a county patrol truck sat at the far corner of the building. Cole stared at the coupe and the truck, his heart pounding.

A long time passed before he was able to move his legs. He stepped out of the woods and walked unsteadily across the yard. He stopped in front of the back stoop, two concrete steps up to a little porch with black wrought iron railings on each side, a back door, a window to its right.

He climbed the steps and stared at the door, mist glistening on its rust-red surface, its doorknob round, brass, ornate, with little raised ridges and curlicues. He stood there without moving, afraid to open the door.

The rain picked up. Water dripped off the brim of his hat. His shirt clung to his flesh.

On the other side of the door, the voices of a man and Carrie murmured, muted by the sound of the rain.

Cole grasped the railing to steady himself and turned his back on the door. He watched the water beading on the hood of the car he'd bought Carrie because she complained of being lonely and housebound.

Lightning lit up the sky; a clap of thunder boomed; and the rain came down in torrents.

Cole walked down the steps. Water puddled in a little depression where he stood. Rain pattered the back of his neck as he looked down at the puddle. He looked over at the woods.

Go back to the car. Drive away. Talk to her when your blood isn't running high.

The sound of faint laughter came from inside, near the window. He looked over at it for a long time. Then he stepped around the stoop, edged along the wall to the window, and stopped just this side of it. He looked at the patrol truck, water rolling off its hood in sheets.

Don't look inside. Walk away. Confront her at home.

He wiped water from his face with his hand. His brow felt warm, almost feverish. He took a step toward the window and looked inside.

Through the rain-streaked pane, he saw Jim Lloyd lying on a bed on his back. Carrie sat astride him, leaning forward, the palms of her hands on his bare chest, her body moving up and down rhythmically, her breasts swaying with the motion, a wedge of red hair covering one eye, the other eye closed, her lips parted.

All the air went out of his lungs. He collapsed to the ground and sat with his back against the church, his head bowed.

A panorama of scenes of Carrie and Cole rolled through his mind and faded away to be replaced by Carrie and Jim in the church window.

Lightning flashed. A peal of thunder crashed in the woods and slowly rumbled away.

The image of Carrie and Jim exploded blinding white in his mind's eye and then went dark.

HE LURCHED AWAKE, still sitting on the ground, his back against the church wall. He leaned over and retched.

He wiped his mouth with his sleeve and looked around. He didn't know how long he had been out. The rain had died down to a steady drizzle. His clothes were soaked through. His hat was over-turned on the ground beside him, its crown a pool of water.

He didn't remember drawing his service revolver, but it lay in his lap. He grasped it with both hands and stroked the barrel. It was cool to the touch and beaded with rain water.

The faint ripple of Jim's laughter came again from inside. The soft tones of Carric's voice.

He clicked off the revolver's safety, gripped the walnut handle, put his finger through the trigger guard, and closed his eyes. He saw them on the bed. He saw himself open the door, point the gun at Jim, fire, and turn the gun on himself.

He opened his eyes and gazed at the Chevy coupe. Lonely and housebound, she had said. His vision blurred with tears.

He allowed himself to weep silently for only a few seconds. Then he forced himself to gather all his strength. Even at that moment, in the depth of his despair, he knew what he would do. He would work his way through the pain. He would heal the wound. He would make her love him again. Even more than before. And he would get rid of Jim.

He wiped the tears away, holstered the gun, crawled on hands and knees to the stoop, grabbed the railing, and pulled himself up to stand. He gripped the cold, wet wrought iron bar tightly and pulled himself together.

He looked up at the slate-colored sky. The rain had stopped. The storm had moved on. He steadied himself and walked back to the unmarked car.

Chapter Thirty-Nine

THE RECKONING

March 10-11, 1967, Friday night–Saturday morning

AT TEN O'CLOCK on the night Jim Lloyd attacked Reba, Cole drove over the dirt road through the poplar forest to Blood of the Lamb Church. He parked his car short of the clearing behind a clump of brush near the spot where he'd parked thirty years earlier. He got out of the car and walked along the edge of the trees to the rear of the church. The black Dodge 100 was not there. He went back to his patrol car and waited.

He'd been thinking about nothing but Jim Lloyd since the meeting at headquarters. When Sheriff Musgrove hired Cole as a deputy, he assigned Jim to shepherd him through the training process. They quickly became friends and over the seven years they worked together their bond intensified. When Cole saw Jim and Carrie in the church window, it almost killed him, but he later came to understand Carrie's infidelity. Jim's betrayal was a different matter. He was pure evil, a Judas who pretended to be like a brother to Cole while scheming behind his back to seduce his wife.

Three years ago, Jim had returned and killed Carrie. Now he had returned to kill others, as well as Cole, and Cole was the only one in Selk County who knew him well enough to analyze where he would go and what he would do.

Jim was a smart man, careful, strategic, and deliberate. He had always gone about his business as a deputy sheriff like a chess player. He planned his moves way in advance, and when his adversary checked him, he implemented his backup plan and resumed his attack.

Renting the Jolley place was a smart move. Remote and secluded, it gave Jim a home base well off the radar screen, but Cole was certain Jim had anticipated his cover might be blown and he had no doubt that Jim had devised a backup plan, a retreat to a safe place where he could hole up while he plotted his escape from the county.

The safe place Jim would choose came to Cole quickly. Jim's father's church, Blood of the Lamb. It was as remote and secluded as the Jolley place. Vacant most of the week. Familiar ground for Jim. He grew up in the church. He knew every square inch of the building and its surroundings. And it was the last place anyone would look for a murderer on the run.

Unless the murderer was Jim and the man searching for him was Cole.

Cole had pretended to review the case files all afternoon. He left headquarters at six, assuring Mabel he was headed home, and drove to Sally's Diner for a light supper. He then drove to the town square, stared at the fountain and the park bench, and thought about Carrie. At nine, he drove out of Jeetersburg, checking his rearview mirror to make sure none of his men had followed him.

It didn't worry him that Jim wasn't at the church when he arrived there. He was confident Jim had chosen it as his hiding place and that he would return to it.

Cole waited in his patrol car patiently. At one-thirty, transmissions about the attack on Reba came over his radio. Toby Vess called for an ambulance for Reba and Floyd Spivey and put out an alert for all available personnel to report to Hukstep's Trailer Park. Karson Deford and Will Garrison responded to the call. No one else checked in.

Molly Ruebush's grainy voice came over the airwaves. "Dispatch to County One." Silence. She repeated the call. Another silence, then, "Cole? . . . Pick up, Cole. We've got an emergency and we're shorthanded. . . . Cole? You there?" The alarm buzzer in Cole's home office sounded off to awaken him in such emergencies. Molly had to be wondering why he didn't respond.

Cole shut off his radio, got out of the car, walked to a spot in the woods where he had a view of the back door, and waited.

Fifteen minutes later, headlights tunneled through the forest and emerged in the clearing, washing over the church. A black Dodge 100 glided across the churchyard with moonlight playing on its windshield. It rounded the church and parked by the back stoop.

Jim opened the door and eased out one leg. He almost fell as he stepped down off the running board, grabbing hold of the door to keep his balance. He leaned over and rubbed his knee.

Tall and thin with silver hair and a beard, he looked older than the thirty years he'd added since Cole saw him last. He wore a heavy blue coat that came down to his knees. The .357 Magnum that killed Carrie rode in one of its large side pockets, Cole guessed.

Cole raised his service revolver and put the gunsight on Jim's chest, but his hands shook so badly he couldn't hold it there. He lowered the gun, breathing hard.

Jim reached inside the truck and backed out of it with a stick in his hand. He leaned heavily on it and caned slowly to the stoop, barely able to put weight on his left leg.

Cole raised the gun again, but again he couldn't hold it on target.

Jim climbed the steps and went inside.

Cole dropped the gun to his side and wiped sweat off his brow, his hands shaking violently.

A light came on in the little room behind the sanctuary and poured out the window, casting a wedge of amber over the hood of the truck.

Calm down. Control your rage. Use it to your advantage.

He stood at the edge of the forest for five minutes. When the adrenaline had ebbed, he walked across the churchyard to the stoop and stopped in front of it, the pain pulsating at his iliac crest. The hell with the pain. He climbed the steps and looked at the door, now green, and the doorknob, now plain metal, smooth. Cole looked at the window. Years had passed; the world had turned ten thousand times; but what he had seen in that window would never fade away.

He kicked the door in, crashing it against the wall. Jim sat on the bed, a bandage on his arm, his pants leg rolled up above the knee, an ice pack on the bed beside him, his winter coat draped over the back of a desk chair ten feet from him. He looked up at Cole, startled.

Cole crossed the room in three quick strides and put all his might into a sidelong slashing blow with his service revolver to Jim's head just above the ear. Blood flew across the room and splattered on the wall. Jim fell over on the bed. Cole put the barrel to Jim's temple, gripping the gun with both hands, and pushed his head down hard against the mattress.

Kill him! Kill him now!

Jim shoved him backwards. Cole stumbled, righted himself, and thrust the gun at Jim with a two-fisted straight-armed grip.

Jim sat up on the bed slowly, trembling, blood sliding down his face. "Pull the trigger!" he shouted. "Do it!"

Cole took a step back, breathing hard, still holding the gun on Jim. "Why did you kill her?" he choked out.

"You're the one who killed her. You killed her when you wouldn't let her go."

"She didn't want to go with you," he said. "She chose me over you."

"She didn't choose you. You threatened to take Peter away from her. She chose Peter over me."

"She wanted to stay with me," Cole said, his voice breaking. "She loved me."

"She hated you! You and your almighty quest to become sheriff!" Jim placed his bloody hand on the bed to brace himself, struggling to stay upright. "She loved me," he said in a low voice.

Jim's words struck Cole like a hammer blow to the heart. He backed up to the desk and put his hand on it to steady himself. An image of Carrie from thirty years ago, even more painful than his memory of her and Jim in the window, came back to Cole—Carrie sitting at their kitchen table, her head down, weeping softly.

"Look at me," Cole had said.

She had looked at him, her big brown eyes full.

"Do you love him?"

Tears had streamed down her cheeks. "Yes."

Her answer broke Cole's heart back then, and in the little anteroom thirty years later, his heart broke again. He sat down heavily on the desk chair. "She loved me before you came along," he said, his voice low and quavering. "She loved me again after you left. Even more than before."

Jim smirked. "She hated you. For good reason. You loved only yourself."

They were quiet for a long while. Cole thought about all he had gone through. Jim stole Carrie's love from him. He had won her back. Thirty years later, Jim had returned to Selk County to kill her. Cole had to know the reason. He pointed the gun at Jim. "Why did you kill her?"

Jim put his bloody hand over his eyes. After a long silence, he said, "They fired me. I was sixty-two. No wife. No children. No life." He dropped his hand into his lap and gave Cole a menacing look. "All because you wouldn't let her go."

"That's a reason to hate me, not Carrie."

"There's a lot you don't know."

"Tell me."

Jim touched the wound above his ear, looked at the blood on his hand, rubbed it between his fingers. "When you found out about us, she cut me off. She wouldn't talk to me." He took a kerchief out of his pants pocket and pressed it against his wound. "I went to your house when you were at headquarters. Forced my way inside. She cried. Said she loved me but she couldn't leave Peter." He swayed, put his hand on the bed to hold himself up, and sighed heavily. "She said it hurt too much to be near me and not be with me. She begged me to leave, to go far away and never come back. She told me to put her out of my mind and move on with my life." He tossed the bloody kerchief on the floor and rubbed his hands on his thighs, his eyes full. "I went away. For her sake. But I couldn't put her out of my mind."

"That all went down thirty years ago," Cole said. "You killed her long after."

Jim's tired eyes settled on Cole. "I loved her through all those years. I had no one else. Cared for no one." Jim looked down at his knee and rubbed it. "After they fired me, I called her. Asked her to meet me. She refused. I wrote her a letter. Poured my heart out. Begged her to run away with me and make the most out of what time we had left."

He stopped rubbing his knee and looked at Cole. "Her answer came in the mail. Two sentences. 'I don't love you anymore. Don't ever contact me again.'" His face grew hard. "I didn't blame her when she pushed me away the first time, but this last time around, Peter was long gone. She shouldn't have shut me out."

"You killed her because she turned you away after thirty years?" Cole said, his anger almost strangling him.

Jim glared at Cole. "I planned to kill you, but she came home first. She looked at me like she hated me. 'I told you to stay away from me,' she said. Hard-hearted. Cru—" His voice failed him. He swallowed and cleared his throat. "All the years of trying to forget her. The loneliness. The heartache." He put his hand to his eyes. "I lost control. I don't even remember firing the gun." He dropped his hand and glowered at Cole. "She would have run away with me if you hadn't taken Peter hostage. You forced her to stay with you against her will. You broke her and turned her into someone hard and cold. I didn't kill her. You did."

"You're lying to yourself," Cole said. "You killed her because she didn't love you anymore. You killed her because you couldn't have her. You're a Judas. You betrayed me to steal Carrie, and when she rejected you, you betrayed her. You'll burn in hell for what you did to us."

Jim's face hardened into a mask of pure hatred. They glared at each other for a long time.

Then Cole noticed a gradual shift in Jim's demeanor. A subtle change, Jim's hatred morphing into something less malevolent, but still lethal. A determined look came into Jim's eyes and his body tensed.

He's looking for an opening, Cole thought. Jim, the chess player, in check for the moment but ever vigilant. Cole suspected Jim's handgun was in the pocket of the coat draped across the back of Cole's chair, but Jim always had a backup plan.

This is it, Cole told himself, the moment of reckoning. Give him a chance and he'll seize it.

Pretending he was so distraught that he'd lost his focus, Cole bowed his head and slumped in the chair, relaxing his gun arm, allowing it to dangle toward the floor.

In a swift, fluid motion, Jim reached under the bed, withdrew a rifle, and pointed it at Cole.

Cole raised his gun and fired one round. The bullet hit Jim in the forehead, dead center. As the force of the bullet knocked him backward, Jim's rifle exploded, blowing a hole in the beadboard just above Cole's head. Jim fell back on the bed, blood and brain matter spraying the windowpane behind him. The rifle lay across his chest still in his grasp. His legs twitched and went still.

Cole kept his gun trained on Jim for a long time. Then he stood slowly, walked over to the bed, pried the rifle out of Jim's hands, and looked down at his corpse.

"She loved me," Cole whispered. "She loved me."

Chapter Forty

THE PASSENGER

July 22, 1967, Saturday morning

FOUR MONTHS after Cole Grundy killed Jim Lloyd, Deputy Toby Vess turned his old blue Ford pickup off Whiskey Road onto a dirt driveway and stopped. Someone had staked a sign beside the mailbox. Black letters on a white field: For Sale by Owner.

Toby urged his truck over the rutted road and emerged from the brush and scrub pines into a clearing. He parked in the driveway and looked at the house.

The metal stake still stood beside the stoop with a chain snaking away from it under the house. Toby looked over at his passenger, who had his head held high, his jutting chin emphasizing his severe underbite, his yellow eyes fixed on Toby. Toby got out of the truck and looked back at the dog. He didn't move. "You'd best come on now."

The brindle pit bull hopped across the seat and out the door to land at Toby's feet. He sat on his haunches and looked up at Toby. Toby squatted beside him and scratched the soft spots around the stubs where his ears had been before the sons a bitches cut them off with a pair of scissors so the dogs they made him fight couldn't get a jaw-grip on them. The pit bull closed his eyes and groaned.

The door to the house opened. Walt Ballard stepped out on the stoop, leaning heavily on a cane.

Toby stood and faced him.

Walt came off the stoop awkwardly and limped through the weeds toward the truck. He stopped about ten feet from the dog and Toby. "Buck," he said.

The dog stood up, furrowed his brow, and wagged his tail.

Walt leaned over and patted his thigh. "Come, Buck."

Buck looked up at Toby and then at Walt.

"Go ahead," Toby said.

Buck trotted over to Walt and looked up at him uncertainly.

Walt offered his knuckles. Buck sniffed the hand, tentatively at first and then with growing enthusiasm. His tail wagged furiously. He barked and jumped up on Walt. Walt steadied himself with his cane and laughed. He patted Buck's big flat head that was now adorned with a crimson scar that parted his short hair down the middle.

Toby watched the pit bull jump around on his hind legs while Walt played with him. He took a deep breath and walked over to Walt and the dog.

Walt knelt on his good knee with his bad leg stretched out stiff to the side and put his arm around Buck's shoulders. Buck licked his face. Walt laughed. "I missed you, Buck, you old rascal, you!"

"Is that his name?" Toby said. "Buck'?"

Walt struggled to stand. Toby helped him up. Walt leaned heavily on his cane. "Buck's what I named him. What do you call him?"

"I call him P.D."

"What do the letters stand for?"

"Nothing. They just seemed to fit."

Walt laughed. "He looks good, Toby. Looks like you fed him plenty. He's put on weight. I can't thank you enough for taking care of him. Cole told me the pound was twenty-four hours away from putting him down when you stepped in and took him home. You saved his life."

Toby watched P.D. prance around Walt with his tongue hanging out and his powerful jaw slack in a wide dog-grin. "It didn't seem right," Toby said in a sandpaper voice. "He didn't do anything wrong, but they said they had to put him to sleep because no one would take him."

P.D. continued to jump around Walt, as happy as a puppy. Toby turned toward his truck, squinted up at the sun, swiped at his eye, and looked down at the ground. "Anyway, he's back with you where he belongs."

"Thanks, again," Walt said.

Toby waved his hand in the air and walked back to his truck, doing his best to resist the urge to look back at the dog. He opened the truck door and hesitated, trying to come to terms with the end of his time with P.D. As he stood there, the pit bull brushed by Toby's leg, hopped up in the truck, and sat on his haunches by the passenger window with his head held high and his underbite exposing his two lower canine teeth, his yellow eyes fixed on Toby.

Toby looked back at Walt and then at P.D.

Walt caned over to the truck. He looked at Buck for a long moment. He ran his hand across his mouth and looked off at the scrub pines bordering the clearing. When he turned to Toby, his eyes were full. "I wasn't gonna ask you cause I know it ain't fair to you, Toby, but I need a big favor."

Toby faced Walt.

"I reckon you heard I'm selling the place and moving in with Reba."

"I saw the for sale sign. I didn't know about Reba, but I'm mighty glad y'all are getting back together."

Walt looked down at the ground. "Had to get myself damned near killed before she decided to take me back. It's a hard way to court a woman. I don't recommend it."

Walt was quiet for a few moments. He seemed to be searching for words. Then, "Thing is we won't have room in her trailer for a big smelly dog like Buck." He glanced at Buck, then looked away at the brush again, and bit his lip. "I know it's a burden, but I was hoping he could stay with you." Walt looked down at his cane. Its walnut handle was a carved rabbit's head with red glass beads for eyes. "I'd be forever grateful if you'd take him off my hands."

Toby started to speak, but his voice caught in his throat. He licked his lips and said, "You sure about this?"

"I'm sure," Walt said, still looking down. "It's hard on me, but it's the right thing to do for Buck."

"It's no burden on me. He's a good dog." Toby looked at P.D. "Gets lonely at my place sometimes," he said under his breath.

He turned back to Walt. They shook hands.

Walt ran his sleeve over his nose, looked at Buck, and caned back to the stoop.

As Toby turned the truck around and drove out toward Whiskey Road, P.D. looked back at Walt standing on the stoop until the scrub pines closed around the old Ford and blocked his view. Then he turned and looked out the windshield at the road ahead. Toby reached over and rubbed his big shoulders.

Chapter Forty-One

THE BRACELET

July 22, 1967, Saturday morning

THAT SAME MORNING, Cole sat at his kitchen table, thinking about Carrie.

On warm summer nights, she and Cole used to sit in their Adirondack chairs in the front yard, drinking iced tea and talking. She called it their quiet time. Three weeks after her funeral, sitting alone out there on a moonlit night, he saw a shadowy movement in the woods at the edge of the yard and heard the faint sound of Carrie's laughter. He went down to the trees and looked. No one was there.

A few weeks after that, he awoke in the dark in bed, and he heard her whisper his name. He reached out for her. His hand fell on her pillow. It was warm. He got out of bed and turned on the light. Her side of the bed was undisturbed.

She came to him again and again. He felt her breath on his cheek. He heard the murmur of her voice in the silence before dawn. He felt the light brush of her fingertips on his brow. He heard the soft tread of her step on the porch in the night.

His doctor said these experiences were common among widowers. Cole's subconscious perception hadn't caught up to the reality of Carrie's death. Give it time, he said.

And so it went. As time passed, she came to him less frequently. She hadn't visited him in more than a year when the jay called from the big white pine on Bobcat Mountain and he lurched to his left and the shooter's bullet whizzed by his jaw. For a few days, he thought maybe Carrie's spirit gave breath to the jay's cry at that crucial moment to save his life.

When he learned Jim Lloyd had fired the shot, he changed his mind. He didn't know if she would have intervened to save him from Jim. He hoped so, but he wasn't sure. That was when he decided he had to try to come to terms with her death.

Mabel Lucas sat at the kitchen table across from Cole that Saturday morning. "Every closet and dresser drawer in this house," Mabel said, "is chock full of her things. Dresses, blouses, sweaters, winter coats, jackets, shoes. Even the bathroom cabinets are filled with her cosmetics and medications. You've kept everything she ever touched. It's as if she still lives here."

Her tone was sympathetic, but Cole felt defensive. "She does live here. In a way."

Mabel reached across the table and took his hand. "You know that's not true, Cole," she said gently. "That's why you asked me to help you go through her things."

Cole looked down at his coffee mug and said nothing.

She squeezed his hand and released it. "I called Goodwill. They're sending a truck on Monday."

He tightened his grip on his coffee mug and kept his head down.

"You don't have to part with everything," she said. "Is there anything special you want to keep?"

He paused, thinking.

"What about her rings?" she said. "Her wedding band? Her engagement ring?"

"They're on her hand."

"Oh," she said in a small voice.

He put his hands over his eyes and rubbed them. "There's a bracelet," he said. "Silver. With our names engraved on it."

"Where is it?"

"Top left-hand drawer of the bureau in my bedroom in a black leather case."

She pushed her chair back from the table and got up. Cole watched her walk across the kitchen to the hallway. Tall, strong, plain. Galumphy saddle shoes, white athletic socks, a shapeless, billowy black dress designed to swallow up her big-boned frame.

He knew he couldn't let go of Carrie without help, but he'd never opened up to anyone about her. The list of candidates he could talk to was short. Chase was like a son to him; Toby an older brother. But he couldn't bring himself to show them his vulnerability. Mabel was the daughter he never had. If anyone could draw him out, he thought it was this smart, sensitive young mother of seven, who loved him.

She came back to the kitchen, sat down, and placed a square black case in front of him.

Cole opened the box. The sun glanced off the sterling silver cuff lying in red velvet. He took it out. A quarter-inch silver band with a seven-inch circumference, in pristine condition. He read the inscription on the inside rim in what the jeweler called Angel Tears font: "Carrie, I will always love you, Cole."

He held it in the palm of his hand for a few moments, then set it back in the case and closed the lid. He took a sip of coffee and looked out the open window. A light breeze carried the scent of jasmine inside.

The yard was eerily quiet. No birdsong in the woods. All twenty birdhouses were strangely vacant.

He felt Mabel's eyes on him. She knows I need to talk, he thought. She's waiting.

He looked at a long low birdhouse hanging from the maple tree by the driveway, a red house with white letters he had crudely paint-brushed across its green tin roof: Carrie's Diner.

"She had an affair," he said in a gritty voice.

He kept staring out the window at the birdhouse, but in his peripheral vision, he saw Mabel lean forward.

"It was my fault." He pulled himself together. "Sheriff Musgrove was about to retire. Toby, Jim Lloyd, and I were the likely successors. Toby said he didn't want the job. Jim didn't step up and go for it." He took a deep breath and let it out. "I worked double shifts every weekday, spent every weekend at training seminars and community outreach projects, volunteered for every out-of-town assignment. After I was elected sheriff, I spent every waking hour trying to prove I deserved it. For four years, all I thought about or cared about was my work."

The weight of Cole's regret bore him down. It took him a few moments to summon the will to go on. "I had built this house and moved her out here in the country away from all her friends. She didn't know anyone in the hollow and we had no close neighbors. I isolated her. Then I abandoned her. She tried to tell me, but I was deaf to everything but my job."

He looked at Mabel. She sat very still.

"She was lonely and miserable. She thought I stopped loving her."

Cole folded his hands on top of the table. Mabel cupped her hands around his.

He nodded toward the leather case. "I gave her that bracelet two months after I saw her . . . after I found out about the affair. I told her I knew it was my fault. Told her I still loved her and I wanted her back." He took in another deep breath. "She refused to take it. Said she loved . . . someone else."

Mabel rubbed his hands. Neither of them said anything for a long time. Then Mabel said, "How long did it take to win her over?"

His mouth was dry. He licked his lips. "Five years."

"Long time."

"She didn't trust me." He hesitated and then said, "I did some harsh things in the beginning to keep her with me."

Mabel nodded. "You fired Jim Lloyd."

Cole was surprised. "How did you know?"

"The timing fits," she said, her caterpillar eyebrows knitted.

He averted his eyes. She could read his mind and he didn't want her to see all the dark places he had gone.

Outside, the wind blew through the shade trees, their leaves glittering lime green in the bright sunlight, the hanging birdhouses swaying gently.

"You're still trying to prove you love her," Mabel said.

He looked at her.

"You lost her because she thought you didn't love her. You spent the rest of her life trying to convince her she was wrong." She opened the leather case, held it up to the light, and stared at the inscription. "I will always love you," she read aloud. She looked at Cole. "It's a promise." She looked out the window and then back at Cole, her black eyes shining. "You're still trying to keep it."

Cole felt a fist-sized rock inside his chest begin to break apart.

Mabel turned the bracelet over in her hand. "It looks brand new," she said. She looked at Cole, her heavy brow furrowed, and understanding dawned in her eyes. "She never accepted it, did she?" She swallowed hard. "She never wore it."

Cole took the bracelet from Mabel's hand, laid it gently in its velvet bed, closed the lid, and covered the case with his hands. "She said it reminded her of the bad times between us." He paused for a long time and then said, "But I thought maybe she . . ." his voice trailed off and died.

"You thought maybe she didn't believe your promise," Mabel said, her voice quavering. "You thought maybe she never really trusted you again." Mabel leaned back in her chair and stared at him, her eyes full. "Oh, Cole," she whispered.

He looked down at the case. Neither of them said anything for a long while.

Then she stirred, and he looked up. "You made a mistake thirty years ago," she said. "It was a heart-wrenching time for you and you didn't handle everything perfectly, but you did your best to show Carrie you loved her." She reached across the table, pried his hands from the case, and held them. "You did your best, Cole. It's time to let go of the guilt." She squeezed his hands. "It's time to let go of Carrie."

The rock inside him fragmented slowly, piece by piece. He pulled his hands away from Mabel, caressed the case for a few moments, then slid it across the table to her, held on to it for another long moment, and then let go.

Chapter Forty-Two

THE SINS OF THE FATHER

July 31, 1967, Monday afternoon

A WEEK after the Goodwill truck took Carrie's things away, Cole stood at the kitchen phone and dialed his son's number. Peter's wife answered. A short, perky blonde with boundless energy and optimism, Linda was a tax lawyer in Philadelphia until she got pregnant with the twins, Carrie and Quinn, now three years old. Loquacious and articulate, Linda had always been easy for Cole to talk to, but that day she met his attempts to make conversation with a closed mouth. He gave up and asked to speak to Peter.

She hesitated and then said, "Didn't he tell you we're separated?"

Cole went still. "I didn't know. I'm sorry."

"So am I."

It took him a few moments to absorb the impact of the news. Then, "When did you separate?"

"He moved out in January. I filed for divorce in March."

It was almost August now. Cole's back ached. He leaned against the counter and rubbed it. "I know I've been a stranger to you and

Peter. I'll understand if you don't want to tell me, but I'd be interested to know what caused the breakup."

"Peter's boundless ego. He doesn't care about anything except the hospital. Never here with us. No husband to me. No father to the girls. I couldn't convince him to spend time with us no matter what I said or did. I've been a de facto single parent for three years. I decided to make it de jure."

One of the twins cried out and a high-pitched wailing duet followed. "I've got to go," Linda said. "I'm sorry he didn't tell you. I guess he doesn't care any more about you than he cares about us." She hung up.

Cole put the receiver in the cradle and stared at it.

He found the hospital's number and dialed it. He asked the switchboard operator if Peter Grundy was on duty. She put him through to the third floor nurses' station and he asked to speak to Peter. "Who's calling, please?" A crisp, efficient-sounding voice.

"Coleman Grundy, his father."

"Hold, please."

He held for a full minute. Then another. And another.

The telephone finally crackled to life. "I'm sorry," the same voice said, but with a softer tone. "Doctor Grundy is with a patient. He can't come to the telephone."

"Can't or won't."

"I . . . He's with a patient."

Cole put his hand over his eyes and gathered his wits. "I'm sorry, ma'am. I don't mean to trouble you, but could you please tell him I spoke to his wife and I need to talk to him?"

She was quiet for a few seconds and then said, "Hold on."

He was on hold longer this time. Then, "I'm sorry, Mr. Grundy. He told me . . . He said he has nothing to say to you." She paused. "He told me to use those exact words."

At the base of the cabinet door above the phone, the painter had applied a brushstroke with too much reddish-brown stain. A line of air bubbles remained petrified under the surface. Cole ran his thumb over them, as he had done a hundred times over the years, the little bumps pleasant to the touch.

"Thank you for your time, ma'am. I'm sorry I troubled you."

"It was no trouble at all, Mr. Grundy," she said softly.

He returned the telephone receiver to its cradle, placed his hands palm down on the counter, and looked over at the doorway that led down the hall.

Thirty years ago, the night after he saw Jim and Carrie in the church window, he confronted her in the kitchen. She sat at the table. He stood in the center of the room, facing her, his back to the door to the hallway.

He told her he knew about Jim. She sat with her head bowed and her hands clasped in her lap. She didn't deny it or try to explain it. He wanted her to say it was just a fling, that it didn't mean anything, that it was a mistake she regretted, that it was all her fault and she was sorry. But she said nothing, and that fueled his jealous fury. He lashed out at her. Most of what he said was a blur in his memory, but he remembered telling her in graphic detail what he had seen in the church window and calling her a whore and a slut. In the midst of his tirade, she looked past him and her eyes widened. He turned to see Peter standing in the door to the hallway, seven years old, pale, trembling, tears rolling down his cheeks.

Peter worshiped his mother, and Cole had been an absentee father. Peter had hated him from that night forward.

Years later, after Cole and Carrie had reconciled, she tried to heal the breech, but Peter refused every attempt Cole made to reach out to him. Eventually, Cole stopped trying.

Now Peter was thirty-seven; they had no relationship and he was making the same mistake Cole made thirty years ago.

Cole rubbed his back and looked at the telephone for a long time. Then he picked it up and dialed the hospital. The switchboard put him through to the nurses' station again and the same voice answered. "I know I've already caused you too much trouble, ma'am, but I'd appreciate it if you'd do me one more favor. Would you please tell Dr. Grundy I'm coming to Philadelphia? I'll be there in the morning. I'll meet him at the hospital or wherever and whenever he wants. If he can't see me tomorrow, I'll stay there until he can see me. Tell him I won't leave there until we talk." His back clenched. He leaned over and the tightness eased. "I'm sorry to trouble you with my problems, but would you please be so kind as to give him that longwinded message?"

"I'll tell him."

"Thank you, ma'am." He started to hang up.

"Mr. Grundy?"

"Yes, ma'am."

"Good luck."

"Thank you, ma'am."

He straightened up, placed the telephone in the receiver, looked at the doorway, and blew out a long breath.

Chapter Forty-Three

MABEL'S REPORT

August 16, 1967, Wednesday morning

COLE SAT at the kitchen table drinking coffee looking out the window at a cloudless azure blue sky. A pair of robins had taken over Carrie's Diner and their wings fluttered as they pecked at seed in its front-porch trough.

Mabel Lucas's patrol car climbed the slope and rolled to a stop near the car shed. Mabel had visited often in the past two weeks. She'd given him advice about talking to Peter, and she consoled him when Peter told him to stay out of his life. "You made a start. That's what's important. Keep trying. You'll break through eventually, but if you don't, you'll know you did your best."

She walked toward the house carrying a valise. She looked smart in her tan county uniform, the sun glancing off the badge pinned to her shirt, her wide-brimmed hat shading her face as she stopped to tighten the belt holding up the service revolver holstered on her hip.

Cole met her at the front door and led her into the kitchen. He poured her a cup of coffee and they sat across the table from each other. "How's your back?" she asked.

"Not much pain anymore. The last shot they gave me seemed to help more than the others." He knew Mabel thought facing up to Carrie's death and confronting Peter had improved his outlook, and his doctor seemed to agree. "The doctor says stress made my back worse. He thinks the pain may not come back so fast this time."

She smiled. "I'm glad you're better." She unzipped the valise. "Kennie told me you were sleeping in this morning," she said, referring to her replacement as Cole's secretary. "Thought I'd drop in and give you a report on my way out to the firing range."

"How's the training going?"

"I can't hit the side of a building at twenty paces. Toby says it might help if I would keep my eyes open when I pull the trigger."

"You'll get the hang of it."

"Can't get any worse." She withdrew a folder and set it on the table. "Remember how Dolley Madison told us they couldn't find a hospital record of a small-caliber gunshot wound around the time of Reba's twelfth birthday?"

Cole nodded.

"I talked to the lady who runs the hospital's archives last June. Turns out they don't have a rational filing system for records dating before 1948. They just dumped them heebie-jeebie in a big old record storage warehouse off Route 29 South. I didn't want to give up on finding that record without a fight so I've sent Jefferson State summer interns over there to rummage through the warehouse off and on since June. Yesterday, one of them hit pay dirt." She took a document from the folder and handed it to Cole. "April 6, 1937, was one month after Reba's twelfth birthday."

Cole read the document. It said Dolley Madison treated a man for a small-caliber gunshot wound at one A.M. on that date. The name of the patient took his breath away. He laid the document on the table and looked out the window and tried to recover. The pair of robins hopped along the porch of Carrie's Diner. One of them darted inside the nesting hole. Cole lifted his coffee cup to his lips, but his hand trembled so badly he set it down again.

He didn't look at Mabel. He didn't want her to read his mind, but apparently she didn't need eye contact to glean what he was thinking.

"I didn't live here in 1937. I've never heard of this man, but you know him, don't you, Cole?"

He nodded. He looked down at the document again, read it all the way through, then folded it into a square and put it in his shirt pocket. "Don't tell anyone. Don't write up a report."

There was a long silence. Then Mabel said, "We can't let him get away with this."

"You know me better than that."

Mabel looked uncertain.

"I'll make him pay for what he did," Cole said.

"You'll arrest him? Turn him over to Wiley for prosecution?"

Cole wrapped his hands around his coffee cup and looked down at it. "A public prosecution would hurt innocent people."

Mabel looked even more uncertain. "I don't understand."

He reached across the table and took her hand. "Trust me. Keep this man's name a secret between you and me, and I'll make him pay. Privately. In a way that doesn't hurt anyone else. "

Mabel stared at Cole for a while, then put her hand over his and squeezed it. She put on her hat and stood. "Let me know if I can help."

He heard the front door close and the clump of her boots across the porch. From the window, he watched her walk over the flagstone to her car and open the door. She stopped and looked back at him. Then she got in the car, turned it around, and headed out to Whippoorwill Hollow Road.

Cole held his hands up in front of him. They were shaking as badly as the night he killed Jim Lloyd.

Chapter Forty-Four

PERMISSION

August 16, 1967, Wednesday afternoon

COLE DROVE to headquarters and spent the day considering alternatives. Late afternoon, he settled upon a plan of action he thought would protect the innocent from further harm, but he didn't feel he had the right to implement it on his own say-so. He called Reba Emley and told her he needed to talk to her.

"Kelly's Place at seven," she said.

"That won't work. We need to talk alone."

She was quiet for a few moments. "You found him," she said. "You found the snake. I can hear it in your voice."

Cole paused, not ready yet to tell her all of it. "I know who he is," he said, "but there's a problem. I need your help with it."

She was silent for a few beats. Then, "Fox Run Schoolhouse. Now."

"I'll be there in thirty minutes."

As Cole pulled his patrol car into the schoolyard the sun was setting behind the old schoolhouse, painting the clouds above it crimson, orange, and pink. Reba's Impala sat in the long shadow of the building. She stood leaning against the driver's door wearing jeans and a red short-sleeved shirt, her arms crossed over her chest.

He parked beside the Impala and Reba got inside the patrol car. He noticed lingering signs of Jim's attack. She'd lost weight from having her jaw wired shut for six weeks. Her chin bore a faint fish-hook-shaped scar, and her jaw was slightly off kilter.

"How did you find him?" she said.

He took Dolley Madison's report out of his shirt pocket, unfolded it, and handed it to her.

She held it up to the fading sunlight with shaking hands. Her eyes widened when she saw the name. She read the rest of the report, reread it a second time, handed it back to him, lit a Kool, and looked out the window at the schoolhouse, her eyes glistening. "I didn't expect it to be him."

"I didn't either."

She looked across the road in the direction of Leland Mundy's grave and looked back at the schoolhouse. "It ain't fair." She bowed her head and pinched the bridge of her nose. "I hate to think . . ." Her voice trailed off. She took a deep drag on the Kool and blew smoke out the window. "You said you need my help. What kind of help?"

He told her what he wanted to do. He laid it out carefully and in detail, so she'd be sure to understand. When he finished, he gave her some time to think. Then he said, "There's a big disadvantage with doing it this way."

She stubbed out her cigarette in the ashtray and looked at him, waiting.

He set his hat on the bench seat between them and ran his hand over his bald head. "People like him don't ever get better. He didn't quit when you shot him. There are little girls who came after you. If we do what I want, no one will ever know their names. Their stories," he paused and wiped sweat off his brow, "and your story will never have a voice. No one will know what he did. He won't be judged. He won't be sentenced. He won't be punished."

She stared at him, her brow knitted, still waiting.

"I need to know if this is all right with you," he said. "Without your permission, I can't bring myself to do it."

She was quiet for a long time, staring at the rusty swing set and the dead locust tree. A hot breeze swirled powdery dust across the yard and then died out. A crow cawed in one of the pines on the other side of the road.

"Go ahead with it," she said. "It's the best way to end it. No more pain. No more hurt."

He let out a long breath.

"One condition," she said. "When it's done, I want to know what you told him, what he said, what he did about it. I want to know every detail. Don't leave nothin out."

He nodded. "I'll tell you all of it."

She lit another Kool, pulled smoke into her lungs, and blew it out the side of her mouth. Tears beaded in her eyes. "I hope it works," she said softly.

"Me, too."

Chapter Forty-Five

THE VELO DOG

September 7, 1967, Thursday

OVER THE NEXT THREE WEEKS, Cole investigated. In 1943, the man named in the medical record bought Langham Properties, a small company in Charlotte, North Carolina, and built it up into a commercial real estate powerhouse. Three years ago in 1964, he sold Langham for a rumored mid-eight-figure fortune and "retired" to a plantation-style manse perched on a knoll overlooking the Pee Dee River near Cheraw, South Carolina. Within months after his retreat to the twenty-acre estate, he formed a new company and began to invest in real estate in Chesterfield and Marlboro Counties.

On a warm, humid, sunny afternoon, Cole sat in a burgundy barrel chair facing an antique cherrywood desk with a green inlaid leather top covered with deeds, mortgages, liens, title reports, surveys, construction blueprints, and plat maps.

Tall and slim, Charley Hix sat behind the desk, smoothing down his wispy gray hair with delicate pale fingers, an almost unde-tectable tremor in his hand.

"I fired Jim Lloyd during my first term as sheriff," Cole said. "Did he tell you that when you hired him?"

"He worked in security for my company in Charlotte, deep in the bowels of the organization. Someone in that department hired him. I had nothing to do with it."

Charley's voice had changed with age, Cole noticed, from the firm tenor of his younger days when he was married to Kelly McNiel to a high-pitched, reedy, tremulous whine.

"So you had no contact with him at Langham Properties?" Cole asked.

"I might have dealt with him on some minor matter, but if I did, I don't remember it."

"Interesting." Cole withdrew a document from his briefcase and slid it across the desk to Charley. "That's a record I found in Jim's personnel file at Langham."

Charley only glanced at the document. "Those records are confidential."

"Buster Dillon gave me access to all the company's records."

A telltale sheen of sweat glistened on Charley's brow.

"That document lists Jim's job title as 'Security Specialist,'" Cole said. "Under job description it says 'Special Projects.' What caught my eye, though, is the reporting relationship. Everyone in security reported to the general counsel. Everyone except Jim. He reported directly to the chief executive officer, Charles M. Hix."

Charley pushed the document back across the table, giving Cole a tight smile. "After I sold Langham to Dillon, he ran it into the ground. He needs a scapegoat to appease his investors. To save his hide, he sued me. He claims I defrauded him. You can't believe a word he says about me."

Cole returned the smile. "I suppose that explains why he's been so cooperative, but your close connection to Jim doesn't depend on Dillon's word." Cole pushed the document back across the desk. "The date on this personnel record is January 14, 1957, seven years before you sold Langham to Dillon."

Charley's eyes narrowed and the muscles in his face tightened into a look of menace he never showed Cole in the old days. "Quit playing games. Cut to the chase. Why are you here? What do you want?"

Cole gave Charley a long, cold stare. He stood and crossed the plush maroon carpet to look through a set of French doors flanked by floor-to-ceiling windows. Charley's office was on the second floor of his manse and opened onto a widow's walk that overlooked the Pee Dee River. Sunlight glistened on gentle ripples along the river's muddy-brown back.

"After you sold Langham and pulled out of Charlotte," Cole said, his back to Charley, "Dillon fired Jim. Last fall, he landed in Selk County. He set up a false identity and deposited twenty-five thousand dollars in the Jeetersburg branch of the First Virginia Bank, a healthy sum of money considering he'd been unemployed for three years."

Cole looked at the white railing enclosing the widow's walk. The paint on the ornately carved spindles was new, unblemished by the winds rolling in off the river.

"On Christmas Day," Cole continued, "Jim murdered a woman. Over the next few months, he committed two more murders and four attempted murders. He planned to kill two more people, but they died before he could get to them. The odd thing is most of his victims had no connection to him and he had no personal motive to attack them."

Cole turned and looked at Charley. "I figure he was a contract killer. He worked for someone who wanted those people dead." Cole crossed the room and stood beside Charley's desk, looking down at him. "Jim worked for you, Charley. You paid him to kill Hazel Emley, her daughters, and the men they confided in."

"That's preposterous," Charley said evenly. "I didn't pay Jim Lloyd to kill anyone." Charley stood. "I won't have you come into my home and insult me with scurrilous accusations. Get out. Now."

Cole didn't move.

Charley reached for the telephone on his desk. "Get out or I'll have my men throw you out."

Cole withdrew another document from his briefcase and extended it to Charley.

Charley didn't even glance at it. He put the telephone to his ear. "Lonnie, put me through to James."

"If you don't hear me out," Cole said, "I'll go public with this document. You'd be wise to take a look at it before you summon your thugs."

Charley glared at Cole. "Hang on for a minute, James," he said into the telephone. He took the document and read it, and his hand started shaking slightly. He laid it on his desk and covered the mouth of the telephone receiver. "This proves nothing," he said, his voice tight and strained.

"It proves you sought treatment for a small-caliber gunshot wound at Dolley Madison Hospital on April 6, 1937, at one A.M. It proves Reba Emley shot you that night. It proves you're the man who molested her when she was a little girl."

Sweat trickled down the side of Charley's face. "I . . ." His voice broke. He cleared his throat. "I shot myself. I was cleaning my gun. It fired accidently."

"Our ballistics tests will say otherwise."

Charley started to say something, then seemed to decide against it.

"Hang up the phone, and I'll tell you why your lie won't work."

Charley hesitated. "I'll give you one minute. Then I'll call my men." He placed the receiver in its cradle.

"Reba shot the pedophile who raped her with a Velo Dog, a little pocket revolver known as a bike gun. A Frenchman invented it for bicycle riders to use against dog attacks. It fires such a low-energy round that there are cases where people had to shoot themselves in the head twice to commit suicide. When Reba shot you with her bike gun, the twenty-two-caliber bullet didn't go all the way through. According to the intern who treated you, it lodged in the external oblique muscle of your back. I guess that's why you took the risk of going to Dolley Madison. If the bullet had gone through, you could have nursed the wound yourself, but when it got hung up in your back, you knew the infection could kill you so you had to go to the hospital." Cole gave Charley a hard look. "And that's what did you in. The intern who removed the bullet retained it, and Reba still has the Velo Dog that fired it. I'll be handing them over to Frank Woolsey next week for ballistics tests. How do you think the tests will come out?"

Charley leaned forward, put his hands on the desk, and bowed his head. He sat down slowly, leaned back in his chair, and put his hand over his eyes.

Cole picked up the documents and returned them to his brief-case. "When the ballistics analysis is done, I'll hand everything over to Wiley Rea. You remember him. He went to school with us. Judge Blackwell appointed him as commonwealth's attorney in January when Nate Abbitt resigned. He'll stand for election for the first time next year. He's looking for a way to make a name for himself, a platform to run on. Prosecuting a high-profile, wealthy pedophile will garner statewide publicity, maybe even national press. There's no statute of limitations on the criminal prosecution of child molestation in Virginia, so there's nothing to hold him back. He'll come after you hard."

Charley looked up at Cole, his eyes tired, hollowed-out, tortured.

"Next Friday, a week from tomorrow," Cole continued. "I'll hand Reba's little bike gun and the bullet off to my forensics team. What happens from there on will be out of my control."

Cole walked back to the French doors and looked outside. A string of seagulls flew over the river heading east. Cole lingered at the doors to give Charley time to absorb the full import of every-thing Cole had told him. He watched the birds shrink to little white dots and then disappear in the distance.

Cole turned and looked at Charley, who was still slumped in his chair with his hand over his eyes.

"I put a timeline of Reba's story together with your history in Selk County," Cole said. "You started molesting Reba in 1935 when she was ten years old. She shot you in 1937. At first I figured you left Kelly and Rachel right after she shot you, but the records proved me wrong. You didn't walk out on them until six years later in 1943." Cole paused. "I wondered what made you run away then."

Charley dropped his hand to his lap and looked at Cole, his eyes full.

"Rachel was nine years old in 1943," Cole said, "a year younger than Reba when you first molested her." He paused for a long time and then said, "I'd like to believe some small spark of decency lay inside you back then, down deep under all the slime." Cole walked over to Charley's desk and looked down at him. "Your daughter's a successful lawyer. The best attorney in Jeetersburg. She has a great future ahead of her." Cole softened his voice. "Unless something comes along that breaks her down."

Cole picked up his hat and put it on. "I'm hoping that small spark of decency is still alive," he said. "I'm hoping it will protect Rachel from the beast that lives inside you one more time." He gave Charley a knowing look. "You have until next Friday." He turned and headed toward the door.

"Wait," Charley said.

Cole looked back at him.

"Are you saying you might not go to the prosecutor?"

"That depends on you."

Charley leaned forward. "I have to know with absolute certainty." He hesitated, apparently searching for the strength to continue. "What will you do if . . . something happens to me?" His voice shook.

Cole locked eyes with him. "I'll close the case. Burn the file. Tell no one what I found."

Charley held Cole's gaze for a long time. Then he swiped his hand across his brow and looked out the windows, his chin quivering, his eyes clouded and fearful.

"Goodbye, Charley."

Cole walked out of the office and closed the door behind him.

Chapter Forty-Six

THE NEXT OF KIN

September 13, 1967, Wednesday morning

A WEEK after Cole met with Charley Hix, he got a phone call at headquarters from the sheriff of Chesterfield County, South Carolina, who he'd met with before he went out to see Charley. In his forties, short and stout with wavy blond hair and a perpetually flushed face, Curly Dodson had given Cole a rundown of Charley's three years in the Cheraw area, and Cole had been impressed with his knowledge and professionalism.

"Charles Hix is dead," Dodson said over the telephone.

Cole sat behind his desk, looking out the windows at Beacon Hill shining pale blue in the sunlight. "How did he die?"

"Passed away in his sleep. Housekeeper found him in bed Sunday morning."

"What killed him?"

"The coroner says he had lung problems, a respiratory ailment of some sort."

Lung problems. Visceral congestion, severe pulmonary edema, petechial hemorrhage of the lungs, Cole guessed.

He was surprised Charley chose such a hard way to die. Maybe he didn't know what succinylcholine would do to him. He wasn't a doctor and the publicity about the Coppolino case didn't dwell on the horrific last moments of the drug's victims. Or maybe Charley had found some courage in his final days.

The greater puzzlement to Cole was how Charley managed to dispose of the syringe and vial. According to Shirley, paralysis set in from thirty to sixty seconds after an injection. He had help, Cole guessed, a henchman like Jim Lloyd, who would keep silent about an assisted suicide in exchange for a big fee.

"Grundy? You still there?" Dodson asked.

"I'm here."

"His housekeeper said he seemed perfectly healthy the day before he died. You see anything wrong with him when you met him?"

"Nothing obvious."

"Strange."

Cole didn't comment.

Dodson said, "Reason I called is the housekeeper says the only kin Hix ever talked about was a daughter name of Rachel lives in your county. I need to notify her of her father's death, but I can't find any record of a Rachel Hix up your way."

"Her mother filed legal papers years ago to change her name. She's Rachel McNiel."

"That explains it. Can you give me her contact information?"

"Might be better if I notify her. She hasn't heard from her father since she was a little girl, and they didn't part on good terms."

"Okay by me. These calls are never easy."

Cole hung up the phone and looked down at the file on his desk marked "Hix, Charles." He opened it and reread Mabel's research on Reba's Velo Dog. Manufactured in 1904, the little French "bike gun" was extremely rare. That's what gave Cole the idea to tell Charley that Dolley Madison retained the bullet. The gun was so unique that its bullet would have identified Charley as Reba's molester beyond any doubt. Ironic, Cole thought, that a shrewd multimillionaire real estate mogul whose entire life was built on lies had chosen to kill himself because of a lie he didn't question.

Cole took a last look at the documents, closed the file, and marked it for the burn barrel.

Chapter Forty-Seven

SWEET TEA

September 13, 1967, Wednesday afternoon

THE MANAGER at Kelly's Place told Cole that Kelly didn't plan to come in until two, so he drove out to her house at noon. Mature maples and oaks cast shade over the sidewalks along Buford Street in Jeetersburg's "old town," where stately Gilded Age homes with gables, cupolas, cut-glass windows, tin roofs, and wraparound porches sat back from the street on expansive manicured lawns adorned with flowerbeds and neatly trimmed hedges.

Kelly was in her home office, listening to the stock market report on the radio, dressed in her bartending uniform, a tight, tailored three-quarter-sleeve red blouse and a black leather skirt that came to midthigh. Most sixty-year-old women wouldn't dare to wear that outfit, Cole thought, but she looked good in it.

He told her he needed a few minutes of her time. She led him out to the porch. He sat in a rocker and she went inside for a pitcher of sweet tea, then settled in the porch swing.

"Rumor has it you might not stand for reelection next year," she said.

"I considered retirement for a while, but I've decided against it. My back got better and I . . . I'm in a different frame of mind." He fell silent.

"You've come with bad news," she said. "I can see it in your eyes."

He looked out at the quiet street. A crisp breeze moved through the shade trees. Gold and cardinal leaves floated in the wind and came to rest on Kelly's lawn. "Charley's dead," he said.

Kelly's eyes widened slightly, then returned to normal. "How did he die?"

"A respiratory ailment."

She was quiet for a while and then said, "I haven't heard from him since he walked out on me. I have no idea where he lived."

"He owned a real estate business in Charlotte. A few years ago, he sold out and moved to a house on the Pee Dee River outside Cheraw, South Carolina. That's where he died."

She took a sip of tea. "It's strange. I grew up with Charley. I was married to him for ten years. I had a child by him, but I don't feel a sense of loss. It's as though he was someone I never met."

"I'd be surprised if you felt anything for him after what he did to you and Rachel."

"I suppose." She looked across Buford. Cole followed her gaze to the porch of a pale yellow house where a small elderly man in a wheelchair had a plaid blanket over his legs. A stout, busty middle-aged woman with long frizzy red hair wearing a tight tank top and red short-shorts came out on the porch carrying two glasses of lemonade. She set one on a table by the old man and kept the other for herself. She said something to him. He didn't respond. She sat in a rocking chair next to him, crossed her meaty thighs, and talked to him between sips of lemonade. The old man stared straight ahead, as still as a statue.

"I loved Charley when we got married," Kelly said, drawing Cole's attention back to her. "He pretended he loved me, too, but after his father died and he took over the family's real estate business, he dropped his act. All he cared about was the almighty company. He left for work before I got up in the morning and came home after Rachel and I were in bed. Some nights he slept on the sofa in his office and didn't come home at all. At least, that's what he told me. He could have spent those nights in the arms of another woman for all I know. I tried to reach out to him, but he didn't want any part of me." She set her tea on the table. "I had no feelings for him by the time he left me. We hadn't touched for more than a year."

Cole looked down at his glass. He'd decided that telling Kelly the truth about Charley would hurt more than it would help, but he didn't know if he was right. Since Betty Lou Mundy's murder, Cole had lost his moral bearings. In his lowest moments, he considered himself a murderer. He shot Jim Lloyd in self-defense and Charley Hix committed suicide, but he set them both up to die. No judge or jury decided their guilt. He alone sentenced them to death. He had played God, and now he was playing God again, deciding what was best for Kelly and Rachel, but God was omniscient and Cole was not. He couldn't find a clear line between right and wrong anymore.

A peal of laughter brought him out of his thoughts. Across the street, the redheaded woman wiped the old man's chin with a napkin. A yellow stain the size of a baby's bib had spread across his white shirt. She dabbed at it, cackling away. The old man stared straight ahead, seemingly oblivious to everything around him.

Cole's thoughts returned to the purpose of his visit. "Rachel is Charley's next of kin. The Chesterfield County Sheriff wants to talk to her about the disposition of his body, funeral arrangements, and the like. I told him I'd let her know, but I thought you might want to speak to her first."

Kelly brushed a strand of auburn hair out of her eyes. "I'll tell her tonight." She looked into the distance pensively. "A few months ago, the news of Charley's death might have opened old wounds for Rachel that had never healed, but lately she seems to be in a better place. Stronger. More sure of herself. I don't think Charley can hurt her now."

"I hope not."

They sat quietly for a while. Then Cole set his glass on the table. "Thanks for the sweet tea." He stood and put on his hat. "Let me know when you've told Rachel and I'll put her in touch with Sheriff Dodson." He walked across the porch to the top of the steps.

"Cole."

He stopped and looked back at her.

She stood, picked up the tray with the pitcher and glasses, walked over to the screen door, and faced Cole. She started to say something, stopped, looked down at the tray, then looked up at him again. "Are you lonely?"

Her question caught Cole off guard. Before he could think of anything to say, Kelly said, "That's the question Rachel asked me a while ago. 'Are you lonely, Mom?'"

Cole stared at her curiously. "What was your answer?"

"I told her I'm fine. I'm happy. I love my work."

Cole thought about that. "I suppose that would be my answer, too."

She fell silent. Their eyes locked, and he felt uneasy. She broke the tension. "You mind grabbing the door for me?"

He reached around her and opened the screen door.

She stepped inside and started across the room, but she hesitated. She turned around and locked eyes with him again while he held the door. "I lied. I love my work, but it's not enough." She paused and then said, "You're lying, too, Cole."

His throat tightened. "Kelly—"

"Carrie's dead."

He froze.

"You can't bring her back by pretending she's still here."

Cole started to speak, to deny that he was in denial, but the words didn't come. He stood transfixed, mute.

The sunlight played in Kelly's eyes, changing them from hazel to caramel and back to hazel again. They were beautiful. She was beautiful.

"I'm lonely, Cole," she said, "but I won't stay lonely. If you don't make a move, I'll find a man who will."

She turned around and walked across the parlor and went through the swinging doors that opened into the kitchen. He watched them swing shut and come to rest. He let go of the screen door. Its slack spring pulled it closed gently.

He stood on the porch for a long time, staring at the swinging doors through the screen mesh, pondering Mabel's words about the bracelet he gave Carrie and its inscription: I will always love you. It's a promise you're still trying to keep.

Through the screen door, Cole stared at the parlor's oak floor where it met the edge of an oriental rug with navy blue, yellow, and maroon patterns. He shook his head and sighed, then turned and walked to the top of the steps. He stopped there and looked across Buford. The redheaded woman had gone inside the house. The old man sat in his wheelchair, alone, staring straight ahead at nothing.

A dog barked at the end of the street. A child laughed in the house next door. Cole looked up at the topaz sky. His eyes returned to the old man who was sitting still as a corpse.

Cole turned around, opened the screen door, and went inside. He walked across the rug and stopped at the swinging doors. Oak, fine grain, lacquered with a rich dark stain.

Fear waged a war inside him with loneliness. Continuing to love Carrie was safe. She couldn't hurt him. It took courage to love the living.

He stood there for a long time. He put his hands against the doors, which were smooth and cool to the touch. He hesitated for a moment, then pushed them apart and walked through.

The End

Acknowledgments

In preparation for a writers' conference several years ago, I drafted the first fifty pages of a proposed novel. It began with Sheriff Coleman Grundy's discovery of Betty Lou Mundy's corpse at dawn on a cold February day in 1967.

My good friend, the accomplished writer Pamela Fagan Hutchins, critiqued my work. She liked the first few chapters and panned everything that followed. She was right on all counts.

Fellow authors Felicia Little, Patty Flaherty Pagan, Heidi Dorey, and David Welling reviewed my first ten pages and gave me their feedback. Their enthusiasm for the beginning of the story helped me survive the chaotic creative process that followed.

Despite what I thought was a good beginning, I couldn't seem to spin out a compelling story. My wife, Cindy, nursed me through a long, dark period, repeatedly reviving my comatose morale and feeding me ideas to save the storyline.

My editor, Meghan Pinson of My Two Cents Editing, raised *The Judas Murders* from the dead twice with fresh ideas when I'd almost given up, and her encouragement about early drafts kept it on life support. Without her guidance I would never have finished it, and as always, her editing skills took the story to a much higher level while preserving my style and voice. Simply put, she completes my work. For my money, she's the best developmental editor anywhere.

And she and Rhonda Erb, fact-checker and proofreader extraordinaire, also of My Two Cents Editing, are the best copyediting team in the free world. It's a pleasant bonus that they're also great fun to work with.

Fellow SkipJack author Marcy McKay read a late draft of the manuscript and offered several insights, two of which were critical to the final product. Her tips were invaluable and her encouragement was another turning point for me. She's not only a great writer, but also a great tutor of writers.

Having midwifed the birth of the story, Pamela Fagan Hutchins read and critiqued a late draft, making several key suggestions about perspective and plot line that made the finished product so much better.

SkipJack Publishing assistant and fellow author Bobbye Marrs is a versatile superstar who brought all of her talents to the table in researching several complex issues. She directed me to the Coppolino case and gathered information about succinylcholine while somehow convincing a doctor she cold-called for advice that she is not a serial killer. She reviewed a late draft, gave me helpful suggestions, and steered me away from critical substantive mistakes. In her spare time, she designed and created the book cover, formatted the text for the print and e-book publications, and managed the distribution process while simultaneously pumping out my newsletter and maintaining my website and blog. Told you she was a superstar.

I greatly appreciate the essential help I received from several experts. Catherine E. DeMonte, LMFT, gave me insight into the personality and behavior of pedophiles, explained the devastating impact of child molestation on its victims, and referred me to resource materials that expanded my understanding of both. Dr.

Peter Fagan reviewed sections of the book involving succinyl-choline and schooled me on the drug's traits and the effects of an overdose on the mind and body. Tracy Antoon critiqued sections of the book that referred to the sale and distribution of pharmaceutical drugs. Ryan Weeks, a U.S. Marine and expert rifleman, gave me advice about long-distance rifle shots, firing ranges, tripods, and guns. I did my best to set the story within the framework of the information the experts gave me, but any and all errors are my fault alone.

Last but not least, without the ongoing support and encouragement of Pamela and Eric Hutchins, I doubt I'd still be writing. Thanks so much for all the help over the years.

About the Author

Ken Oder was born in Virginia in the coastal tidewater area near the York and James Rivers, where military installations during World Wars I and II fueled the growth of urban centers like Norfolk, Hampton, and Newport News. His father worked for the Navy Mine Depot in Yorktown and later as a Hudson dealer until he heard his calling and became the minister at Mount Moriah Methodist Church in 1960. The family moved to White Hall, Virginia, a farm town of about fifty people at the foot of the Blue Ridge Mountains. The mountains and the rural culture were a jarring contrast to the busy coastal plains, but once the shock wore off, Ken came to love it there. He found the mountains and hollows spectacularly beautiful and the people thoughtful, friendly, and quietly courageous. White Hall became Ken's home, and his affection and respect for the area and its people have never left him.

Ken and his wife moved to Los Angeles in 1975, where he practiced law and served as an executive until he retired. They still live near their children and grandchildren in California, but a piece of Ken's heart never left White Hall. That place and time come out in his stories.

Please visit www.kenoder.com and connect with the author on Goodreads for news and new releases.

Fiction by SkipJack Publishing

KEN ODER

The Closing

Old Wounds to the Heart

The Judas Murders

BOX SET

Murder, They Wrote: Four SkipJack Mysteries,

by Pamela Fagan Hutchins,

Ken Oder, R.L. Nolen, and Marcy McKay

PAMELA FAGAN HUTCHINS

Act One

Saving Grace

Leaving Annalise

Finding Harmony

Heaven to Betsy

Earth to Emily

Hell to Pay

Going for Kona

Fighting for Anna

Searching for Dime Box

Bombshell

Stunner

Knockout

MARCY MCKAY

The Moon Rises at Dawn

Stars Among the Dead

Pennies from Burger Heaven

Bones & Lies Between Us

REBECCA (R.L.) NOLEN

The Dry

Deadly Thyme

ANTHOLOGIES

Tides of Possibility, edited by K.J. Russell

Tides of Impossibility, edited by K.J. Russell and C. Stuart Hardwick

Made in the USA
Monee, IL
24 January 2020